ISLAND SHIFTERS

BOOK THREE

AN OATH OF THE CHILDREN

VALERIE ZAMBITO

Copyright © 2012 Valerie Zambito
All rights reserved.
ISBN-13: 9780988457522
Cover Art by Nick Deligaris
www.deligaris.com

OTHER TITLES BY VALERIE ZAMBITO

ISLAND SHIFTERS - AN OATH OF THE BLOOD (BOOK 1)

ISLAND SHIFTERS - AN OATH OF THE MAGE (BOOK 2)

ISLAND SHIFTERS - AN OATH OF THE CHILDREN (BOOK 3)

ISLAND SHIFTERS - AN OATH OF THE KINGS (BOOK 4) - SOON!

ANGELS OF THE KNIGHTS - FALLON (BOOK 1)

ANGELS OF THE KNIGHTS - BLANE (BOOK 2)

ANGELS OF THE KNIGHTS - NIKKI (BOOK 3)

ISLAND SHIFTERS SERIES REVIEWS

"FROM THIS BOOK'S FIRST PARAGRAPH, I WAS HOOKED UNTIL THE VERY END."

"I HAVE TO SAY IT HAS BEEN A VERY LONG TIME SINCE I READ A BOOK AND GOT GOOSE BUMPS!"

"I WAS SWEPT AWAY BY THE COLORFUL CHARACTERS AND BRISK PACING OF THE BOOK, ALMOST COMPELLED TO KEEP TURNING THE PAGES AS ZAMBITO'S ACTION-PACKED STORY CARRIED ME ALONG."

"WITHOUT A DOUBT, THIS IS, BY FAR, THE BEST BOOK I HAVE EVER READ IN MY ENTIRE LIFE. AS SOMEONE WHO HAS READ OVER 780 BOOKS IN THE LAST 20 YEARS, THAT'S SAYING SOMETHING."

Map of Massa

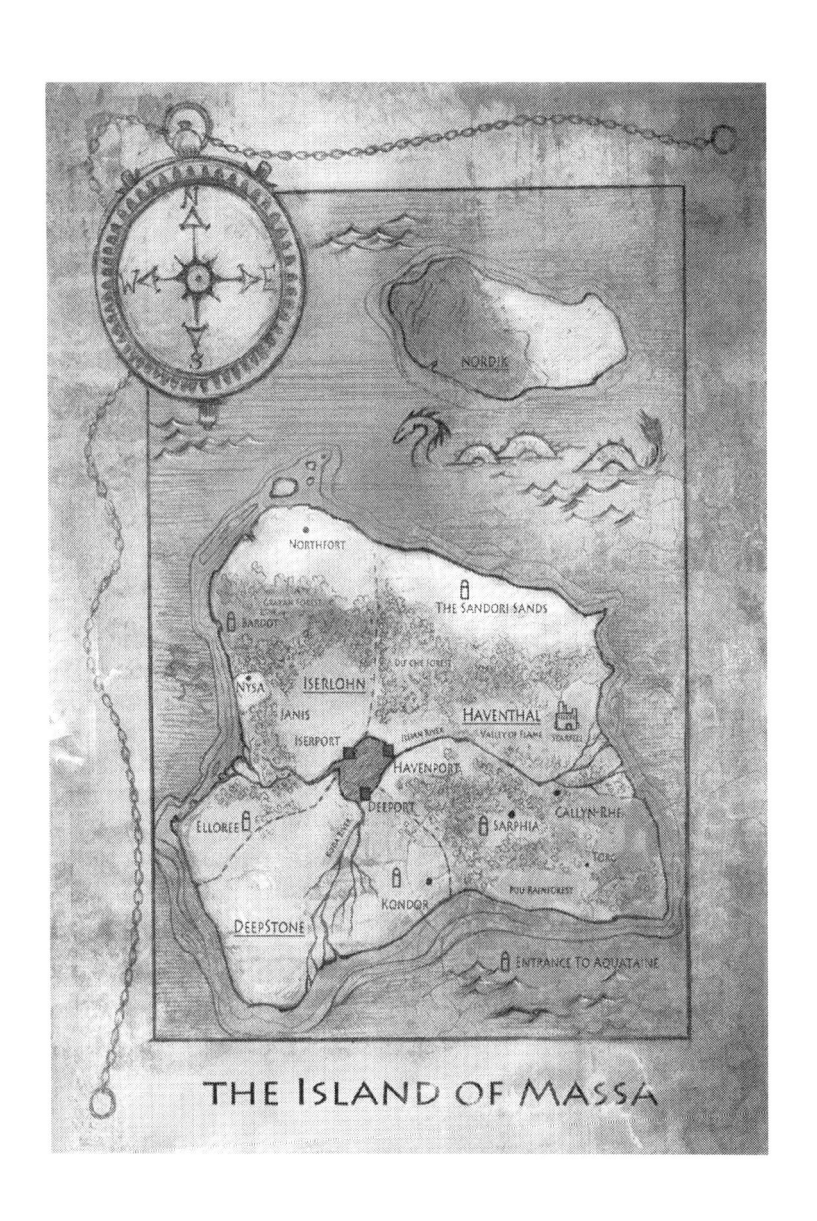

Table of Contents

	Prologue	1
1	The Departure	10
2	Crones and Crows	19
3	A Proposal	28
4	Growls in the Night	37
5	Blood Thirst	44
6	Betrayal	52
7	Baya's Sorrow	61
8	Birthrights	71
9	Dangerous Waters	80
10	The New Order	88
11	The Mayor's Gala	96
12	Immunity	106
13	Trapped	118
14	Blood Supply	127
15	A Tightening Web	135
16	Predator and Prey	145
17	Up in Smoke	150
18	The Island of Ellvin	159
19	Shattered Innocence	169

20	Gifts	177
21	Bloodbath	188
22	The Feast	197
23	Gooseberry	203
24	An Arrow Through the Heart	210
25	Surrender	216
26	A Beacon of Hope	222
27	Concessions of War	229
28	Dark Legacy	237
29	An Arrow Through the Back	244
30	The Short Stick	254
31	Battle at the Gates	264
32	An Oath of the Children	272
33	Calm Before the Storm	279
34	Airstrike	286
35	Release From Darkness	294
36	The Return	302
	Ruling Nobility of Massa	309
	About the Author	312

Prologue

The boy knew he would be punished. That much was certain. All that remained to be seen was what form it would take.

A tremor of fear raced up his spine as he ran, and he fought back the urge to cry. The Shiprunner had been very clear in his instructions to deliver the letter unopened and with all due haste to the Premier. Anyone with sense would have done just that but curiosity got the better of him, and after examining the rolled parchment, he felt confident that he could manipulate the wax seal back into shape so that it would appear undisturbed.

He had been wrong.

Even he could see that the Premier would know immediately that the letter had been opened.

Clutching the damning evidence tightly in one hand, his anxiety propelled his steps faster as he raced through the streets of Ellvin.

Papa often warned him that his inquisitiveness would get him into trouble, but surely, his father could understand how all of the gossip in the villages had built his hopes so. With worry for Mama weighing on his mind, the temptation had proved too much.

Despite the reprisal sure to be handed down on him from the Premier, a surge of excitement coursed through his body as he recalled the written words of the missive. The rumors *were* true. People from far away were coming to the island to meet with the Premier, and they were bringing precious wormwood plants with them.

The boy shook his head in disbelief. *Bringing them here to the island! Maybe now Mama will be able to take the draught she so desperately needs.* He knew there was a long waiting list for the meager supply of wormwood left on the island, but if these new visitors brought enough, it was possible that his mother could be moved higher on the list.

With renewed hope, the boy ran faster, dodging around carts and pedestrians, his long black hair flowing behind him.

If he was going to suffer lashes for opening the letter, he didn't need to add any more by being late. Pumping his arms furiously, his small feet kicked up a trail of dust from the dirt road leading to the Premier's compound. Passing through the caste villages along the way, he didn't stop, even when friends of his called out for him to join in their game of marbles. With a curt shake of his head, he pushed on. Not just because of the lashes, but because he wanted Mama well again and the sooner the Premier received the letter, the sooner the foreigners would come.

"Letter for the Premier!" he shouted out as soon as he descended on the front gates of the compound. He waved the parchment in his hand at the two Battlearms standing guard. "Quickly now, let me in! Important letter for the Premier!"

One of the slender guards on duty thrust his spear out toward the boy in order to stop him from advancing further. The other reached out and rang a large, bronze bell.

The Premier's Adjunct, his white tongor flowing around his ankles, strode across the courtyard to the gates. He grabbed the iron bars and peered imperiously down at the boy. "What is it?" he asked impatiently.

The boy held the note up. "A message for the Premier, sir!"

The Adjunct pushed his spectacles higher on his nose with one finger and looked at the parchment, but made no move to take it from him. "Is it from the ships?"

"Aye, sir."

"Very well, come with me."

The fighter opened the gate to allow him passage. "Maybe I could just leave it—"

"You heard me, boy," the Adjunct snapped. "Now come along."

With a resigned sigh, the boy followed behind the Adjunct, renewed trepidation making his feet feel as though they were made of lead. He had never been to the Premier's compound before. In truth, he wasn't even a messenger. He just happened to be playing at the docks when the Shiprunner grabbed him by the back of the neck and ordered him to deliver the note.

He looked down at the wax seal in one last desperate glance to determine if there was anything he could do to fix his mistake, but there was nothing.

Swallowing back his fear, he climbed three flights of stairs behind the Adjunct and then followed him down an opulent arched corridor with large curved windows lining the sides. The hallway reminded the boy of a tunnel, only this tunnel held magnificent tapestries, vases, and golden statues the like he had never seen in his entire life. He tried not to gawk, but it was impossible. The value of the items in this hallway could probably feed his entire caste for a year. It always puzzled him why moneyed folk purchased meaningless trinkets when they could buy more practical things like food and tools and, of course, the draught. Did the Premier not realize that many people on the island were struggling to feed their families and to get their names on the lists? The boy shook his head. If *he* was the Premier, he would sell all of these items and give the profits to the people that needed it the most.

Walking swiftly along the endless hallway, he realized that the Premier's compound was also much larger than any of the other homes in his village. And, eerily quiet. Again, he had to wonder why the people that needed the least space lived in the largest houses. He would change that, too, when he was the Premier. To his way of thinking, the largest families should have the largest homes. It just made sense, so he wondered why no one thought of it yet.

Listening to the whispered hush of the Adjunct's slippered feet on the lavish tile, he grew more nervous with each step. He wished he had stopped at his hut beforehand to get Papa. With his father by his side, he wouldn't be feeling so afraid.

He wiped away a tear that suddenly fell from his eye and straightened his back. He was twelve now and boys of twelve years did not cry. At least that is what Papa always told him.

Up ahead, the Adjunct stopped before a set of double doors at the end of the corridor and guarded by two more fighters in their crisp white tongors with gold trim. One of the fighters opened the doors without a word from the Adjunct. As personal aide to the Premier, he must not need special permission to enter.

Just inside the door, the Adjunct turned to him. "What is your name, boy?"

"Tatum, sir."

"What caste are you?"

"Ironfingers, sir."

The Adjunct grabbed his hands and inspected both sides. "I do not see the scars of the blacksmith upon you."

"I am only twelve, sir. My apprenticeship will not begin until next year."

The Adjunct shook his head. "What a pity. So young."

Tatum didn't know what he meant by that, but decided he should not ask.

The man turned back to the dark interior of the room and announced, "Your Eminence, a messenger is here to seek an audience with you."

Standing behind the Adjunct, Tatum tried to peer around him, but it was difficult to make anything out in the dark recesses of the candle lit room. They waited in silence for several long moments before Tatum heard a rustling of movement.

"Send him in." The voice was deep and confident and could only be that of the Premier.

The Adjunct stepped to the side and placed a hand on the small of Tatum's back, urging him forward. He went nervously with the note held out in front of him as though it were a talisman that could keep him safe. Tatum kept his eyes forward as he walked the aisle between massive pillars toward the figure sitting upon his throne and bathed in candlelight.

"Come closer boy."

Tatum hurried to the Premier and stretched the parchment out toward the leader of the Ellvin people.

A long fingered hand appeared out of the folds of a richly embroidered robe.

After releasing the note, Tatum immediately knelt with his head down, but his curiosity piqued once again and he glanced up from underneath his eyelashes.

Just as Tatum feared, the Premier looked carefully at the seal and frowned before he unfurled the rolled paper and began to read.

The seconds ticked by. The room was deathly quiet as the Premier's eyes glided over the words. Finally, he looked up and steely, black eyes latched onto Tatum. "Did you open this, boy?"

Tatum suddenly felt the urge to lie. Some deep-rooted preservation instinct inside his body was telling him that in order to live, he must lie. But, with the Premier's gaze boring into his skull, he found that he could not. The Premier's Ascendancy was the strongest on the island.

"Aye, Your Eminence."

"Why?"

"I...I was curious, Your Eminence."

"Can you read?"

"Aye."

He held up the parchment. "What does this say?"

"It says that...that people are coming to Ellvin and they are bringing wormwood plants with them."

"I see. And, this interests you?"

"Aye, Your Eminence. My mother is plagued."

The Premier scoffed. "We have many plagued on the island, young man. What makes yours so special?"

His small shoulders tightened and he was afraid he would cry again. "She is special to me, Your Eminence."

"You would like her to receive the draught?"

"More than anything," he whispered.

The doors in the back of the room opened and the Premier released Tatum from his penetrating stare. Tatum let out a small breath, relieved for the short reprieve from the Premier's attention.

He peeked over his shoulder and recognized the woman hurrying down the long aisle toward them. It was Samara, the Caste Second of the Eyereaders. She appeared to float as she glided closer, her long black hair hardly stirring as she moved. By the look of health in her face, Tatum realized that she, like the Premier, did not suffer in the least from lack of the draught.

Samara glanced briefly at him before kneeling in front of the Premier. "Your Eminence."

"You may rise, Samara." He gestured with his chin. "This boy has just delivered a message from the ships. Is the news as good as I have just read?"

"Better, Your Eminence."

The Premier snorted. "What could be better than the arrival of wormwood plants, Samara? The Ellvin people have just been saved from obliteration!"

Can it be? Tatum wondered. *All on the island saved?*

Samara glanced once more at Tatum before continuing, but the Premier urged her on.

"Blood."

"Blood?"

"It is an island of magic, Your Eminence. Almost every soul I encountered in Massa had some spark of magic." Her eyelids fluttered. "It was exhilarating."

The Premier sat forward on his throne. "Are you sure of this, Samara?"

"I am, Your Eminence."

The Premier came off his chair and stood before the Eyereader. "It has been many, many years since we've had the blood. I was starting to believe that there was no magic left in the world."

"There is an abundance of magic in Massa, Your Eminence. I can assure you of that fact."

"Oh, Samara," he breathed in excitement, "to obtain our sustenance from blood instead of the wormwood draught? I can hardly dare to believe it's true!"

Samara's thin eyebrows arched higher. "You do understand the repercussions?"

"Of course, I do!" the Premier snapped. "Not everyone will condone such an approach, I realize that."

"No, I am afraid not, Your Eminence."

The Premier turned and walked back to his throne and sat. "I think it goes without saying that we cannot disclose this information to the population just yet. It could cause untold turmoil if people knew a cure was on the way. Folks with loved ones who are ill will do just about anything to save them." Black eyes turned his way once again. "Don't you agree, boy?"

"Aye, Your Eminence." Tatum smiled broadly at the handsome face. How could he have ever thought him to be frightening?

"You may go now."

Tatum stood. "I...I can go?"

"Aye, you may go."

What? No lashings? He could hardly believe his luck. *And, Mama is going to receive the draught she needs to be well again! Wait until Papa hears about this!*

Tatum bowed one last time to the Premier and turned to walk down the aisle. It felt strange to be walking without an escort, and he suddenly felt an icy itch between his shoulder blades. Ignoring the peculiar feeling, he kept walking and did not turn around. If he had, he would have seen the brief nod the Premier gave to his Adjunct standing in the shadows. He would have seen the small crossbow appear in the man's hands, and then he would have known that the bad thing he had done would not go unpunished after all.

Chapter 1

The Departure

"Your daughter is late again," Kiernan felt the need to inform him for the third time.

"Why is she always *my* daughter when she's not doing what she's supposed to be doing?" Beck asked.

Kiernan raised an eyebrow at him as if the answer should have been obvious. He shook his head in good humor and let the conversation drop. After nearly twenty years of marriage to his iron-willed Princess, he knew when to keep his mouth closed.

Instead, as they waited together at the harbor at Northfort, he silently appraised his lovely wife. At thirty-eight years of age, she was still stunning in every regard. Lithe and toned, she had the body a woman half her age would be envious of, but it was more than her physical beauty that captivated him. Right from the very beginning, it was the intoxicating combination of her passion for life, her intelligence, and her strength. She challenged him at every turn whether a simple game of Dragon's Fire, innocent swordplay or a heated debate of political stratagem. Kiernan kept him engaged and excited about life on a level that surpassed anything he could ever achieve alone. No, there was never a dull moment with his warrior bride, and he adored her more today than the day he first met her.

With a satisfied smile, he turned from his wife to glance out to sea. It was hard to believe that where he now stood had once been his homeland of Pyraan.

In his youth, Pyraan had been nothing more than a disgraced land of exiles. A place where every shifter born on the island was forced into cohabitation for the singular purpose of using their magic to defend Massa against outside forces. But, to Beck, it had always been *home*. It was where he had been born, where he lived with his beloved parents, and where he first met Kiernan. Such bittersweet memories and now the entire land lay submerged under the Arounda Ocean.

Just as unstoppable as the shifting tides of the sea, so, too, on land does everything change. Where once, only a small portion of Massa was accessible by the ocean through the narrow Twin Bluffs, this northernmost section of the island had grown over the years to the now bustling port city of Northfort where travel to and from the island was becoming more frequent.

Nordik, the home of the Cyman race of people and located northeast of the island had become a popular retreat for many Massans. There was also the newly discovered land of Damone east of Nordik, and the tiny island of Hiberi south of Damone.

Beck and the other *Savitars* had visited all three islands over the past few years and their efforts resulted in the development of profitable trade agreements for Massa and opened talks for numerous other cooperative ventures. Beck had to admit that he was surprised to find no other shifters or magic users on any of the other islands they visited. He felt sure that Massa was not alone in its magical capabilities, but so far, they had found nothing.

Today, they sailed for the island of Ellvin.

"I don't see them yet," Kiernan complained, craning her neck to see over the large crowd gathered to see the royals off on their latest voyage.

"Stop fussing, they'll be here." As soon as the words left his mouth, a loud murmur raced through the suddenly parting throng and Beck caught glances of white. White horses high stepping in unison. White hair flowing in the wind. The Elves had arrived.

"See? It's Airron, Melania and Izzy."

"Father!" The shout drew his attention to his eldest son, Kellan, striding toward him. Muscular, tall and dark-haired, most people commented, and Beck had to agree, that he was the spitting image of him. Following silently behind Kellan was his second son, Kane. Blonde, like Kiernan, Kane was quieter and much more reserved than his larger than life brother. Shadowing both, were their male Draca Cats, Maks and Jain.

"I looked for Kenley as you asked," Kellan grumbled, "but she is nowhere to be found. You really need to take a firmer hand with her, father."

Beck promptly ignored the pointed look his wife gave him and turned toward the sound of heavy staccato steps striking the cobblestone road signaling the arrival of the Dwarves. Another wide furrow in the crowd formed as Rogan, Janin,

Reilly and Jala appeared at the entrance to the harbor in the midst of a ring of Dwarven Iron Fists.

Another loud cheer roared for the impressive troupe and Beck smiled, anxious to see his old friends again. As the only Mage on the island, it was his duty to seek out new technologies and methods from other peoples around the world and in that effort gratefully accepted the assistance of the other *Savitars* on his seafaring journeys. Given that the trips proved so highly beneficial to Massa, this trek today would be the fourth in as many years ordered by the Council of Kings.

Over the noise on the dock and the streets below, Beck and Kiernan greeted Airron, Rogan and their families as they stepped onto the wide pier.

A tap on Beck's shoulder spun him around to face the Ship Captain, Rafe Wilden.

"She's ready when you are, Your Grace." *She* being *The Wanderer*, a three-masted dinoque of considerable size.

"Thank you, Captain, but we're still waiting for..." Beck let his words trail off when he caught sight of Kirby Nash and Kenley's Draca Cat, Baya, moving smoothly through the crowd. Wherever Kirby and Baya were, Kenley wasn't far behind. "Never mind. We will be ready to board in a few moments."

Years ago, after Roman Traynor's betrayal, both Beck and Kiernan rebuffed the idea of personal guards, and Kirby was reassigned to Kenley. Kiernan trusted no one as much as her former protector for their strong-willed daughter.

The handsome Scarlet Saber jumped up on the dock and knelt before them with his left fist on the ground. "Your Graces."

"Please rise, Captain. Where is Kenley?" Kiernan asked him brusquely.

Kirby rose to his feet. "On her way, Your Grace. You should feel her arrival momentarily." He coughed nervously. There was clearly more on his mind. "Your Graces, if I may?"

"Of course, Captain, speak your mind," Beck told him.

He cleared his throat again. "Are you sure you wish to leave all of the children here on the island?" At the look on their faces, Kirby quickly continued. "Some of the Sabers, Fists and the Gardien have expressed, shall I say, extreme concern over protecting all of the children at the same time."

Beck tried to hide a smile. In the absence of parental influence, the protectors often found themselves on the receiving end of most of the mischief perpetrated by their charges. When those charges also had the use of powerful magic, the pranks took on a whole other level.

Kiernan laughed out loud. "Kirby Nash! Are you going to let a few children get the better of the revered Scarlet Sabers and their counterparts? Battle-hardened soldiers? Afraid of mere children?"

Kirby Nash turned as scarlet as his title, but mumbled under his breath, "There is nothing *mere* about those children."

Abruptly, a gust of air sprang up and Beck's long black cloak whipped around his legs. He lifted his hand to shield his eyes from the blowing sand generated by the swirling wind.

"It's Kenley!" Izzy Falewir announced with an excited shout.

Beck watched as his daughter rode an air current at least sixty feet off the ground, her body bladed for balance and her arms stretched out to the sides. A look of pure joy creased her features as the wind blew her long black curls back from her face.

The crowd went wild when they saw her.

Never one to shun an audience for her skill at airshifting, Kenley lifted her arms above her head and shot straight up into the air like an arrow. At the apex of her climb, she stopped and hovered for a few moments before gently laying back into what looked to Beck like a deadly free-fall.

Shrieks and gasps exploded from the onlookers, but Kenley pulled herself up at the last moment and soared into the sky once again.

Beck observed her continued aerial stunts with his heart lodged in his throat. He only began to breathe normally again when she came out of her spins and descended out of the sky.

As soon as her feet hit the ground, she strode toward them with an enormous grin on her flushed face. She was wearing leather trousers and a tight-fitting leather jacket made especially for flying. Beck had to admit that she was an impressive sight, and in the fifteen years since Kenley's abilities had been made known, another airshifter had yet to be born. She was still unique among shifters.

People shouted to her as she made her way through the path that opened up for her, and she acknowledged all with a polite nod, but did not stop to talk or let them deter her from her destination—the platform where her family waited.

To Beck's left, Baya let out a contented mewing sound, and the bright green eyes tracked Kenley's every step as she moved closer. Even more so than Kirby Nash, Baya did not like to be out of reach of Kenley when she took to the skies.

"Am I late?" Kenley inquired casually as she breezed up onto the elevated wooden pier.

"The better question is, are you ever on time?" Kellan retorted.

Kenley made a face at him as Kiernan grabbed her arm.

"Now, Kenley—"

"Yes, I know mother," Kenley interrupted. "I'm the oldest, so it will be my responsibility to look after the children."

Beck winced at the withering look Kiernan leveled at their daughter, but knew better than to comment.

Kenley knew better, too, and quickly pulled Kiernan into a hug. "You can count on me, mother. Stop worrying."

The gesture softened Kiernan slightly. "We'll be gone almost a month. I expect you to keep them occupied and out of trouble, Kenley."

"Everything will be fine. I promise."

Beck looked with amusement at the looks of sheer terror on the faces of the protectors. The three Scarlet Sabers, Kirby Nash, Gregor Steele and Haiden Lind, stood beside Kenley, Kellan and Kane. Two Iron Fists, Iben Rydex and Dallin Storm, stood next to Reilly and Jala Radek, and the only female protector, Elon Aubry, held the hand of the youngest *Savitar* offspring, Izzy Falewir.

Kiernan held up a finger. "And, no pranks this time!"

Kellan's eyes widened innocently. "Pranks? Why, whatever are you referring to, mother?"

Rogan gestured toward one of the Iron Fists. "Let me refresh your memory, young Prince. Remember when we were away last year? Between your earth and Reilly's water, you buried Dallin in a mud sinking up to his neck! And, then left him there for hours!"

Everyone except the protectors laughed.

Melania Falewir ran a hand down her daughter's hair. "And, what about Izzy sending that falcon after Haiden? The way I heard it, the bird chased and pecked at the poor man every time he dared to step outdoors. He had to run with his arms covering his head for three weeks straight!"

Haiden smirked at the reminder, but that was as much as he would give up.

Captain Wilden interrupted the storytelling. "It really is time, Your Grace."

Beck nodded and after hurried goodbyes, ushered Kiernan onto the lowered gangplank of the dinoque and once aboard, toward the bow of the ship. The Massans in the harbor waved and shouted while the sailors on board rushed to man the capstan to reel in the heavy mooring ropes.

Beck stood beside Kiernan at the rail as the large vessel slowly pulled away from the dock and was surprised to see a frown on her face. She typically loved these adventures to other islands much more than he did.

"I hope they will be all right, Beck."

"Who? The children? Of course, they will." When she simply grunted, he grabbed her chin so she had to look at him. "There is nothing to worry about. Between six protectors, three Draca Cats, and their own abilities, the children will be fine."

"I know, but *that* is a very bad omen," she murmured as she looked past him back toward the harbor.

"What is?" he asked, confused.

She pointed at a large, black crow perched on one of the wooden pilings on the pier, and its beady little eyes seemed to be staring directly at them.

Beck laughed. "I didn't know you were superstitious, my love."

She put an arm around his waist and buried her face in his chest. "I hate crows."

"I thought you hated snakes?"

"Them, too."

He chuckled again and held her tighter.

"I can't explain it. I just have a bad feeling." She looked up at him, her green eyes laced with concern. "You aren't worried at all?"

He shook his head. "No."

"Why?"

"Because I haven't seen or heard from the Oracle in fifteen years. When that old woman reappears in my life, *then* I will start to worry."

Chapter 2

Crones and Crows

Captain Nash leaned in close to Kenley's ear to be sure she heard him over the swell of noise in the harbor. "Don't even try it, Princess."

She turned her back on the rest of their large party to face him. "Captain, I can assure you that while in my custody, the children will be on their very best behavior."

His loud snort caused the others to look at them. He grabbed her arm and steered her away. "I don't want a repeat of last year, Kenley. You will set an example for the children and keep them out of trouble or..."

She glared at him under her upraised eyebrows. "Or what, Captain?"

"I...I will take you over my knee, that's what," he growled at her.

"My, my, Captain, that sounds suspiciously more like a proposition than a threat." When his face flushed red, she threw her head back and laughed. "Don't worry, Captain, your honor is safe with me."

He mumbled something unintelligible under his breath, but she was already turning from him to gather the children. A fluttering movement out of the corner of her eye caught her attention, and she turned back toward the extended pier where the dinoque had been docked only moments ago.

A black crow sitting on one of the pilings squawked and beat its wings causing a loud ruckus. Kenley shuddered. She hated crows. She was about to turn away, when she noticed an old woman standing by herself directly beneath the agitated bird staring after the departing ship and shaking her head.

Kenley paused, deciding whether to approach, and then the woman turned toward her. She sucked in a quick breath. The woman's eyes were completely white. Even though it should have been impossible for the woman to see, there was no mistaking that direct gaze. Kenley had no doubt that the woman could see everything around her. And, then some.

"I'll be right back," she said to Kirby and walked over to the woman. The old lady did not look away as Kenley approached. "Pardon me. My name is Kenley, and I was just wondering if you required assistance."

"I know who you are," the woman replied in a deep, gravelly voice.

Kenley wasn't surprised. Most people on the island knew who she was. Usually by her green eyes, but sometimes by her distinctive, long black curls. She tried again. "Are you looking for someone?"

"The Mage."

Kenley pointed to the ship now making a graceful turn to head out into open water. "I'm afraid you just missed him. He is on his way to the island of Ellvin and will not be back for three or four weeks."

"Interesting."

"Can I help you?"

A thoughtful frown crept into the woman's face as she looked out to sea. "For years, I have wondered why it will not be the Mage who fights and at long last I have my answer."

"Pardon?"

The woman did not answer at first and Kenley thought perhaps she had not heard the question, but then she finally turned back and moved her white eyes up and down Kenley's body as though measuring her up in some way.

"Interesting," was all she said for the second time and then shuffled away toward the platform steps that led to the streets below.

Very strange. Shrugging, Kenley turned away from the mystery to the more pressing matter at hand—the children.

Reilly, a watershifter, at nineteen was a year younger than she was and his sister, Jala, a fireshifter, was a year younger than Reilly. The twins, Kellan, an earthshifter, and Kane, a sightshifter, were both fifteen and little Izzy Falewir, a feralshifter, was the youngest of their group at the age of twelve. The six progeny of *Savitars,* and all extremely powerful in magic.

Kenley clapped her hands together as she walked back to the group, and the protectors tensed in high alert. They had been through this before.

"All right, it's time to head back to Bardot. We will proceed in an orderly fashion and..." Five pairs of eyes glinted at her mischievously. "Oh, what utter nonsense! Let's do it!"

With one last apologetic glance at Kirby Nash, Kenley waved her hand in a circle and the air around her began to stir. She felt Izzy Falewir's small hand slip into hers.

"Kenley Atlan!" It was Kirby, and he sounded furious.

The air gusted in the form of a mini tornado on the platform, and Kenley's hair whipped around her head. She carefully kept her magic directed at the six protectors and watched them disappear behind a cloud of dust.

Kenley jumped off the platform and took off running through the cobblestone streets of Northfort, the others close on her heels. When they were far enough away, she risked a look back over her shoulder and giggled in amusement as her hapless victims tried to breach the gale force winds holding them back.

Was that really necessary, Princess?

Baya's reprimand cut through her joy.

We're just having a little harmless fun, Baya.

And, the protectors are just trying to perform their duty. Why must you make it so difficult for them?

Because I wish to be free, Baya! Do you really not understand? How would you like to be followed around everywhere you go? For Highworld's sake, I can't even go to the privy on my own without a Scarlet Saber shadowing me!

It is for your safety, Princess. Surely, you realize that by now.

What do I need to be protected from? If anyone tries to harm me, I can take to the skies! she declared forcefully. Staring into eyes the color of her own, she made her tone deliberately softer. *Besides, I have you to protect me. That is all I need.*

True.

No one can stand against the ferocity of a Draca Cat.

Not if they wish to live.

Humans and beasts of every size tremble at the very mention of Callyn-Rhe.

Baya clicked her tongue. *Your flattery is far too transparent, little one.*

But, working?

Yes.

Kenley hugged her best friend tightly around the neck. *Thank you for understanding, Baya.*

Know now that I will not interfere with any punishment Captain Nash deems appropriate.

I understand.

Go then. Have your fun, but just for a few hours mind you. We have a long journey ahead of us.

Maks and Jain, who were younger and far more playful than Baya, let out an excited howl as they loped to the front of the group to cut a path through the people on the streets.

I remember when you used to be like that, she reminded her friend.

Never.

Kenley smiled at the outright lie.

Reilly spoke up. "Now that we have a few hours of freedom, how about we go to the lake? My gills are starting to dry out."

"You don't have gills!" Jala scoffed.

"Not yet," Reilly murmured in disappointment and, since he was a Surface Dweller, it was unlikely that he ever would develop the physical traits so predominant in the watershifters that lived below ground in Aquataine.

"Swimming with a watershifter! Count me in," Kellan shouted.

Jala and Izzy quickly agreed. Kane as usual was silent, following anywhere his twin brother wished to go.

"To the lake it is," Kenley confirmed, and the party continued to maneuver through the throng toward the outer gates with most people giving wide berth to the enormous Draca Cats padding imperially out in front. Some shouted out their greetings from afar, almost all dropped to a knee as they passed.

Sharing some of her father's aversion to crowds, as soon as they were through the gates, Kenley shifted the air and rose a few feet off the ground. "I'll meet you there!"

"Show off!" she heard Kellan shout.

The wind gathered beneath her, pushed her off the ground, and she shot into the air once again. *Now, this is freedom!* Fierce exultation thudded through every nerve of her body as the wind sliced over her and she climbed higher into the sky. Nothing gave her as much joy as the thrill of flight, of manipulating the elemental power to which she was bound to propel her through the air. Here, in the rush of wind, she did not have to worry about royal protocol. In the sanctuary of the clouds, she did not have to worry about having her every action scrutinized.

She felt a momentary pang of regret for deceiving Kirby, but quickly put it behind her. He just didn't understand her need to be on her own. The protectors thought these forays mischievous pranks, but each of the descendents of the *Savitars* felt different. To them, it was a few days of peaceful anonymity. A rare opportunity to just be children for a change instead of prodigy shifters or royals in waiting.

Spotting the children and Dracas below her running swiftly toward Lake Tear just west of the Sandori Sands, she shook her thoughts away and descended to the ground in front of them in a full sprint. Her companions caught up quickly and their laughter warned her.

Out of the corner of her eye, she saw an enormous stream of water shoot toward her in a torrent meant to knock her from her feet. She only just managed to take to the air in time to avoid a soaking.

Reilly Radek!

With a wolfish grin, she spun toward the five children below her and watched them stop in their tracks, realizing their mistake in getting so close to her. This was a game they played often, and one in which she always won. But, the children were becoming more powerful and it was increasingly difficult to defeat them all at the same time.

With a commanding spin of her hand, she unleashed her magic at Reilly and turned his own water stream back on him, pinning him to the ground.

Next, she went for the strongest of the group, Kellan, but she wasn't fast enough. He thrust out his hands and disappeared under a protective dome of earth. At the same time, Kane multiplied and she watched five images of her younger brother sprint off in different directions. Which one was the real Kane? She could no longer tell. She growled in frustration.

The whine of a shifted fireball caused her to turn toward the hurtling glow, but she easily snuffed it out with air and sent Jala reeling back. Little Izzy had already summoned a Grayan wolf to her side and was climbing onto its back to make her escape, but Kenley swept them both aside with a wind funnel. Once the wolf regained its feet, it took one look at the Draca Cats and sprinted back into the forest. Izzy let him go.

That left her two brothers.

Zooming in close to Kellan's dome, she peppered it hard with air until it disintegrated. He erupted out of the ground and frantically called forth a coat of earthen armor. She watched the dirt and stones on the ground roll up and over his body. Realizing at the last second that she was floating too close to him, she only just managed to avoid one of his powerful swings.

Laughing, she cast her arm out and sent him flying.

There was only Kane left now, and he was the tricky one. She had always been able to pick out her brother from his replicas, but she could no longer do so. In the past few years, her brother had grown exponentially more adept in his magic and his illusions were incredibly realistic.

Still, she started to pick off the Kane images and one by one, they vanished in a puff of smoke. She felt proud when she defeated the first three and searched wildly for the last two. She flinched when she saw Kane standing directly below her with a satisfied smirk on his face. She landed on the ground, ran at him and spun, launching a kick meant to take him off his feet.

To her surprise, her foot sailed through nothing but air, and she fought to keep her balance. A tap on her shoulder twisted her around awkwardly. The real Kane! He grabbed her around the neck and slammed her to the ground.

She winced, but smiled up at her brother in admiration. With golden eyes glowing in the afternoon sun, he reached out his hand to help her to her feet. He was too polite to gloat, but Kellan didn't have any problem in that regard.

"Now, that is a first! Well done, Kane! It seems our sister is getting a little slow in her old age."

She grabbed Kane's outstretched hand and stood. "Not too slow to blow your measly defenses apart," she shot back.

The Radeks and Izzy laughed when they joined them, and the Draca Cats watched all of the activity with bored aplomb, but Kenley knew that green, blue and golden eyes missed nothing.

"Come on," said Reilly. "Who wants to be the first on a water slide?"

With enthusiastic response, they walked together toward the lake.

Still unnerved by her encounter at the harbor, Kenley asked the others if any of them had seen the old woman standing on the dock.

None had.

Kenley shivered, although she could not say why. Maybe it was the woman's critical gaze and the way she seemed to be judging Kenley in some way.

Far more likely, it was the woman's eerie, all white eyes.

Chapter 3

A Proposal

The casual laughter around the table in the palace kitchens cut off abruptly when the doors banged open. Kirby Nash's face was crimson with fury.

Eyes grew wide in fright and utensils clanged to the floor as the cook and servants dropped what they were doing to dart into one of the back rooms.

Kirby's eyes locked directly on Kenley.

"Out!" he thundered to the children as he strode angrily to their table.

"But—"

"Out, I said! Now!"

Chairs scraped back as the children complied with his order.

Kellan bent down and whispered in Kenley's ear, "Good luck, sister."

Kenley nodded and sat calmly, waiting for the storm she had been expecting for three days. Her face a mask of serenity, she set down her teacup and looked up at the Captain planted in front of her in his red and black uniform and shiny saber hanging low on his hip. If she thought to escape, there was no chance of that now.

Baya peeked up at the commotion from her place by the back door, but then closed her eyes again, obviously holding true to her word not to interfere with Kirby's wrath.

Kenley rose to her feet in the modest space offered between the wall of Kirby's chest and her chair. "Captain."

"Do I ask for that much, Kenley? Do I?"

"No, not really..."

"Why then? Why must you continue to torment me?"

"Do I torment you?" she asked innocently.

He turned away from her and ran a hand through his hair. "You know you do," he whispered.

"It's late, Captain. I think he should continue this conversation in my chambers. I do not wish to be overheard."

He simply nodded.

Baya?

The cat barked out a snort that told Kenley she was on her own and made no move to rise.

With a glint of victory in her eyes, Kenley made her way along the palace corridors and up the stairs to the third floor, her heart thumping wildly in her chest. She had never seen Kirby this angry before. As he strode silently behind, she could almost feel the heat rolling off him in waves against her back, but she did not dare turn around.

When they reached her suite of rooms, he stalked ahead and opened the door. After she passed through, he entered and kicked the door shut.

"Look, Kir—"

She let out a surprised yelp when he swung her up into his arms and lurched toward the side table. With one brutal swipe, he sent the wine decanter and glasses crashing to the floor and flung her on top. A husky growl escaped his throat as he leaned into her and covered her mouth with his. With a self-satisfied moan, she laced her hands through his blonde curls and hungrily returned the kiss, wrapping her legs around his waist.

Kirby's hands explored her body roughly as though trying to excite and punish her at the same time.

"The bedroom," she murmured breathlessly and with a wordless snarl, he lifted her and strode out of the sitting room, his lips never leaving hers.

At the foot of the bed, he set her on the floor and ran his hands over the silken folds of her red gown. In one swift motion, he gathered the material at her hips, drew it over her head and tossed it aside. He took a step back to admire her naked body brazenly before gently pushing her back onto the bed. She absorbed his gaze unabashedly. She had loved this man heart and soul for as long as she could remember. Her body was his for the taking.

"Do you realize what you do to me, Kenley Atlan?"

Her mouth crept up at the edges. "If it is anything near what you do to me, Captain, then stop talking and show me instead."

With a roguish grin, he removed his sword belt and undressed. Even though they had been lovers for over a year now, the sight of his muscled chest gleaming in the candlelight still caused her heart to race. His handsome face, so strong and serious all of the time, took on a loving, intimate cast as he edged his way up her body and hovered over her.

When he finally lowered his body and began to move against her, slowly at first and then more urgently, she gave herself over completely to his demands. Somewhere in the deep recesses of her mind still capable of thought, she wondered how in the Highworld Kirby could ever refer to this as torment.

～

"Oh, Beck, look!" Kiernan's eyes lit up at the sight of the dolphins swimming playfully alongside *The Wanderer*. Standing on the tips of her toes on a plank wedged in the bow, she leaned over to get a better look.

"Careful," Beck said, standing directly behind her, his strong arm snaking around her waist in a tight grip.

She let him pull her back upright and leaned back against his chest, letting the sun's rays beat down on her upturned face. "This is heavenly," she murmured.

Beck nibbled on her neck. "Me or the sun?"

"Both. I just love to sail, Beck. All my worries just seem to fade away on the sea."

"Including the crow?"

"Including the crow, you brute!" She breathed out a content sigh. "Out here, I can relax and just be myself. Not Princess Kiernan Atlan. Not *Savitar* Kiernan. Just Kiernan." She closed her eyes and grinned at the sky. "I feel so free."

He laughed. "You sound like Kenley."

She smiled when she realized he was right. Kenley took to the skies whenever she wanted to be free of her protectors, and Kiernan took to the water whenever she wanted to be free of her duty. It appeared she and her daughter were more alike than she realized.

"Perhaps," she admitted.

He hugged her tight again. "You were only two years younger than Kenley when I fell in love with you twenty years ago. And, truth be told, you still look exactly like that girl of eighteen."

"I think it's time you were fitted with spectacles, my love."

"My eyesight is just fine, and you know it's true. Everyone speaks of your beauty."

Her emerald eyes twinkled. "If that is true, then I can only attribute it to being madly in love."

They remained locked in each other's arms as *The Wanderer* sliced through the ocean, the spray misting pleasantly on their faces. After several moments of comfortable silence, Beck said, "I wonder if Kenley will ever find the kind of love that we share. Don't you think it's about time for her to be thinking of that?"

Now, it was Kiernan's turn to laugh.

"What?" he asked. "Why are you laughing?"

"For a Mage, my dear husband, you really can be quite unperceptive when it comes to matters of love."

He pushed her away and held her at arm's length. "What does that mean?"

"Your daughter has been in love since the age of twelve—if not before."

"What?"

"Yes, Beck, your little girl is in love and has been for a very long time. It is time you knew."

"With who?"

"Kirby Nash."

Beck's mouth fell open. "Kirby Nash? He is her protector! She cannot possibly be in love with him. He has his duty." He shook his head. "No, Kirby would never let that happen."

"He loves her, too."

Beck threw his hands up. "And, how do you know all this?"

"All you have to do is look at the two of them to recognize how they feel about each other. Not all men are as slow to realize these things."

"I was *not* slow to realize with us." He stopped. "Was I?"

"About two years too slow. But, I forgave you for that a long time ago."

Beck ran a hand over his chin. "Kirby Nash? Really? If I can put aside the fact that he should have been protecting her instead of...of...oh, I don't even want to think about that. But, if I am to seriously consider him, I truly cannot think of a better man for our daughter."

Kiernan shrugged. "I agree."

"But, he *is* at least seventeen years older than she is."

"I don't think it matters to Kenley, so it shouldn't matter to us."

"Allow me to reserve final judgment until we return. Oh, yes, the Saber Captain and I will be having a very lengthy chat when I return to Massa."

༄

Kenley stretched languidly, content to be waking up with Kirby next to her in the bed. She turned on her side and snuggled against him. "Mmm...I should get you angry more often."

He lifted one eyelid. "I don't think it's possible to get me any more angry than you already do."

"Do you want me to tell you I'm sorry when I'm not?" she asked him honestly.

He let out a deep breath and turned toward her. "No. You should know by now that you can always tell me the truth. In fact, I demand it." He leaned in to kiss her gently. "Can you just try to make my life a bit easier in the process?"

She wiggled her eyebrows at him. "I don't know. After last night—"

"Kenley!"

"All right! I promise to try," she said and felt the tension visibly leave him.

He propped himself up on an elbow to gaze down at her. "So, tell me, when are you going to marry me and make an honest man of me?"

Her body stiffened. "Marry you?"

"Yes, marriage. Isn't that what you want?"

She was suddenly at a loss for words. Kirby Nash was all she ever wanted her whole life, but marriage? She was very content with the way things were. Marriage would inevitably lead to children, and in her mind both had always represented just more ties to hold her down. She was an airshifter. She was born to fly!

When she did not immediately answer, he continued. "We should at least tell your parents about us before they find out from another source."

Grateful for not having to answer, she said, "Oh, my mother already knows."

He shot up into a sitting position. "What?"

She shook her head and got out of bed with a mumbled, "Men."

"You told her?" he asked, watching as she retrieved her dress from the floor and stepped into it.

"No, but I can tell that she knows. She is a very perceptive woman, you know."

"I do know. I was her guard for many years."

"In any event, you are right. We should tell them both before long. My father will be very angry if he is the last to know."

Kirby winced. "That, I am not looking forward to."

"Why not?" she asked, sitting on the edge of the bed to pull on her slippers.

"A line was crossed, Kenley! He is going to be very upset about that."

"A line was not crossed, Kirby. As far as I am concerned, there never was a line. You are the only man I have ever, and will ever, love. Besides, my father cares for you just as much as I do, and I know that he will be happy for us. Just wait and see."

She started to stand, but he threw her back onto the bed and she squealed. "Thank you."

"For what?"

"For saying that you love me. I feel the same way, Kenley, I...I guess I always have. Especially, since you left me very little choice in the matter. You are a very determined young woman when you have your mind set."

She smirked. "I take that as a compliment."

His expression sobered. "You are my life, Kenley Atlan. Protector or husband, I vow to shield you and love you and place your needs above mine for all time. Marry me."

The outer door to the sitting room opened, saving her from a reply a second time.

Baya's growled announcement sounded in her mind. *A Saber is here to see Captain Nash.*

What does he want?

Do you really expect me to ask him?

She smiled. *Sorry. I'll be right out.*

"One of the Sabers is here," she told Kirby, and he quickly dressed and together they walked out of the bedroom.

"Captain Nash." The young guard greeted his superior with fist to chest. "We have just had word from up north."

"What is it, Saber?"

"You asked to be notified of any incoming ships while the royals are traveling, Captain"

"Yes, that's right. Go on."

"A ship can be seen approaching Northfort. Although, still too far off shore to view their pennant, it appears to be the same ship that brought the Ellvinians two weeks ago."

"The Ellvinians? Why would they be coming back here to Massa?" Kenley puzzled out loud. "The *Savitar* representatives and the wormwood plants they requested are on their way to Ellvin."

"It is odd," Kirby commented.

"I'll go see what they want," Kenley said. "Flying, I can be there in no time."

"No."

She looked questioning at Kirby. "What's the matter?"

"Nothing," he said, pulling her close. "I just want to be with you, and I can't do that if you fly."

She kissed the tip of his nose. "Fine. We'll take horses."

Baya rose from her place on the floor and gave an approving snort. *Shall we go?*

Kenley glared at her. *You used to be a lot more fun, Baya.*

We all have to grow up sometime, Kenley Atlan.

Chapter 4

Growls in the Night

One by one, they came. Flashes of white in and around the trees scattered the shadowy mist that hung low to the ground. Satisfaction surged in Nazar's chest as he watched the Draca Cats slink into the rainforest clearing. Although he felt their appearance tonight a good sign, the question remained. Were they here to join him or oppose him?

A low snarl developed low in his throat. One way or another, he would be Sovereign of Callyn-Rhe. If he had to shed the blood of his brothers and sisters to achieve that goal, so be it.

Next to his side, he felt his mate clench her muscles in readiness. She, too, was prepared to do what was necessary for him to succeed.

He snapped at her in soft warning. *Rehka!*

The female cat let out a faint whimper and obediently relaxed her stance.

Nazar waited until the clearing was full before walking forward to greet the assembled group. *Brothers and sisters, you have honored me by your presence.*

A young, large male stepped forward. *We came to hear what you have to say, Nazar, but no decisions have been made.*

You speak for all, Muuki?

The youngster realized his mistake and yowled. If Nazar considered his words a challenge, he would have a fight to the death. A fight that Muuki must know he would lose to Nazar's strength and experience.

Muuki cowered to the ground. *No, Nazar, I do not speak for all. Forgive me for speaking out of turn.* The young cat quickly backed away into the crowd with his head lowered in submission.

Nazar did not take his narrowed gaze off the male cat until he completely disappeared behind the wall of Dracas.

Very well. Nazar paced along the line of cats. *You know why I have called you here. The time for change is now. Moombai, with his old ways would have us remain hidden to the world, but I say let us walk free. Let us walk among the inferior races so that all in Massa can witness our strength and fear our wrath. The shifters came out of their exile many years ago, yet Moombai would still have the Draca Cats lie dormant. I say no more! I say now is the time of the Draca Cat!*

Howls of agreement shattered the silent forest. Many, but not all.

A female Draca stepped forward and bent her foreleg in respect. *What you say is true, Nazar, but why? We have everything we need in Callyn-Rhe. Why should the other races concern us?*

Nazar expected this question and was ready for it. *Why, you ask? The answer is simple, sister. Evolution. As a species, we need to shed the stagnation of our self-imposed exile. We need to grow and learn and...*, he paused until every eye in the forest was upon him, *...and, yes, dominate.*

The female blinked large, amber eyes. *Dominate the humans?*

A savage growl tore from his throat. *Yes, rule all who live on the island of Massa! We were born to lead and born to battle! As the oldest race in existence, we have the magic, the intelligence, and the strength to rule. So, why do we hide, brothers and sisters? A Draca Cat in hiding? It is blasphemy! It is—*

Nazar stopped when a nervous keening sounded from several of the cats. A regal Draca strode through a widening gap in the crowd with her head held high and her eyes on Nazar.

Again, Rehka tensed beside him.

Felice, he greeted with a shallow bow of his head.

Nazar. She did not bow.

What brings you out to the woods at this late hour, sister?

You, Nazar. Whispers have reached my ears, and I have come to see if they are true.

What whispers would that be?

That you wish to begin a revolution. That you wish to overthrow the rightful Sovereign of Callyn-Rhe.

Agitated howls and yips lit up the night. The loudest of which was his. *Yes! And, it will be so, Felice! The Draca Cats shall become the dominate species and rule the island of Massa through our Kenley bond!*

Cries of distress rippled through the cats. Even Nazar grimaced at the painful effect of his own words.

The Dracas have an unbreakable oath of protection to the Kenleys! How dare you suggest them harm!

I do not suggest them harm, sister. As soon as he thought the words, the pain subsided. *They will be our voice of rule. We will use them to our advantage.*

Felice looked around at the other cats and bared her teeth. *I cannot believe what I am hearing! Do all here agree with this madness?*

Nazar noticed with satisfaction that most of the cats nodded their agreement. Some remained infuriatingly silent, but he was no longer concerned with them. He now knew he had the majority with him.

We begin now, Felice! The Sovereign must step aside.

He will never consent to this! He will fight you to the death, Nazar.

Nazar stood to his full height. *It is a challenge I will accept.*

Then, you are a fool. She turned her back on him. *I go now to tell him of your plans.*

Nazar lifted his lips in a snarl. The best chance he had against the Sovereign was the element of surprise. If he allowed Felice to walk away from this clearing and warn Moombai, all would be lost. All along, he knew it would come to this, and he was prepared. He had to prove to the Dracas the strength of his power and commitment. Taking advantage of the retreating Draca, he pounced.

Felice roared in pain when he landed on her back and bit deep into her neck. She twisted and rolled, snapping at him with her powerful jaws.

The Dracan crowd moved back as he took her to the ground in a hissing, spitting tangle. Felice used her hind legs to run her talons across his underbelly, and he let go of her throat with a distressed screech.

Felice wobbled to her feet and tried to escape, but he charged her again and they crashed into one of the centuries old trees of the rainforest, bark and fur flying.

Weak from the blood leaking from her throat, she did not move when he pinned her to the ground and held her there.

You will not get away with this, Nazar, she warned softly.

I already have, sister.

Lifting his head, he howled his victory into the night and then sank his canines into the open wound on Felice's neck.

She cried in mortal agony as he ripped her throat out.

∾

No!

The shout in Kenley's mind startled her and she dropped the saddlebag in her hands. She rushed to Baya's side. *Baya! What is it?*

The white Draca Cat paced anxiously just outside of the stables where Kirby and the royal groomsmen readied their horses for the journey to Northfort.

Something is wrong.

With Maks or Jain?

No, at home in Callyn-Rhe. Baya lifted her head to call to the younger cats. *Maks! Jain! Come to the stables at once!*

Baya continued to pace, and Kenley was unsure how to help her. *Did someone speak to you from home?*

No, the distance is too far, but I felt violence happen.

Within seconds, her brothers' male Draca Cats skidded around the low wall surrounding the stables.

We are here.

Baya shook her head as if trying to rid her mind of a disturbing image. *I think Felice, my mother, has been injured.*

Injured? How? asked Maks.

I do not think it was a chance injury. It felt like she was fighting for her life when it happened.

A Moshie? They all knew that the Moshies were the sworn enemies of the Draca Cats. They knew not the why of it—only that it was.

I do not know, but I have to go there.

Of course, you do, Kenley assured her friend. *You must find out what's wrong, and I will go with you.*

Baya nodded her snowy head gratefully.

Kenley turned to Kirby with a sad smile. "I am afraid I have to leave you."

He grabbed her arm. "Kenley..."

She held her hand up. "I have to go with Baya to Callyn-Rhe, and since you are not able to travel through Aquataine, I must go without you."

"What has happened in Callyn-Rhe?"

"I'm not sure yet, but Baya feels there is something very wrong and I trust her instincts. You know I can't leave her in her time of need. She may need my assistance."

He let out a heavy breath. "Kenley, I have taken an oath to your protection. I promised your parents to stay by your side at all times, and I will remind you of your promise to try and make my life easier."

She smiled and reached up to cup his cheek. "Kirby, my parents could not possibly have known there would be an urgent situation in Callyn-Rhe. It is unfortunate that you can't travel the waterways, but it's a fact we can't get around."

"I don't like it."

"I will be back soon, I promise."

He pulled her close and kissed the top of her forehead. "If anything ever happened to you..."

"Nothing will happen." She lowered her voice. "You must know that I don't want to be away from you any more than you wish to be parted from me." She leaned in close to his ear. "Especially, after last night."

She never understood how his ears could turn so red, but he did seem reassured by her words. He directed a meaningful glance at Baya.

The Draca Cat snorted. *Assure him what he already knows. I will protect you with my life.*

Before Kenley could translate, Kirby said, "Tell Baya I am grateful."

Kenley opened surprised green eyes. "How did...?"

"Years of observation." He turned toward Baya. "And, friendship. Thank you, my friend."

"Now, that the two of you have had your conversation, I must ask for a favor. Please take the children and go to Northfort to find out why the Ellvinians have returned. I will take Reilly with me as he can help Digby watershift our craft to Haventhal."

Kirby nodded. "All shall be as you command, my Princess."

"Thank you. Come, Baya. It is time Callyn-Rhe had a long overdue visit from a Kenley."

Chapter 5

Blood thirst

"So, what do we know about the Ellvinians, Beck?" Rogan asked and handed his empty dinner plate to the young crewman assisting their meal.

The cook peeked out of the galley. "Would you like anything else this evening, Your Graces?"

Beck shook his head. "No, thank you, but if you would, please have Captain Wilden join us when he has a moment."

"Yes, Your Grace."

Beck leaned back from the large wooden table bolted into the floor of the ship's hull. "To answer your question, Rogan, very little. I know that the island of Ellvin, roughly twice the size of Massa, lies due west of here. Lars Kingsley, the mayor of Northfort, mentioned that the ambassador who visited two weeks ago as well as his crew all appeared to be of Elven descent."

Airron spoke up. "They *are* Elves." When all eyes turned incredulously his way, he quickly continued. "Well, at least I think they are. I have been researching Elven history in King

Thorn's private library and found tomes that very few know survived the Mage War. The Ellvinians are mentioned in writings that date back hundreds and hundreds of years."

Melania's flabbergasted look was not missed on Airron.

"What?" he asked. "I *can* read, you know."

"I know you *can* read. I'm just surprised you did."

The friends laughed, but Airron tossed his long white hair over his shoulder and forged on. "As I was saying, if they are the same people, I think these Ellvinians once lived on Massa. According to Elven lore well before shifters were exiled in the Mage War, the Elves fought bitterly over magic with the majority wishing to ban its use completely. When a compromise couldn't be reached, hundreds of Massan Elves left the island to start anew elsewhere where magic could be practiced out in the open. No one ever knew what happened to them after that, but there is a record that *Ellvinian* was the name they chose for themselves before leaving."

"What makes you think they are of Elven descent, Beck?" Kiernan asked.

"According to Lars, the ambassador had the pointed ears characteristic of the Elf, but unlike the silver hair and purple eyes of Massan Elves, both his hair and his eyes were black."

Airron shrugged. "The books never mentioned them having black hair. Maybe they aren't the same people after all."

"So, why are we bringing them all of the wormwood stashed below?" Rogan inquired.

"According to the Ellvin ambassador, whose name was Chandal by the way, his people are in dire need of the plant for medicinal purposes. He has traveled far in his explorations for the plants and when he sailed to Nordik and discovered that Massa had opened its borders to travelers, Chandal immediately changed course for a visit."

Janin shook her head. "I never heard of using wormwood plants as a curative."

"Actually, some of the Elves in northern Haventhal call wormwood the blood plant and swear that it produces plasma instead of nectar."

"That can't be true, is it?" Kiernan asked.

Beck leaned forward and interlaced his hands together on the table. "I have no way to analyze it, but the flowers on the plants do secrete a thick red fluid. I cannot imagine that it is actually blood, but I have seen stranger things in my life. And, it doesn't taste like blood. It has a sugary, sweet flavor."

Kiernan scrunched her nose in distaste. "You tried it?"

"Yes. I was curious." A knock on the door cut their conversation short. "Come in."

It was Rafe Wilden. All wiry, corded muscle throughout his chest and arms from working all of his life on ships, his hips and legs looked abnormally thin and narrow in contrast. Beck nodded at the Captain he first met many years ago when he was a ferryman in Iserport and transported Beck to Elloree when he was searching for Kiernan. The world was in chaos at the time with the treacherous scheming of Adrian Ravener, and Rafe ended up abandoning Beck in Elloree, but Beck understood why Rafe made the choice he did. The world was in turmoil and he had been worried for his family. It was hard to hold that against a man.

"You wanted to see me, Your Grace."

"We did not get much of a chance to speak earlier, Captain. How long do you think before we reach Ellvin?"

Rafe stuck a finger in his short, white hair and scratched. "If the map the Ellvinian Captain provided is any good, we should arrive in a week's time."

Beck nodded, wishing it could be sooner. Although Kiernan felt relaxed and carefree on these goodwill voyages, he was always anxious to return home. He enjoyed the time with his dear friends, but intangible ties pulled him back toward Massa. The children first and foremost, but also his concern over the Oracle's foretelling all those years ago. A fight was coming to Massa at some point in his future, of that he was certain.

"Thank you, Captain. That will be all."

Rafe bowed his head and went back through the galley door.

Beck turned back to his friends. "Before I forget, if I ever use the word *gooseberry* on this trip, I want you to repeat it back to me instantly without question, without hesitation."

Rogan blinked. "Gooseberry? What is a gooseberry?"

"It is a small green berry, but what it *is*, is not important. However, if I ever use this term, repeat it back to me."

"Oh, I get it, fireball," Airron said and wiggled his fingers in the air. "Beck is doing the whole enigmatic Mage thing right now."

Beck smiled. "Humor me."

"Gooseberry?"

"Yes, gooseberry."

When he extracted promises from all of his friends, Beck leaned back on the wooden bench. "Now, let's get to a more pleasant topic. How do you think the children are doing?"

"The better question is," Kiernan mumbled, "how do you think the protectors are doing?"

Hendrix Bane hated this walk. Fortunately, he rarely had to make the effort. For the most part, the medical technicians tended to the creature and that was fine with him. He would rather forget the thing was even alive. But, he could never do that now. After hundreds of years of tending to the Vypir, it had suddenly become relevant.

As always, his Battlearm Second, Emile, walked by his side. After this visit, they would go before the other Seconds and inform them of the imminent arrival of the wormwood plants. Before the news was shared with the populace, however, the solicitation of new bribes would commence and new lists would be devised.

Hendrix laughed to himself. Let them fight over the draught. According to Samara, *he* would soon have the blood.

Emile interrupted his thoughts. "When are the Massans due to arrive, Your Eminence?"

"Oh, we should not see them for a while yet."

"But, it should only take—"

"The map that Chandal provided," Hendrix interrupted, "will take them off course and at sea longer than necessary." He glanced over at his confidante. "You would not have them catch sight of our Shiprunners making their way to Massa now, would you?"

Emile bowed his head. "No, Your Eminence."

A white-robed technician rushed along the white corridor to intercept them. "This way, Your Eminence, Second Emile."

The technician directed them into an unfurnished white walled room. The only disruption to all of the white was the large observation window across from the door.

Hesitantly, Hendrix walked to the glass window and gasped aloud. The emaciated white-haired Vypir looked nothing like it did the last time he saw it. Lying on its back on a narrow table, the protracted chest heaved as the creature struggled to breathe, its rib cage clearly visible under dry, translucent skin. The knuckles of its long arms rested motionlessly on the floor on both sides of its body, and its long legs, muscle and sinew bulging, were bent at the knee and perched on the tips of its clawed feet. But, it was the face that had shown the most change. The skin was pulled so tight over its skeletal features that the narrow lips were unable to cover the sharp teeth protruding from its mouth.

It was hard to believe that this creature was once one of the most powerful Magi to ever have lived.

"What's wrong with it?" he asked the technician.

"It requires blood, Your Eminence. The Vypir is engineered to seek out and consume magic-laced blood. We don't have any here on the island to give it."

"Tell me something I don't know," Hendrix snapped. "Is it still eating food?"

"Very little."

Suddenly, the Vypir leapt off the table and hurled himself against the window with a blood-curdling scream. Hendrix shrieked and stumbled backwards. With strength the Premier did not know it possessed, the creature banged its head on the glass leaving streaks of blood as the skin ruptured from the contact.

A technician ran into the room to subdue the beast, but it evaded the soporific dart from the small crossbow and used its long arms to envelop the technician and pin him to the ground.

The Vypir's long tail sprang up from behind him, and Hendrix shrank back from the two tiny fangs that clicked together inside the opening at the end.

The creature swung the appendage down onto the neck of the technician and latched on. The man's eyes bulged and small rivulets of blood trickled down his throat as the Vypir's tail suckled greedily.

Emile ran from the room.

"Has it ever done that before?" Hendrix asked in whispered horror to the technician in the white room with him.

"No. He should have no desire for normal plasma."

As though he heard the exchange, the Vypir's purple eyes jerked up toward the window and the look of satisfaction was unmistakable.

Hendrix gulped. "I have a feeling that blood was taken for revenge, not sustenance. How are we going to control it outside the confines of its room?"

"Emile can control it. It takes direction from him and only him."

That was interesting news, thought Hendrix. He had not realized Emile had been involved so closely with the Vypir.

Three technicians appeared at the door to the Vypir's room. One held another crossbow and he hastily shot off a dart and it sank deep into the Vypir's neck. The Vypir rolled off the drained corpse on the floor and took a step toward the technicians, but did not make it far before falling face first onto the floor.

"Tolah!" Emile entered the room and immediately ran to the Vypir. "Help me!" he ordered.

The technicians rushed to obey and helped Emile carry the unconscious Vypir back to the table.

Hendrix turned toward the technician. "Tolah?"

The technician shrugged. "That is its name. I believe it was the original name of the Mage before...before he became the Vypir."

Hendrix was repulsed by the beast and did not want to know it had a name. Did not want to be reminded that it had once been a living, thinking individual. He only wanted the abomination to stay alive long enough to drain the magic users sailing for Ellvin shores.

He turned toward the technician and grabbed him by his tongor under the throat. "I am counting on you to ensure that nothing happens to that creature. If the Vypir dies, you die."

As soon he let go, the technician swallowed and bowed low to the ground. "Aye, Your Eminence."

Chapter 6

Betrayal

Afternoon shadows offered little relief from the heat as Kellan rode his mount next to Kirby Nash. He glanced over his shoulder at the others in their party spread out behind. After two days of travel from Northfort to Bardot just the day prior, an unexpected trip back to the port city was the last thing he wanted to do. And, with the protectors and horses to slow their progress this time, it would take closer to three days.

He reached for the water bag hung around his saddle horn and took a long drink. After wiping his mouth with the back of his hand, he looked at Kirby. "What do you think, Captain?"

"Hmm?"

Kellan shook his head, wondering why the Royal Saber seemed so preoccupied ever since the trip began. "The Ellvinians. Why do you think they are here?"

The Saber shrugged his shoulders. "Could be anything. Maybe they were having trouble at sea and it was easier to return to Massa for assistance rather than continue on to Ellvin."

"After all this time?"

Kirby waved a hand in front of his face irritably. "Regardless, we will get our answers soon enough."

Kellan looked over his shoulder at his twin brother riding directly behind him, the sword of Iserlohn peeking up over his shoulder. Like most earthshifters, Kellan did not carry a weapon, but Kane chose to bear the family heirloom that their mother once wore.

Surprisingly, Kane jerked his chin toward Kirby.

Kellan glanced back at the Captain, and saw him trying to swat away a very large bumblebee that continued to try and land on his nose.

"Demon's breath! Get away from me!" the Saber bellowed, arms windmilling around his head.

Kellan smiled. It was unusual for Kane to use his magic. Whenever pranks were pulled on the protectors, his twin preferred to stay in the background and rarely participated. In fact, he rarely spoke to anyone at all except him and their mother.

Kellan's guard, Gregor Steele, nudged his horse close and pointed ahead. "Your Grace, a rider is approaching."

Kellan stood in his stirrups for a better look. It was a single rider and he was coming fast. Faster than the rutted dirt road allowed. "He's going to kill himself! Jala, send up a warning signal for the rider to slow." If that did not stop him, the four shifters, five guards, and two Draca Cats should do it.

Jala wove her hands in the air and let loose a fireball that screamed into the air above their heads and exploded in a loud pop.

The rider pulled up on the reins of his horse, but instead of evading the large group, continued directly toward them. As the rider drew closer, Kellan could now see that it was a young boy. When the boy's gaze fell on the Draca Cats, his eyes widened in surprise and he slid from the still moving horse and fell to a knee. "Thank the Highworld, Your Graces."

Gregor dismounted and grabbed the bridle of the boy's horse before it caught scent of the Dracas and bolted.

"What is the matter, boy?" Kirby asked.

"Ships, sir! Ships have come to Northfort! My father told me to ride for Bardot."

Kirby held his hands out to calm the boy. "We have already had word, lad, and are on our way to Northfort now to receive the visitors. Now, run along and for Highworld's sake, slow that horse!"

Kellan straightened in his saddle. "Wait. How many ships?"

"I'm not sure, Your Grace. My father dispatched a message to the palace in Bardot earlier, but when more ships appeared, he sent me to request the presence of the royals."

"Who is your father?" Kellan asked.

"Lars Kingsley, Your Grace. The mayor of Northfort."

More ships? An inexplicable twinge of unease pricked at Kellan. He looked at Kirby. "It would appear that your trouble at sea theory is becoming more implausible by the moment."

"Let us not forget," Kane said softly from behind, "that the last time an armada descended on Massa, war broke out."

Kellan ran a hand through his hair as he considered his brother's ominous reminder. "How many soldiers are stationed at Northfort?" he asked the Captain.

"Good question, Your Grace. One hundred or so, but that number suddenly seems dangerously low." He turned to the boy. "Ride on to Bardot as your father asked. Seek out an Iserlohn soldier and tell them Captain Nash has ordered three hundred troops to Northfort immediately."

"Yes, sir." The boy jumped to his feet and mounted his horse.

"Hold on!" ordered Kellan. "We will need watershifters, too. Tell the soldier to have a dozen watershifters meet us at the harbor."

The boy nodded and Kellan watched him dig his heels into the horse's ribs and gallop south.

"It could be nothing," Kirby reasoned.

"Or, we could be in a whole lot of trouble," Kane pointed out.

Kane might not speak often, but when he did, Kellan was inclined to listen.

※

Kenley stepped off the raft in the Aquatainian village of Marboro beneath the Sarphia grate and stretched, sore from the days of traveling. She smiled at Reilly. "Unless you are trying to soak me, I really don't get enough opportunity to see you watershift. Your skills are truly exceptional."

"Tell me about it!" Digby exclaimed. "I might as well have not even been here at all. I've never seen anything quite like it."

The young Dwarf reached up to pat the lanky Digby on the shoulder. "I have learned from the master."

Digby waved a webbed hand dismissively. "Bah, you were born with more power than I will ever have."

Baya jumped off the raft onto the sandy beach and shook out her magnificent coat.

"Reilly," Kenley said, "I'm not sure how long I will be, but with Iben left behind in Bardot, it would give me peace of mind if you just stayed here until I returned. Do you think you can do that?"

She expected an argument, but Digby quickly interjected. "Don't worry, Your Grace. I will keep the lad in good company until you return." He leaned in close to the Dwarf's ear. "I know a few pretty watershifters that have been very anxious to meet you."

A grin to rival Airron Falewir's appeared on Reilly's face. "Well, my friend? What are we waiting for?"

The issue settled, Kenley bid her friends goodbye and led Baya toward the limestone stairs that would deliver them just outside of the Haventhal capital city of Sarphia. Long ago, her father showed her a much shorter way through the tangle of magic encapsulating the mystical land of the Draca Cats, Callyn-Rhe. Still, it would take most of the day for her and Baya to navigate the Puu Rainforest.

Kenley climbed out of the cool subterranean underground, and winced as the thick humidity of the forest swathed her like the weight of a heavy blanket. The lower canopy of the oversized trees and plants left little room for air movement and as a result of the trapped moisture, all she could see was a screen of mist that clung low to the ground in wispy tendrils and all she could hear was the steady drip of water rolling off the leaves.

She immediately stripped her cloak and stowed it in her bag.

Baya issued a low, warning growl and a Gardien appeared out of the fog like an apparition.

"Good day, Gardien. It is Princess Kenley of Iserlohn and Baya."

The young Elf's face registered excitement when he saw Baya. For some reason she had yet to learn, the Elves revered the Draca Cats of Callyn-Rhe as a sacred entity. Anywhere outside of Bardot, it was very rare to get a glimpse of the legendary cats so this was quite likely the first time the soldier had laid eyes on one. "It is an honor to meet you both."

Baya clicked her tongue in satisfaction very well aware of the Elves high regard for her race.

"We are passing through on our way to Callyn-Rhe. I hope that does not pose a problem?"

"No, no. You are more than welcome to continue on your way."

"Thank you."

The Gardien bowed low to the ground in front of Baya as they passed.

Stop your preening and come along now, she told her friend.

I do not preen.

No? I cannot see your eyes for the lift of your nose.

The cat ignored the taunt and followed her onto the narrow path that cut deep into the rainforest. The pervasive dampness pressed down on Kenley and she soon began to sweat. *Keep your eyes out for dangers from above,* she warned.

The Moshies, Baya growled.

Yes.

They continued forward throughout the day without incident. At one point, Kenley noticed slithering movement in the limbs above her head, but whatever it was quickly vanished back into the heavy foliage. They stopped once to eat, and Baya called out to Felice to no avail.

I do not like this, Princess.

I have to agree with you. The silence is unnerving.

After several more hours of walking, Kenley and Baya turned onto a bend in the path and, seemingly out of thin air, the wall of Callyn-Rhe appeared before them behind the haze.

They left the path and skirted the perimeter of the wall until they came to the concealed entrance. Kenley ducked inside the arched stone tunnel that led to the Dracan land and after a short walk, a light appeared up ahead.

After the dim interior of the rainforest, Kenley had to shield her eyes as she emerged from the tunnel and stepped out into the bright sunshine of Callyn-Rhe.

She had traveled to the land of the Draca Cats with Baya several times, but the sight never failed to enthrall her. The sun cast long shadows on a lush patchwork of greens and browns and blues. Tall savanna grasses waved and thrashed before a strong breeze that carried the scent of dry soil to her nose.

This time, however, the scene was unlike any other visit.

There were no Draca Cats.

Usually, the landscape teemed with cats running and playing or lazing in the sun on the few scattered boulders dotting the landscape. Now, it was completely empty.

Baya stood still. *What is this? Where are the Draca Cats? Felice!*

Kenley could hear panic begin to take root in her friend's thoughts.

Let's go to the caves where Moombai lives, Kenley suggested. *He will know what has happened.*

I do not understand, Baya mused as they picked their way carefully through the eerie stillness toward the caves at the northern border of Callyn-Rhe. *How could the Draca Cats just vanish?*

Kenley didn't have any answers for her. And, it was not just the cats that were missing, Kenley realized. She didn't hear or see any rustling of small animals and even the birds were gone. Something happened here. Something dreadful enough to chase away all of the creatures that made this place their home.

Suddenly, Baya lifted her head and her nostrils flared as she picked up a scent on the wind.

What is it, Baya. What do you smell?

Death.

The Draca sprinted forward and Kenley followed. It wasn't long before she smelled what Baya had already picked up.

Blood.

When Baya skidded to a stop abruptly and yelped in pain, Kenley almost ran into her. Dodging around the Draca, she saw the source of her friend's distress. Dead Draca Cats. Hundreds of them. Their beautiful white coats stained red.

Dear Highworld.

While Baya remained frozen in grief, Kenley crept closer to the grisly scene. It was apparent that a terrible battle occurred here. Animal against animal, she could easily discern from the teeth and claw marks that raked each corpse.

Her hand flew to her mouth when she spotted the body of Moombai. She ran to his side and prodded his thick fur, checking for any signs of life. There were none.

"Who could have done this, Baya?" she moaned aloud.

Draca Cats.

But, why? Why would they kill their Sovereign and all these others?

Finally, Baya stood and padded closer to the carnage. *Power, revenge, jealousy. It could be any or all of the above. The Dracas are not immune to the sins that plague humans.*

Were you aware of any strife?

Baya shook her head. *No, it is not often that I take interest in the affairs of the Draca Cats. This is not my world.*

Kenley continued to walk around the horrific site hoping she would not find the mother of her friend. It would take some time to know for sure if Felice was among the dead, but Baya asked the question anyway.

Is Felice…?

I do not see her.

Baya's snowy head whipped toward the south and a snarl escaped her raised lips. *Be prepared for a fight, Princess.*

Kiernan crouched already weaving a ball of air in her hands. *A fight? Where?*

Baya gestured to the path they had just followed out of the Puu. *Draca Cats poured out of the forest.*

Draca Cats stained with the blood of the pride.

Chapter 7

Baya's Sorrow

At the sight of the bloodstained Draca Cats, Kenley shifted the air and a swirling vortex sprang to life between her and Baya and the threat.

The front row of Draca Cats tumbled backwards from the force of the wind and the others howled and cowered from the dirt and stones kicked up by the churning air. Head lowered against the gusts, a large male fought the strength of the currents to step ahead of the group. *Wait! We mean you no harm!*

Baya snarled. *How can you say that with the blood of our brothers and sisters still upon you?*

Baya! It is me, Muuki. Tell the daughter of Kenley to lower her screen.

Kenley waited until Baya nodded before letting go of the magic. As soon as the winds died down, Baya rounded her shoulders aggressively and stalked toward the Draca Cat.

I have known you a very long time, Muuki, but today I wonder if you stand before me as my friend or my enemy.

Your friend, Baya, and so are all with me. This was not our work. We are the survivors of this massacre.

Tell me what has happened.

Muuki came closer, walking with a slight limp. *It was Nazar.*

A deep rumble rose from Baya's throat. *Nazar has always been too ambitious for his own good, but to kill the Sovereign? To kill so many of our pride? For what purpose, Muuki?*

He desires power for the Draca Cats and has left Callyn-Rhe to seek it in the land of Iserlohn.

Power? Over the humans? Kenley asked in astonishment.

Yes, daughter of Kenley

How?

Through the Kenley bond. Muuki paused as though shamed to continue. *Once the humans have been cowed to his satisfaction, he plans for the Kenleys to be our voice to the slaves.*

Ridiculous! Baya snorted. *What nonsense is this?*

He killed Moombai and has named himself the new Sovereign. He feels that the Draca Cats have not evolved as a race. That we have become too idle through our isolation from the world. He seeks knowledge and power through conquest.

Baya turned to look at all of the dead bodies. *What I do not understand is how he convinced so many to go along with his plans. We are Draca Cats, Muuki! We have an unbreakable bond to protect humans.*

No, our bonded oath is with the Kenleys, not all humans.

Yes, but our ancestors have always regarded the role of the Draca Cats as that of protector. We have always stood side-by-side with humans to battle evil.

Nazar has changed all of that. He wants more and is not afraid to kill to achieve his goals.

Kenley clenched her fists at her sides at the thought of her friends, the Draca Cats, prowling through Massa and killing innocent people indiscriminately. *We have to stop him, Baya. He is on a rampage to terrorize the people of this island and I cannot allow that.*

Of course, we will stop him. Muuki, where do you stand in this? Are you with us?

We are of like mind, sister.

How many are with Nazar?

All except those that stand with me today.

Kenley counted. There had to be less than a hundred cats with Muuki. That meant Nazar led a force of close to one thousand Draca Cats.

What of my mother, Muuki? Baya asked hopefully, stretching her neck to see past him at the band of Draca Cats. *Is she with you? Is Felice among your followers?*

She is not here. I will take you to her.

Not here? But, where—

Silently, Muuki turned from her and the crowd parted as he walked slowly back to the entrance to the rainforest. Baya and Kenley had no choice but to follow behind.

As Kenley walked, she prayed fervently that Felice was alive and well. That a happy reunion with her mother awaited Baya.

But, it was not to be.

Kiernan paled at the sight of a broken Felice curled up against the base of a gigantic Ficus tree. A red stain at her throat told the story of how she had been killed.

Kenley instinctively reached her hands out to Baya, but her friend was already moving away toward Felice, her stride slow and unsteady.

Mother!

Kenley covered her mouth as she watched Baya nudge Felice's shoulder with her nose to try to urge her to stand.

Get up, Mother! I came! I am here, Mother!

Baya pawed frantically at the dirt next to Felice.

Princess! Help me get her up!

Baya...

A high-pitched whine escaped Baya's mouth when the truth she must have already known became too hard to ignore. Her head fell heavily between her shoulders, and she sagged to the ground.

Kenley turned away helplessly when her friend crept closer and laid her head gently across her mother's lifeless form.

❧

Kellan wondered why so many people were gathered in the city square just inside the Northfort gates and then realized by the scattering of nervous conversation that drifted his way that the crowd was there to glimpse sight of the dark-haired strangers that had returned to Massa.

A tense energy infused the throng, but as soon as they spied the shifter royals, a sense of calm seemed to restore the mood.

"Look! The Princes!"

"Thank the Highworld! The Princes are here!"

Startled by the shouts, Kellan straightened his shoulders in the saddle. Never before had he been expected to assuage the fears of the people. All his life, it had been his parents to whom people looked. Even Kenley to some extent when his parents were otherwise occupied, but never him. Now, the citizens of Northfort were taking comfort from *his* presence and plainly believed in his ability to keep them safe. *Am I worthy of their confidence?* For the first time in Kellan's life, he was feeling the weight of his mantle.

Gregor Steele and Haiden Lind took the lead as they passed underneath the thick curtain wall, shouting out at people to step back from the gates. When some had difficulty hearing the orders of the Royal Sabers over the commotion, Maks and Jain leapt into action, and the twin roars of the Draca Cats scattered the milling crowd like leaves in a strong wind.

Kirby leaned in close so Kellan would hear him over the noise. "I will go find the mayor and meet you at the harbor."

Kellan nodded his acknowledgement and watched as Kirby pressed his horse along the cobblestone road that led to the mayor's estate and wharf district beyond. With the Scarlet Sabers and Draca Cats still out front and the Dwarven and Elven protectors behind, Kane, Izzy, and Jala urged their mounts forward to ride next to him for the ride to the docks.

Air thick with the scent of salt and fish battered at him and all around the clatter of activity rippled through the city. People shouted greetings, tradesmen yelled out orders, merchants plied their wares, animals bellowed and wagons rumbled.

Visitors and tourists gaped at sight of the Draca Cats. Kellan noticed giant Cymans walking among the much shorter and darker Damonians. Hiberians in their colorful scarves and billowing silk trousers bartered with native Massans at the multitude of shops and stands that lined the docks.

"Whoa! Whoa!"

A horse drawing a cart on the opposite side of the road suddenly reared in its harness when it caught scent and sight of Maks and Jain. Izzy quickly threw out her hand and the horse immediately settled, blowing out contentedly through its large nostrils.

Kellan gave Izzy an approving nod, and her violet eyes lit up at the praise.

Gregor waved Kellan forward. "We should stable the horses here and continue on foot. There will be too many people in the wharf district marketplace for the horses."

"Do you have a place in mind?"

"I do."

Kellan nodded and followed as Gregor steered them off the main road to a well-kept establishment tucked in along a side street. The strong smells of hay and manure preceded their arrival at what the sign out front proclaimed to be The King's Horses Stable. The harassed looking stable owner appeared as soon as they rode into his yard, waving his hands, and insisting to Gregor that he was full and could not accept any more horses. When the Saber told him who the request was for, the owner's face blanched and he yelled out for his two young grooms. After a bit of juggling in the stalls, room was made available for their mounts and the anxious owner steadfastly refused payment of any kind.

On foot now, Maks drew in close to his side and Kellan ran his fingers through the white fur. Blue eyes, identical to his own, peered up at him.

I know you do not like the crowds, Prince.

No. Most earthshifters do not.

Let us see what these Ellvinians are about then and leave as quickly as we can.

My thoughts exactly.

Kirby Nash, accompanied by Mayor Lars Kingsley and a dozen Iserlohn soldiers, reached them just before the docks. Kellan had met the mayor several times in the past and he seemed to grow a bit wider with every visit, the vest around his ample belly hard pressed to stay buttoned.

Kellan nodded to the mayor in greeting. "Mayor Kingsley."

The man wrung a black hat in his hands nervously as he knelt. "Your Graces. Thank you for coming so quickly."

"Of course. Please rise."

Lars lurched to his feet and began to ramble anxiously. "I didn't know what else to do, Your Grace. I couldn't find any bodyshifters to get word to you faster, so I sent a messenger and then my own son on horse. I have not given permission for the ships to dock, but I have my doubts now that it was the proper thing to do. I—"

Kellan held up a hand. "Mayor Kingsley. As mayor of Northfort, you have received many ships to the island, and I am sure you followed the correct protocol. What has you so anxious about the Ellvinians?"

"I will let you decide for yourself, Your Grace," the mayor said and motioned to their group. He led them down another side street and then back to the main cobblestone road that offered an unobstructed view of the endless blue of the Arounda Ocean. "What do you think, Your Grace?"

Kellan's fist tightened in Maks' fur coat.

Kane slid into place beside him. "I'm thinking that three hundred soldiers are not going to be enough."

As usual, Kellan had to agree. He had expected to see two ships, possibly even three, but it was an entire fleet. At least a dozen, three-masted warships that looked as though they could easily hold one hundred men or more on each. Twelve hundred Ellvinians. Over a thousand strangers of whom Kellan knew very little about. His thoughts naturally ran to the fact that if the Ellvinians were here to cause harm, now would be the perfect opportunity with the *Savitars* off the island.

The mayor scratched his head. "How strange. I seem to remember now inviting the Ellvinians to return to Massa for a visit this week, but cannot for the life of me remember why I would do such a thing."

Curious now to see these mysterious visitors for himself, Kellan crossed the street and walked up onto the same platform where he stood and saw his parents off less than a week ago.

The ships waited several hundred yards off shore waiting for a signal from the Massans for permission to come ashore. Kellan glanced at the large nautical flag still in its holder on the piling next to him and paused. But, why? His parents were at this moment on their way to the island of Ellvin. An ambassador for the Ellvinians had already been received with positive response, and the mayor himself admitted to inviting the Ellvinians back for this visit. So, why was he hesitating? There was nothing in the actions of the Ellvinians to assume they in any way had ill intentions.

There were just too many of them, Kellan decided, and he could not shake the notion that if waved that flag, he would be inviting an enemy into their midst.

His fingers twitched toward the flag and he wrapped his hand around the pole. Then, a sudden swirling motion under the docks startled him, and he sprang back in alarm as a wall of water arose out of the ocean between the ships and Massa. Twelve heads popped out of the sea with their arms lifted toward the sky as they danced on the waves.

The watershifters had arrived.

A young woman wearing a form-fitting water suit, emerged from the ocean to stand on the extended portion of the dock. Kellan recognized her as Digby's daughter, Alia.

She faced out toward sea and lifted her arms. With fluid movement, her hands and body undulated as she directed the watershifters in a synchronized display of shifting. The wall of water fell back to the ocean and twin colossal pillars shot into the air and bent into graceful arcs. Ropes of smaller streams of water gushed from the sea and twisted and coiled around the pillars, swirling together like living things. Kellan did not know if Alia planned it or not, but when the sunlight hit the moving droplets of water just right, a refracted prism of color burst into existence above the arc. The bystanders on the harbor cheered in delight at the sudden appearance of the enormous rainbow.

The strength of the raw power surging through the water was staggering, and Kellan wondered what the Ellvinians thought of the intimidating spectacle. All he knew was that he was in speechless awe. It was not often that he had the chance to see the watershifters use their abilities, and he was hugely impressed at their skill. It also put his mind at rest. If the Ellvinians had any preconceived notion of doing harm to the people of Massa, the threat in that demonstration was abundantly clear. They did not stand a chance.

Alia dropped her hands and the water pillars splashed down.

The watershifters plunged out of the water once again, created a defensive line, and faced the ships, their bodies raised out of the water to their knees.

Alia turned, hurried to Kellan's side and knelt. "You summoned us, Your Grace?"

"Please rise, Alia." When she did, he took her in his arms and hugged her. "You cannot know how good it is to see you."

She stepped back and smiled. "You as well, Prince Kellan."

He pointed to the ships. "As you can see, we have visitors. I would like you to send the watershifters to the ships and grant permission for six Ellvinians to come ashore. The rest can remain at sea until we determine their purpose for being here."

She bowed her head. "As you wish, Your Grace."

Chapter 8

Birthrights

All was deathly quiet within the Puu Rainforest as thousands of amber eyes viewed the strange activity of the Elves. *Look at their caves, Nazar! How do they make them? I have never seen the like.*

I see, Rehka.

And, the stars! How do they cast the stars from the sky to twinkle in the trees? She paused. *I think they must not be stars at all, but magic.*

Yes, magic, Rehka! Are we not creatures of magic by our very existence alone? Do other creatures of our kind have the intelligence we possess?

Of course not.

No, and our magic is what allows us to see the stars in the trees.

When Rehka fell silent, Nazar thought on his words. He only half-believed them himself. He was not certain how the Elves used their magic and that was the very reason for this uprising. Knowledge. It was time for the Draca Cats to better understand the world in which they lived, and time for them to take their rightful place in that world. First, they would need the assistance of the Kenleys, and in order to do that, they must convince their Draca bondmates.

What do we do now, Nazar? Rehka was the one to ask, but he could feel the same question on every mind behind him.

He gazed again at the swarm of industrious Elves going about their peculiar tasks and wondered at the strength of resistance they would present. Nazar lifted one corner of his lip. There was only one way to find out. His destiny lay in the land of Men somewhere to the west and to get there, he had to first travel through the land of Elves.

Now is the time, Dracas! Follow close behind! If we must fight our way past, then that is what we will do!

The importance of the moment was not lost on Nazar. For the first time in centuries, he was leading the Draca Cats out of seclusion and into civilization among the other races.

He started forward, head held high.

The first Elves that caught sight of the procession of Draca Cats stopped what they were doing and stared.

Nazar let out an aggressive roar and waited for the most dominant of the Elves to challenge him. Instead, the Elves dropped to one knee and lowered their heads in a submissive stance very well known to him. *What is this?* he demanded of no cat in particular.

Cautiously, Nazar continued to lead the way, wary of a surprise attack, but it never came. Instead, he watched as one by one, the Elves bowed down to him and his followers.

Nazar, look!

Nazar turned. In the center of the path up ahead, stood a stone image of a Draca Cat. Proud and elegant and fierce.

He had been right.

In this very moment, he knew without a trace of misgiving that his act of violence against Moombai had been justified. The stone reproduction proved that the Draca Cats of Callyn-Rhe held a place of honor among the Massans and this is where they belonged, out among their subjects.

Nazar nodded majestically to the Elves he passed, accepting the due of his birthright. All was as it should be.

Do not harm the Elves! They know the truth of it. They are our disciples! Let us now go to the land of Men. We shall see if they also know the truth. If they do not, we must teach them.

꧂

"Careful now, you bumbling idiots!" Hendrix shouted from inside the closed palanquin. "For Netherworld's sake, you are not carrying a pig to slaughter!"

In response, the fighters adjusted the long wooden poles on their shoulders and the ride smoothed out once again. Hendrix leaned back on the cushioned bed, brought the draught to his lips, and took a long pull of the life-sustaining liquid. He peered outside through the diaphanous curtains at the long lines of people waiting at the infirmaries for their daily ration of wormwood. Many of those in line would be turned away empty handed. If their name was not on a list, there would be no draught for them today. And, it was not just the poor any longer who were in dire need of the elixir. Hendrix also noticed several affluent merchants in line. It was an unavoidable fact. As the supplies diminished, the lists shortened, no matter how much money you had to spend. The system of bribery that the wealthy depended on—and notoriously circulated more coin than any legitimate commerce on the island—had dried up along with the wormwood.

Most of the Ellvinians ignored the convoy of fighters that carried him or, worse, shook their fists his way. They blamed him for not being able to reverse the failing health of the people, but he recalled a time not too long ago when his presence elicited loving gazes and shouts of adoration. Now, he was met with openly hostile looks as the people on the street glared at him through eyes bleak from wormwood deficiency and cold from hatred. They could tell by looking at him that he did not suffer their same fate. But, why should he? He was the Premier!

Very soon, he would be their beloved champion once again. First, though, he needed to inform the Seconds. Chandal of the Shiprunners and Samara of the Eyereaders were actively carrying out his plans in Massa, and Emile of the Battlearms, of course, was at his side. That left Jarl of the Ironfingers, Balder of the Sagehands, and Anah of the Coinholders. The wormwood they would welcome with open arms, but what would they decide about the blood?

The bearers came to a stop and lowered him to the ground. Hendrix set his empty cup on a shelf and adjusted his tongor.

Emile peeled back the curtain. "We have arrived at the Consulate, Your Eminence."

"Very well." Hendrix accepted the Battlearm's outstretched hand, stepped out of the palanquin, and hurried up the stairs and through the doors of the Consulate before the people were of the mind to start hurtling objects his way. It had happened once, and he did not wish a repeat of that humiliating incident.

The fighters at the doors stood motionless as he passed them, their blank expressions giving away nothing.

Hendrix blinked in the dim interior of the Consulate and smiled inwardly when he saw the Seconds already waiting and seated on cushions under the domed ceiling of the circular room. His Adjunct rushed forward and guided him to his seat, and he lowered himself onto his pillow. Crossing his legs, he accepted the Chero pipe handed to him and inhaled deeply of the cannabis smoke before passing the pipe to Emile who sat down on the pillow to his right. It did not escape Hendrix's notice that Emile passed the pipe to Balder without imbibing.

Hendrix smiled at his Seconds. "Good afternoon. Thank you for gathering with such short notice, but I think you will agree that what I have to say could not wait until our regular session meeting."

Balder passed the pipe to Anah and sat up straighter on his pillow. His eyes were already glassy from the cannabis. "You have us waiting with bated breath, Your Eminence."

Anah chuckled.

Fools. I am surrounded by downright bloody fools.

"Before we start, Your Eminence," Jarl began, "I must bring up a matter of importance to my caste."

"Of course, Jarl, the floor is yours."

"It's about the missing boy. His distraught parents, and many others I might add, are still demanding answers."

Hendrix leaned back on his pillow. "What can I do to help, Jarl?"

The Ironfinger lifted his chin and narrowed his gaze. "You can start by telling me where he is."

"Jarl, why would—"

"The boy was last seen entering your compound, Your Eminence. I need to know what to tell his parents."

Before Hendrix could reply, his Adjunct scurried over. "I can explain, Second Jarl. The boy did come to the compound to deliver a message, but he met an unfortunate end when he fell down three flights of stairs. It is with the utmost regret that I must inform you that the poor boy broke his neck." The Adjunct gave a very convincing rueful shake of his head. "Such a shame. I should have come forward immediately but other matters have kept me quite occupied."

Jarl eyed the Adjunct suspiciously. "Is that so?"

Hendrix held up a hand. "Thank you, Adjunct, for your honesty in coming forward. Nevertheless, you will be punished for waiting so long to report this incident and causing anxiety to the Ironfingers."

The Adjunct pushed his spectacles up on his nose and bowed. "Of course, Your Eminence. I deserve no less."

"I think ten lashes is a suitable—"

"Thirty," Jarl interrupted.

The Adjunct swallowed.

"Thirty lashes is quite severe, Jarl," Hendrix tried to argue.

"A boy is dead, Your Eminence. At *your* compound."

Maybe this one is not as big of a fool as the others.

Hendrix looked his Second in the eye and then nodded in agreement. "Aye, thirty it is."

The Adjunct gave a last shaky bow and left to resume his place in the shadows of the room.

"Do we have any other matters to discuss?" Hendrix asked impatiently.

When the Seconds shook their heads, he decided to get right to the point. "I have the most remarkable news to share. An abundant source of wormwood has been located. Hundreds of plants are being shipped to Ellvin as we speak."

Balder choked on the pipe smoke. "What? The rumors are true? I have been hearing stories for days now, but I brushed them aside as wishful thinking!"

"Aye, Balder, they are true."

Anah, the only female in the room, reached for the pipe and took another pull. "Your Eminence," she breathed through the exhaled smoke curling around her face. "This is such wonderful news."

Hendrix shook his head at the feigned interest. He knew Anah and the others cared little for their fellow countrymen. Born into privileged families, none of them had ever had to work a day in their lives. They did not know what it was like to go without the draught. They were spoiled ninnies who cared only about their next pleasure-inducing endeavor and that weakness was exactly what he was counting on.

"Aye, Anah, it is the best news we could have hoped for. Soon, we will have enough wormwood to restore the entire nation to good health."

"Where is this source, Your Eminence?" Jarl questioned.

"Chandal discovered an island where the wormwood is plentiful and the inhabitants are more than happy to share what they have with us. From the new plants that are delivered, we will be able to begin harvesting once again."

"What about the Titsu bug that destroyed almost all of our wormwood crops?" Balder asked.

Does this idiot ever listen to what is discussed in these sessions?

"As you should very well know, Balder, a repellent has been developed to treat the wormwood. With proper care of the plants, we should never find ourselves in this predicament again."

"Oh," Balder said, around another mouthful of smoke.

"There is more," he said and paused. "This island that Chandal discovered is also a harborer of magic."

There, let them stew on that little morsel. Every hazy eye in the room turned toward him. He had their attention now.

"Magic? It is very interesting, but why should that concern us?" Jarl asked, knowing full well why that should concern any Ellvinian.

"The blood, Jarl! The blood." Surely, even these nits could figure out his meaning.

The pipe was put aside. "But, how would we do it?"

"The Vypir."

Balder's eyebrows rose in surprise. "I thought that thing was long dead!"

"Oh, no, Balder. The Vypir is still very much with us and secured in his room in the bowels of this very building."

Jarl stood slowly from his pillow. They had danced around the issue long enough. It was time. "What you are suggesting is murder, Your Eminence."

Hendrix stood as well. "We are Ellvinians, Jarl! We have always had the blood!"

"Oh, come now! It has been centuries since we have had the blood!"

"Not for lack of trying!" He grabbed Jarl's arm. "Think on it, Jarl! Why would you exist on water when you can have wine? Why would you dine from the midden heap when you can have fresh food?"

"Aye, I say!" Balder enthused groggily and lifted his goblet in the air.

"Aye!" Anah chimed in.

Hendrix ignored them. It was Jarl he had to convince. "It is our birthright, Jarl. It is what our bodies require."

"Desire, *not* require."

Hendrix decided to ignore the distinction. "We must make a unanimous decision right here, right now. Magic users are on their way here to the island. Will we reprise the age-old practice of our ancestors? Will our veins once again sing with magic?"

"The blood!" Balder yelled out once again.

Hendrix looked into Jarl's eyes. "What say you, Jarl? We will need to work together to perform the extractions and subsequent disposals. The public will never know."

"They will be so content with the wormwood that I doubt they will care very much about anything else," Anah cackled selfishly.

All waited in silence for Jarl to make his decision. It would not work unless all of the Seconds were in agreement.

Finally, the Ironfinger nodded. "I am Ellvinian. I shall have the blood."

Chapter 9

Dangerous Waters

Chandal pulled the rangefinder from his eye. "Impressive. I wonder if all the Massan magic users are able to move water." When the stunning Eyereader standing beside him did not respond, he glanced at her.

She drew in a deep breath and her eyes rolled into the back of her head. "I can smell them," she murmured.

"Aye," Chandal agreed. He could smell them as well and the scent was intoxicating. "They think to intimidate us with that display."

"No matter, my friend. In the end, we will get what we want from the Massans," she answered confidently.

"We must gain their trust first."

Samara looked at him as if he said the sky was blue. "But, of course. A child knows that first rule of Ascendency."

Color crept into his cheeks. "I meant to say that the Shiprunners can be reckless at times. They are not always known for their subtlety. With the scent so heavy in the air, they will have to be reminded of their duty to prevent them from being overwhelmed with personal desire."

"Are you not the leader of the Shiprunners, Chandal? See that it is done."

Again, she managed to put him in his place. He was a Second, he reminded himself, just as she. In an attempt to cover his feelings of inferiority, he lifted the rangefinder to his eye again. "Shall we...? Wait! The Massans in the water are approaching."

"If your implantation worked the last time you were here, they will be coming with an invitation to come ashore."

"It worked," he replied with certainty. "That mayor of theirs was very susceptible." He watched the water people come closer and it looked as though they were walking on top of the water. "Shall we take them?" he asked, unable to hide the excitement that tinged his voice. He had never had the blood. No living person on Ellvin had ever had the blood, but the stories of its lure had been passed down for generations.

The Shiprunners on board thought their mission here to bring back wormwood plants. They didn't know what the Seconds knew. That the Premier's foremost goal was to kidnap Massans so the Vypir could steal their blood.

The Premier promised Chandal and the other Seconds a new life—a life sustained by magical blood. *Invigorating beyond anything you have ever dreamed of,* the Premier assured him. Now, with the Massans approaching and the addicting aroma growing stronger, he now understood that what the Premier promised was possible.

He heard the eager murmurs behind him, but there was nothing any of them could do to satiate their hunger. Only the Vypir could extract the magic in the blood.

He looked at Samara who was still apparently considering his question. He knew what she was thinking. It would be risky to take so many at one time. Discretion was paramount to their success if they wanted to keep the supply lines of wormwood and blood operating for a very long time. But, she finally nodded. "Aye. We cannot allow this unexpected opportunity to slip through our fingers. Ready the longboat to bring the Massans on board and have twelve Shiprunners ready to control them."

Chandal called out the orders. Immediately, his men hastened to their tasks and a narrow wooden boat was lowered to the sea below.

Samara held out a hand in greeting to the magic users in the water. "Greetings, Massans!"

"Greetings!" replied one of the men. He noticed the boat being lowered. "Do not bother with that. We will not be boarding. Prince Kellan has granted permission for six Ellvinians to come to shore. The rest will remain at sea until further notice!"

Samara locked her eyes on the man. "Thank you for coming out to personally relay the message of your Prince!"

The man nodded respectfully.

"Your water skills are incredible!" she gushed, and even from the distance that separated them, she could see him warming to her compliment. "Please come aboard so we can discuss without shouting to one another!"

"I really must refuse."

"What is your name?"

"Pauli."

"Pauli, you wish to come aboard, don't you?"

He tilted his head. "Why, yes...yes, I do wish to come aboard."

"It is your deepest desire to talk with me, Pauli."

The man nodded woodenly. "Yes, I would like to talk with you."

A female magic user drifted closer to the man. "Pauli! No." She looked up at Samara. "Forgive us, but it is impossible. You may fill your longboat with six people and we will escort you to the harbor."

Samara's laugh echoed over the open water, and she pushed powerfully at their minds. "I am afraid I must insist! You want nothing more than to come aboard this ship! It is your deepest desire to talk with me!"

The female magic user nodded. "Very well, we will come aboard." She looked to the others and motioned them into the boat. Pauli was the first in.

Some of the magic users didn't bother with the boat and instead streams of water carried them over the rail and onto the deck.

Samara clapped her hands in delight. She turned to Chandal and hissed. "Secure them."

He gave a nod and the Shiprunners moved in a circle around the magic users. One by one, their heads popped up and they nodded in agreement at the potent words of suggestion.

"Put them in the hold," Chandal ordered. "As soon as darkness descends, take them to Ellvin."

Samara smiled approvingly and threaded her arm through his. "Are you ready for our debut, Second Chandal?"

⁂

Under the skilled assistance of the harbor stevedores, the Ellvin long boat hauled in its oars and slid smoothly in between the other vessels moored at the docks. A coil of rope was tossed to the pier and tied to the thick pilings at the end of the extended dock.

"Will that be all, Prince Kellan?"

Kellan was so busy watching the boat of Ellvinians arrive that he forgot that Alia was still standing next to him.

"Yes, Alia. Thank you." He looked back out to sea to wave his appreciation to the watershifters, but they were no longer in the water. "I guess the watershifters must have returned to Aquataine. Please thank them for me. I am very grateful for their aid and yours as well."

"You are most welcome," she replied before bending into a deep curtsy for both him and Kane who, in that odd habit of his, suddenly materialized at his side.

After Alia slipped back into the water, Kellan returned his attention to the Ellvinians. Lars Kingsley had already provided a description of the dark Elves, but seeing them in the flesh was a different matter. Tall and thin, the man and woman who approached appeared to glide through the air, their feet barely touching the wooden pier. They both wore white flowing garments, belted at the middle and pinned at the shoulders with broaches. Long, black hair hung in silken strands down their backs.

The woman bowed down at the waist and steepled her hands together in front of her. "Good day, Massan." As soon as the words left her mouth, Kellan froze. That voice! That lovely, captivating voice! Each word a soothing song that filtered through his mind and erased every fear he ever had. The world faded around him, and he only had eyes for the woman standing before him, his deepest wish that she keep speaking and never stop.

Smiling at his obvious distress, she continued her calming lexis. "I am Samara and this," she gestured toward the man with her, "is our Ship Captain, Chandal."

When Kellan still did not respond, he felt a hard shove from behind and Kirby Nash shouldered through him.

"Welcome to Massa, Lady Samara, Master Chandal. I am Captain Kirby Nash of the Iserlohn Royal Guard." He put his hand on Kellan's shoulder. "This mute is Prince Kellan Atlan and standing next to him are Prince Kane Atlan, Kali Jala Radek of Deepstone and Lady Izabel Falewir of Haventhal."

Samara and Chandal both bowed at the waist again.

"If I may be so bold as to inquire as to your purpose here, my lady?" Kirby asked.

She looked into Kirby's eyes. "Why we were invited by the esteemed mayor of Northfort, Captain Nash. Surely, you wish to welcome us here?"

"Of course, my lady," Kirby quickly assured her and bowed over her hand.

"You do wish to make our visit very comfortable, aye?"

"Yes, my lady! But, I will admit that the number of ships has us—"

"The number of ships is of no concern. We are your friends, Captain Nash."

"Yes, the Ellvinians are our friends," Kirby repeated with a brainless grin very out of character for the Royal Saber. Even stranger was the fact that Kellan knew he wore one to match.

"We would be grateful for rooms after our long journey."

"Rooms!" Kirby shouted. "Lars! Lars Kingsley! We will need rooms for our guests!"

Lady Samara smiled at Kirby. "It would make us feel most welcome if we were to stay at the mayor's estate instead of an inn. Chandal stayed with the mayor during his last visit, and after his glorious recommendation, I absolutely must see it for myself."

"Lars!"

Kellan came out of his trance enough to hear Kane mumble something about love struck idiots, but he ignored him. He didn't want to be distracted from hearing Samara's next words.

Lars Kingsley bustled through to the forefront. "Chandal, welcome back, my friend!"

Chandal greeted the mayor in the same singsong voice and repeated Lady Samara's request for rooms at his estate. He explained that the Ellvinian sailors would remain on the ships at sea for their visit, but he would like rooms for the dozen or so in their personal entourage.

"Of course," the mayor exclaimed a little too loudly. "Follow me and I will show you the way."

Kellan watched the departing party with a beaming smile, but cursed when Kane yanked him around by grabbing a fistful of shirt at his shoulder. His brother's golden eyes were ablaze. "What is wrong with you?"

"Stop that," Kellan roared and shoved him away. The effort cleared his tangled thoughts and he ran a hand down his face. "That was peculiar."

"Clearly."

"Did you hear her voice?" Kellan asked his twin. "It was pure magic."

"Her voice was normal to me. Nothing out of the ordinary."

"Izzy? Jala?" Kellan asked.

"I heard it," said Jala. "You are right, Kellan. It was beautiful."

"As did I," Izzy answered.

"Trust me," Kane advised through tight lips, "there is something off about these people and that's not good since a whole lot more of them are coming this way."

Chapter 10

The New Order

Kenley plopped down on a old log lying on the side of the trail and took a long drink of water from the skin around her shoulder. Baya appeared a moment later, padding listlessly along the path, her head hanging low. It broke Kenley's heart to see her friend in so much pain.

Baya looked up and, noticing Kenley waiting for her, simply laid down with a whimper.

Kenley had thought to give Baya time alone to grieve, but she could no longer hold back. She crossed the distance between them and hugged Baya around her neck.

I am sorry, my friend.

It is all just so senseless. Why did she have to die? Why did all the others have to die?

I know. I wish there was more I could do to ease your hurt.

Baya lifted her head and a large tear dripped from one green eye. In all their years together, Kenley had never once seen Baya cry, and that single tear spoke volumes about the tremendous pain she was in. *Even though I did not see my mother as often as she would have liked, we were very close.*

I know.

I never realized how irreplaceable a mother's love is. Now that it is gone, I am terrified. I feel so alone and unsheltered. Is that silly at my age?

No! Of course not. Kenley swallowed back tears of her own when she thought of how devastated she would be to lose her mother. Her confidence, her strength, her sense of well-being, were all gifts from her mother, and Kenley only had to look into the eyes of Kiernan Atlan to know just how much she was loved and cherished. She vowed never to take that relationship for granted ever again. *I know I can never replace what you shared with Felice, but you have shelter with me, Baya, always and forever.*

Kenley buried her head in Baya's soft white fur and held her friend tightly. They remained locked together in silent solace for a very long time.

When, a shadow passed over Kenley, she looked up. It was Muuki.

We should be going, daughter of Kenley.

He was right. After almost two days of trailing the renegade Draca Cats, they were very close to finding them and could not afford to delay. For reasons Kenley did not understand, the Draca Cats went directly through the busy Elven capital of Sarphia instead of taking a more circuitous route. Mercifully, the cats did not harm any of the citizens, but simply passed through and headed west. To find their oath holders, she knew. The Kenleys. According to Muuki, Nazar needed her family to be his voice of rule.

Kenley let go of Baya and searched for the words that would convince her to carry on, but the Draca Cat lurched to her feet without prodding.

Their journey resumed and the day continued wet and humid. Kenley's shirt was soaked through to her skin and her feet ached from the hours of walking. Her legs, covered with mud up to her knees, began to shake from the exertion and she longed for rest, but knew they did not have the luxury of time. Not when they were so close.

Around a sharp bend on the Elven made path, Kenley pulled up short when she smelled a sharp, pungent odor.

Baya! What is that scent?

Fresh blood.

Again?

Her eyes swept the rainforest for any hint of a predator, and then Kenley saw them up ahead on the trail.

Dead Moshies.

The Draca Cats have been through here, Baya said. *They left the Elves alone, but the Moshies were not so fortunate. I cannot say I am saddened by their deaths.*

Kenley cringed. The blood feud between the ape people and the Draca Cats was not something she understood well, only well enough to know that there was nothing she could do to change it. Bitter animosity on both sides had kept the hostility brewing between the two races for many long years.

The band of Moshies lay scattered and broken across the rainforest floor. Kenley looked down at the humanoid face of one Moshie as she passed. She had never seen one of the fabled creatures before, but knew they existed from the stories her father told her as a child. When he spoke of them, it was always with a fond smile for their prankster antics and close tribal ties. The Moshies were childhood monsters for most Iserlohn children, but for Kenley and her brothers, they seemed more like long-lost friends.

It saddened her to see the brutal scene, but she also knew it was just as likely that the Moshies initiated this fight instead of the Draca Cats.

The Illian River is not far from here, she told Muuki.

If there is a river ahead, the Dracas will most likely stop to drink and rest. If they do, we will be able to catch up to them there.

They never discussed what they would do when they found Nazar and his followers, but Kenley would allow Baya to take the lead. This was her fight.

It took another four hours of hard travel to reach the Illian and discover that Muuki had been right. The Draca Cats were spread out along the river and...waiting. *Waiting for what?* Did they know that they were being tracked?

A male Draca Cat with a fresh scar across his muzzle stepped forward as Kenley, Baya and their much smaller group emerged from the Puu.

I expected Muuki and the others, but I must say that I am very surprised to see you, Baya. He nodded toward her. *And, you, daughter of Kenley.*

Kenley did not remember ever meeting this Draca Cat before, but he obviously knew her from her previous visits to Callyn-Rhe.

Murderer! Baya roared. *I name you a murderer, Nazar!*

Nazar did not back down and answered her roar. *If that is what you wish to call it! I killed my jailers, yes! I did not want to kill them and tried peaceful ways for many years, but Moombai clung to the old ways. He was not a good leader for the Draca Cats.*

And, Felice, Nazar? What did my mother do to deserve her death?

The big cat seemed genuinely remorseful. *Felice was an unfortunate victim. Her eyes were closed to the truth, and because of her position within the pride, she could have raised others against me.*

Baya crept closer. *In this new order of yours, do all who oppose the mighty Nazar die?*

Nazar's amber eyes narrowed dangerously. *We cannot afford dissention.*

So, your answer is yes. Let all hear of your tyrannical plans!

Baya! It saddened me to sacrifice the blood of my brothers and sisters in Callyn-Rhe, but they would not listen! We must grow and learn! Become better, stronger, smarter! Why can't you see that?

Kenley watched anxiously as the two cats circled each other.

You say that you wish to rule the humans, Nazar, but what do you know of their world? Can you fight against the magic they command? Can you use the tools they use? Can you sail their ships? Can you speak their language?

Nazar shook his head and growled. *The first humans were naught but animals! Savages! The difference is their leaders strove for advancements while ours embraced complacency. In our idleness, the humans shaped the world according to their strengths! Why cannot we now shape the world to our strengths? We are not mindless creatures, Baya! We have the same ability to make this world over into our image as the human ancestors of old did!*

Baya snapped her teeth toward the Nazar. *You are a fool! All of you! The Draca Cats fought alongside the humans against a tyrant twenty years ago.* Now, you will try to resurrect his evil ways?

Tell me! In the past twenty years, have the Draca Cats evolved? Is anything different today than twenty years ago? One hundred years ago? The answer is, no!

Both cats stopped pacing and faced each other. *Domination is not the way, Nazar.*

It is a start.

I cannot stand by.

I am sorry you feel that way, sister, but I will not shed any more Draca blood. We will go our separate ways.

No.

The watching Dracas whimpered nervously.

Are you challenging me?

I am.

Come closer then, my sister. I am here!

Baya sprang toward Nazar.

Baya, no! Kenley shouted and sprinted forward with the intention of stopping Baya from a deadly fight, but her friend suddenly disappeared into the ground. Kenley tried to skid to a stop, but she couldn't stop her momentum and found herself falling through the air after Baya. She shifted and a cradle of air caught her before she would have slammed into the bottom of a deep pit. Staggering to her feet, she looked up in time to see a heavy grate slam into place over the hole.

Kenley flew upward and grasped the iron bars. With a scream, she tried to move the grate, but it wouldn't budge.

Nazar's face peered down at her. *Who says we cannot use the tools of humans?* the big cat snarled. *This grate will hold you nicely until we return.*

Nazar! What have you done?

My oath prevents me from harming you, daughter of Kenley, so I will be back to release you once we have made our demands known to the sons of Kenley in the place you call Bardot. Try not to think too poorly of me.

"No! Leave my brothers alone!" Kenley yelled. "Muuki! Help us!"

Muuki's head replaced Nazar's at the grate.

I am sorry, daughter of Kenley, but Nazar has convinced me. The old ways truly are gone. It is time for a new order.

❦

Samara flung open the windows in her guest chambers and breathed in deeply. Ah, yes, seawater, roasting chestnuts from the vendor in the courtyard below her room, and...magic. Her body involuntarily shuddered at the seductive haze washing over her.

The Premier had not exaggerated in his descriptions of the addicting scent. Could she continue to exist solely on the draught now that the promised ecstasy of the blood danced tantalizingly over her senses? She could taste it, feel it, touch it, and the anticipation was torturous.

She pushed away from the window with a frown. She was beginning to regret her hasty decision to take the water people yesterday. Surely, they would be missed and it would cast the Ellvinians under a heavy cloud of suspicion, something she was ordered to avoid at all costs.

The Premier's commands were simple. Assimilate into the society, take up residence, obtain employment. Then, in a discrete manner, capture and return to Ellvin a manageable supply of magic users. It was the only way to ensure the

Ellvinians a continual source of the blood with the Massans none the wiser.

She rubbed her arms. *Did I make a fatal mistake?*

If so, the Massans would rise up against them and their first font of blood in remembered history would dry up, and she would not survive the return voyage home. Chandal would see to that.

Wine. I need wine. She walked over to pour herself a glass of spiced wine and downed the liquid with one swallow. What was done was done. It was time to concentrate on finding out more about these Massans.

One thing was quite certain—their vulnerability to Ascendency was strong. She needed very little skill to exert her power of suggestion over them. Unfortunately, that meant that the Shiprunners would also have no trouble as well. Most of the sailors were still among the ships at sea, but several hundred were now in the port city. It could ruin everything if Chandal did not heed her warning and take the steps necessary to control the actions of his caste.

Her own work would start tonight. She convinced the mayor to arrange a gala in her honor this evening. There she would seek out the Prince with the blue eyes that greeted her at the harbor. Once she had him under her influence, he would be only too willing to tell her all about the political structure, military capabilities and magical skill of the island of Massa. Aye, once she had the Prince in her grasp, that young man would tell her everything she wished to know, and more.

Chapter 11

The Mayor's Gala

Kellan pulled on the mayor's borrowed coat and adjusted the sleeves. It was snug in the shoulders, but would have to do. It was all he had.

He walked to the full-length mirror in the small chamber room and grinned. Tonight, he would see her again. He had not seen the Ellvinian woman since yesterday and whenever he thought about meeting up with her at the mayor's gala tonight, his stomach clenched. He would ask her to dance as soon as dinner was over, he promised himself, and the image in his mind of her pressed up close to his body caused him to shudder.

Idiot! What was he thinking? He had never even kissed a girl and yet here he was having bold thoughts about a woman to whom he had barely spoken. If he didn't know better, he could almost believe that the woman cast a spell over him. His father once told him that he had been the victim of a Glamour Spell and wondered briefly if Samara could be a sorceress. It would explain why he heard such poetry from her red lips while Kane heard nothing of the sort.

Maks interrupted his thoughts when he produced a loud yawn from the corner of the room, blue eyes peering at him through half-lidded eyes.

Kellan walked to the window to look out into the courtyard in front of the mayor's estate. Below, livered servants hurried in all directions, presumably preparing for the gala. He glanced beyond the courtyard and toward the merchant's district. Usually, the streets were congested with pedestrians exploring the wares for sale or waiting for a ship to return with loved ones, but it was curiously quiet this evening.

He was about to turn back into the room when his eyes drifted further north to the harbor, and he sucked in a surprised breath. All of the Ellvinian ships were moored at the harbor! All twelve!

What is going on here? He remembered giving the visitors permission for six...or maybe it was a dozen, people to come ashore. So, why were all of their ships in port? No, not all. He counted again. Eleven ships were docked, but he was sure there had been twelve yesterday. Where had the other gone? Back to Ellvin? On another wormwood seeking mission?

The same foreboding he felt on the return journey to Northfort resurfaced and lodged in his throat. So much so that the soft knock that sounded on his chamber door twisted him around in a panic. The floor trembled at his feet with the burgeoning magic that instinctively flared to life.

Maks jumped to his feet. *What is it, Prince?*

Kellan wiped a hand down his face to calm his emotions. *I am not sure, Maks, but be ready. We may have trouble on our hands.*

I've been bred for battle. I am always ready for trouble. An excited growl escaped his throat. *And, I don't get nearly enough for my liking.*

Kellan walked to the closed door. "Gregor?"

"Yes, Your Grace. You have guests."

Kellan slowly opened the door. Kane, Jala and Izzy stood just beyond his guard in the finest clothes that could be procured for them.

"Thank you, Gregor." The three children filed in, leaving their own guards outside with Gregor. Jain made his way over to Maks, and Kellan could hear them having a conversation but tuned it out. Instead, he turned to the expectant faces of his brother and friends. Was he being paranoid? He once again caught a glimpse out the window of the tips of the Ellvinian masts. No. He was not. "I want us to stick together tonight," he told them. "Keep an eye on the Ellvinians and let me know if anything out of the ordinary happens."

"You mean like everyone bowing and scraping to them, their entire fleet now moored at our doorstep, and Kirby Nash turning back the three hundred soldiers he ordered to Northfort? That out of the ordinary?" Kane asked.

"What?" Kellan shouted. "He turned them back?"

Kane went to the window and looked out. "Not only that, there is not a single Iserlohn soldier left in Northfort."

"What? That's impossible, Kane!"

"Unfortunately, no."

"What are we going to do?" Jala asked.

Kellan looked down at the two girls and an overwhelming desire to protect them coursed through his body. Even though Jala was older than him by three years, the dominance of his earthshifting made him a natural born leader and it was purely instinctual for him to take control.

He took Jala's hands in his. "Do not let Izzy out of your sight tonight." He squeezed tightly. "Promise me that."

"I promise."

Despite the age difference, the two girls were the same height and they looped their arms together.

Kane turned from the window. "Galas are not for me. I'm going to go to the waterfront to see what I can find out. You would be surprised by what can be learned by hanging about in the right shadows."

"Take Haiden," Kellan said.

He shook his head. "No, but I will take Jain."

Kellan wasn't entirely sure if he liked the idea of his brother out there alone, but had no other choice. Kane was old enough to make his own decisions. "All right, but take care, brother."

Kane nodded and slipped out of the door with Jain.

Kellan held his elbows out to Jala and Izzy. "I guess it's up to us, then. If you will have me, I would be honored to escort you lovely ladies to the mayor's gala."

The girls took his arms and they exited the room out into the large balconied hallway. As the ranking authority in Northfort, Lars Kingsley's estate was the largest in the waterfront city and included at least thirty guest chambers, a formal ballroom and servant quarters that were home to over a hundred people.

Kellan glanced over the railing at the antechamber below and skipped a step in horror. He had seen the ships, but the sight of the party below spilling over with Ellvinians made his mouth go dry.

Chandal and Samara requested rooms for a small personal retinue, but there had to be several hundred Ellvinians downstairs at the gala.

"Demon's breath," Jala swore, and at that moment, Kellan had never felt so afraid, so young, and so ill equipped to handle a situation. Intuitively, he knew the island was in danger, but his feelings were at odd with the smiles and laughs of the Massans interspersed among the Ellvinians. Kirby Nash, speaking to an Ellvinian male, waved up at him with a broad smile on his face. Kirby was Captain of the Royal Guard. Diligent, mistrustful, and guarded were just a few of the words he could use to describe the Saber, so if Kirby was smiling and at ease, why did Kellan still feel such an overriding sense of doom?

"Remember what I said," he told Jala. "Stay together and do not let Izzy out of your sight."

Jala nodded and they descended the stairs as their names were announced to the crowd.

Colorful garland and twinkling candlelight decorated the antechamber and ballroom beyond. The smells of roasting venison and sweet pies drifted enticingly through the room causing Kellan to realize just how long it had been since he had last eaten. The strains of a buoyant lilt from a pan flute accompanied the soulful timbre of a minstrel as he sang of love and romance, and Kellan wondered when the mayor's servants had time to put together such a lavish fete.

He clutched Jala and Izzy a bit closer as he stepped off the stairs and navigated the crowd, anxious now to find Kirby and find out why he turned back the Iserlohn soldiers.

Every time he thought he spotted the blond curls among the sea of black, an Ellvinian stepped in his way to block his path forward and he lost sight of the Saber Captain. Kellan growled in frustration when another tall guest appeared out of nowhere. "Good evening, Prince," the dark Elf greeted and leaned in close to Kellan.

Kellan automatically moved back. As a Prince, he wasn't used to people being this close to his person. "Good evening," he replied uneasily.

The Ellvinian walked past and Kellan could have sworn the Elf paused to smell the back of his head.

"Why do I suddenly feel like a meal?" Jala asked, voicing his unspoken thoughts.

"Ah, here she is now!" a loud voice announced to the gathering.

Kellan turned.

Lady Samara, dressed in her native white garment—except that this one was cut down to her naval—descended the stairs on the arm of the Ship Captain, Chandal.

An Ellvinian walked by and whispered in his ear. "You will have eyes for no one but Samara this evening."

"What...?"

On the other side, another hushed voice said, "Your heart races for the Lady Samara."

Kellan looked back at the Ellvinian woman descending the stairs and a slow smile spread over his features. Extricating himself from the girls, he started toward the lovely creature that filled so many of his thoughts of late. He heard Jala complain, but ignored her protests, his attention now all on the dark-haired beauty of his dreams.

*

"Where is he going?" Jala demanded with her hands on her hips. "He just warned us to stick together and off he goes!"

"I'm sure he won't be long," Izzy said, trying to sound reassuring but failing miserably.

"How could he just leave us like this? And, where did all these Ellvinians come from?" Jala shook her head. "Let's find Dallin and Elon. It is not like them to leave us among so many strangers." She suddenly felt very exposed as black eyes leered down at her from every direction.

Recalling Kellan's last words to her, Jala grabbed Izzy's hand and held on firmly. Even though Kellan seemed to have deserted them, she had promised she would not let go of Izzy's hand, and she intended to fulfill that promise.

One of the Ellvinians reached out and touched her hair, and she wrenched away from him. His mocking laughter infuriated her. How dare these visitors take such liberty? In a panic now, she twisted her head, but it was impossible to see anything. Where was Dallin Storm? Her guard had followed her down the stairs, she was sure of it. And, Ebon Aubry, the Elven Gladewatcher? That woman would never leave Izzy alone.

Jala spun frantically. Everywhere she turned a black-haired Elf blocked her way.

"I don't like this," Izzy said, her voice cracking in fear.

"Me, either." She looked over at her young friend who reminded her of a delicate white flower in a dark, dense forest. Jala smiled and cupped her face. "I will not let anything happen to you. Just do not let go of my hand. We will go find Kellan or at least Dallin and Elon."

Izzy nodded and pressed her body closer. Jala pushed their way through the crowd. She just needed to find a location to see over the heads of the Elves so she could find their protectors. In all likilihood, Dallin was just as earnestly looking for her as she was him. She could almost hear his lecture in her mind and for once, she would not complain.

Still, try as she might to convince herself that she and Dallin were innocently separated, the blatant facts were difficult to ignore. Her protector would never allow her to disappear into a crowd. Never. That could only mean that her dear Dallin was most likely incapacitated in some way.

She managed to drag Izzy to the far end of the ballroom when she spotted one of the mayor's servants winding her way through the crowd while balancing a tray. Jala quickly ran to her. "Pardon me."

The girl immediately dropped into a curtsy. "Yes, Your Graces."

"I was wondering if you have seen Prince Kellan."

The girl shook her head, obviously frazzled with all of the visitors. "No, Your Grace."

She didn't bother to ask about Dallin or Elon, sure that the girl would not even know who they were.

"Thank you," she said, and the girl scurried off.

Jala made her way back to the corner, but two Ellvinian males in particular continued to eye their progress. She almost called forth a ball of fire just to wipe the smirks from their dark faces. Dark faces that held dark intent, she was sure of it.

"I have had enough of this. We should go back to our rooms," she declared and Izzy quickly agreed.

Suddenly, a tall shadow appeared before her and she was not surprised to see one of the smirking Elves.

"Why, what do we have here?" he asked insolently and reached out to touch Izzy's hair. "I have never seen a white-haired Elf before. You are very beautiful."

"Don't touch her," Jala hissed, pulling Izzy behind her. She glared up at the tall Elf and swallowed, reminding herself that she was safe, that this man was the guest here and help was just a shout or a summons away. She put her arm around Izzy's waist and tried to walk around the man.

He stepped in front of them again.

"Please leave us or I will scream," she threatened, craning her neck to look up at him with authority.

His black eyes grabbed a hold of hers and did not let go. A pure and commanding song drifted from his mouth. "You were just going to return to your room."

"No, I...my, what a lovely song," she commented.

"Your room."

"Yes, come Izzy, let us go now to our rooms." She turned to walk around the Elf, but was yanked back when Izzy did not move.

With a frown, she noticed the man holding onto Izzy's shoulders.

"Your little friend will stay with me while you will return to your room." He reached out and pried Izzy's hand from hers, breaking all contact. "You wish for nothing more than to sleep in your big bed. You are getting very tired."

She started to shake her head, but the song was so beautiful.

"You are tired now and wish to lie down in your room," he sang to her firmly.

"Yes," she repeated, wallowing in the alluring texture of his voice.

"No!" Izzy screamed and clawed for her hand, grabbing it tight once again. The man quickly looked into Izzy's eyes and sang his dazzling cadence in her ear.

"What are you waiting for?" the Elf asked Jala.

"I wish to go to my room now."

"Aye! You do."

Without another word, Jala dropped Izzy's hand, turned and made her way to the stairs forgetting all about her worry of the dark Elves, her young friend, and her promise.

Chapter 12

Immunity

Kellan knew he was acting the fool, but couldn't help himself as he twirled Samara across the cobblestones. The mayor's gala had spilled out through the open arched doorway and into the moonlit courtyard beyond. Flickering torches gave the evening a dreamlike feel as they danced the Stecci. With impeccable timing, they came apart while still holding hands high in the space between them. Eyes locked on each other, they circled three times, took a step back for the obligatory bow and curtsy, and pressed together once again.

Samara's tinkling laugh lit up the night and she leaned in close to sniff his hair. "Mmm..."

Kellan pulled his head back to look at her. "Lady Samara, I must ask why you keep doing that?"

"Because you smell *so* good, Prince Kellan."

Kellan blinked in confusion. While he did wash lightly at the basin in his room before the gala, it had been a few days since his last bath.

She laughed as though she had just read his mind. "It is getting late. Would you mind escorting me to my room?"

"Of course not, my lady." Kellan dropped his embrace and put his hand on the small of her back to guide her into the estate. If anything, it seemed as though more people had gathered and it took several moments to make their way to the stairs.

Climbing behind Samara, Kellan almost ran into her when she abruptly paused and turned on the second floor landing. "What is that?" she asked sharply.

He followed her gaze. "What?"

She pointed to Maks skulking up the stairs behind them, the hackles on his neck standing straight up in the air. "Oh, that's Maks, a Draca Cat."

"Why is it here?"

Kellan's expression softened. "He's here because he is my protector and friend."

"Well, get rid of it," Samara ordered.

When he hesitated, she reached out and roughly jerked his chin toward her until he had no choice but to look directly into her eyes. The song that poured out of her mouth made him weak in the knees. "You wish to send the cat away and come with me to my room. Send the cat away, Prince Kellan."

Kellan turned to obey, but Maks spoke first.

Has the wine addled your mind?

What? No. I...I had one glass of wine and that was all. Why?

I have no other explanation for your foolish behavior.

What does that mean?

Where is Gregor Steel, Prince? He is missing as are all of the other guards.

Kellan looked around. He wasn't even aware the Saber was missing. All his life, the man had been like an extension of his arm or his shadow in the late afternoon. Always there, but not always noticed.

And, where are Jala and Izzy?

Kellan shook his head in confusion at Maks' question. Where were the girls? Maks was right. He had to investigate right away to be sure all were safe. He turned back to Samara. "If you will excuse me, my lady. Maks has reminded me of urgent matters I must attend to."

Her scowl drew her features in tight. "No. You will send that cat-thing away and come with me to my chambers," she insisted. "You wish nothing more in this world than to come with me right this minute."

He nodded mechanically and said to Maks without turning to face him, "Go on, friend. I will come seek you out later."

No! You will act like a Prince of Iserlohn and find your missing friends!

Kellan offered his arm to Lady Samara and continued up the stairs to the guest chambers on the third floor, turning his back on the frustrated growl of Maks.

When they arrived at the door to her room, he suddenly felt nervous. His mind was telling him that he wanted to be here, but his heart was urging him in other directions.

Kellan held open the door and Samara entered the room ahead of him. The white dress she wore swirled around her hips in such a way that made it difficult to look elsewhere.

She approached a side table holding a wine decanter and a plate of fruit. "Wine?" she inquired with a smile over her shoulder.

Kellan gulped, barely able to nod.

Samara laughed, poured two glasses and walked over to hand one to him.

"Thank you," he mumbled, accepting the proffered glass.

She turned to the armchairs by the fireplace. "Sit," she commanded, pointing to one.

Kellan sat down, stiffly, his mind reeling with mixed emotions.

"There is so much I wish to know, Prince, that I am at a loss as to where to start my questioning."

"What do you wish to know?" he asked and took a long drink of wine.

"Let us start with the magic, shall we?"

"The magic?"

"Aye, what kind of magic do the people of Massa have?"

"Oh, well, most of us are shifters. There are a few sorceresses left and, of course, my father is a Mage, but the rest are shifters."

"What does a shifter do?"

He proceeded to tell her about the innate ability of most Massans to manipulate the elements and living creatures around them through the use of magic, and her eyes grew larger and more nervous as he spoke.

"Your people are very powerful, aye?"

"We have the power for great destruction, yes, but we would never harm the innocent." He brought the wine glass to his lips once again and gave her a pointed look over the rim. "Do not worry, Lady Samara. It is only evildoers that need fear the shifters of Massa."

For some reason, her eyes narrowed to slits. "Go on."

He then explained to her what it meant to be a shifter and how the blood oath prevented them from using magic for sinister purpose.

She gazed into the fire for long moments after he was done. "I will share a secret with you, Kellan. The Ellvinians also have an ability of sorts. It is called Ascendency."

"I have never heard of it. What is it?"

"A form of persuasion. It is the power of suggestion laced with hypnosis. Some Ellvinians believe it is magic, but most do not agree. Every Ellvinian has the ability, although some are quite a bit stronger in its use than others."

"Power of suggestion? You can actually make people do what you want, just by suggesting it to them?" he asked dubiously.

She smiled at him and nodded. "Aye, young Prince, that is exactly what we can do."

The events of the last few days flashed through his mind, and his eyebrows pulled together. "Is that what you've been doing here, Samara?"

She simply shrugged.

He was angry now. "Tell me, is your trickery against the Massans for sport or are your plans more malicious in nature?" He stood. "Tell me why you're really here."

She waved him back down. "Oh, Prince, sit down. The Ellvinians are here to discuss a long-term supply of wormwood only. Our Ascendency is a natural part of our make-up, and we could not turn if off if we wanted to. Please sit."

"I think I'll stand."

She steepled her hands under her chin as her gaze ran over him. "You are a very dangerous young man."

"I can be."

"You see, I also have another ability of sort. I am an Eyereader."

"An Eyereader?"

"I have the ability to see into the future. All in my caste have this ability."

"And, you have seen something about me in your future?"

"I have. Just this morning, in fact. Your friends as well, although one is missing. Where is the girl with black ringlets? If my visions do not deceive me, she can use magic to fly."

"What do you want with her?" he growled.

"Let's just say that I want to have a word with her."

His jaw clenched. "I don't think so."

"Have you not been listening to anything I have said, Prince? You will do as I say whether you wish to or not."

∽

Callous laughter accompanied the Ellvinian sailors as they walked in groups along the wooden pier at the wharf. The harbor was suspiciously absent of the late night revelers who typically frequented the taverns along the waterfront in droves.

To avoid notice, Kane pressed closer into the doorframe in the alleyway where he was crouched. He knew Jain was hiding at the end of the narrow corridor, but he couldn't see him.

"It's like taking candy from a child," one of the sailors roared.

One of his companions clapped him on the back in agreement. "I had one chap hopping on one leg until I finished an entire pint of their mead."

The gang laughed.

Not to be outdone, another said, "I told one family to leave their house and go south. I wonder how far they'll get before they realize what they're doing."

"Aye! And, the women!" one boasted. "Although, it does take a bit of the fun out of it for them to be so willing. I prefer my romps far more feisty!"

"Be careful that Second Chandal does not catch you abusing the women!" one warned.

"Bah! He is too busy having galas at the mayor's estate to care what happens out here."

Kane's expression hardened. These pretenders came to Massa under the pretense of friendship and instead exploited the hospitality of his people. The question was, how were they able to convince the Massans into the odd behavior they just described? Did they threatened them with physical harm? Somehow that didn't seem right.

Jain!

Yes, I am here.

I need to get closer to listen in on the Ellvinians. Stay here and wait for me.

I cannot promise that.

You must. I have to find out how these strangers are so easily manipulating the Massans. If you make yourself known, they will feel threatened, and I will learn nothing.

A large snort sounded in his head. *I will try to do as you ask, Prince.*

Not good enough, my friend. You must promise that whatever happens, you will stay concealed. You know that I can disappear if I need to.

If one tries to harm you...

Even then. Remain hidden, Jain, or else I will not have the opportunity again. The safety of the island may depend on what I learn.

The snort turned into a low growl. *It will be as you say.*

Kane stepped away from the doorway and hugged the brick wall to the end of the alleyway. He didn't feel like he was in any real danger, but still wanted to avoid being seen if he could. The sailors would be much more free with their words if they felt they were not being overheard.

Large hanging lanterns spaced along the wharf at intervals provided Kane with the shadows he preferred as he stalked the group. Fat drops of rain began to fall, hitting the wooden pier in staccato splats. Kane cursed silently. Rain was the bane of the sightshifter as the falling droplets would make furrows in magically created images and render them useless.

Lost in his thoughts, it caught him off guard when a hand reached out and touched him. "Kane."

He spun around with a scowl at the interruption that was allowing the Elves to get further away down the pier. His eyebrows rose in shock. "Alia? What are you doing out in Northfort in the middle of the night?"

The girl tossed her long red hair over her shoulder. "Looking for you."

Despite his frustration, a smile tugged at the corners of his mouth. "Now, what could a mermaid possibly want with me?" he teased.

She blushed and straightened a dress that didn't need straightening. Since the watershifters were no longer in hiding, Alia spent much more time in the Surface World than the previous generations and her body had not developed the androgynous quality of so many other Aquatainians.

She was also one of the few people he felt comfortable enough with to let down his guard. At eighteen, she was three years older than him, but his golden eyes never seemed to bother her the way they did others. "Does Digby know you're here?"

"No, he is with your sister in Haventhal." She grabbed his hand and drew him further under the awning of one of the shops lining the pier. "I'm glad I finally found you. I tried to visit at the mayor's estate but was turned away."

"There is a gala there tonight."

"I don't think that would have mattered. These peculiar Ellvinians roaming around seem to be keeping everyone away." She pulled him closer into the shadows. "Kane, the watershifters that I sent to greet the Ellvinian ships never returned to Aquataine."

"What do you mean?"

"They never came home. I checked with the families of all twelve watershifters. They're missing."

His eyes turned to ice as his instincts screamed at him that the Ellvinians were responsible for the disappearances. "It's not safe here, Alia. You really must return home while I look into what you have told me."

To his surprise, she stepped closer and put her arms around his waist, her cheek pressing against his chest. "I feel safer when I'm around you."

His breathing caught in his throat at the unfamiliar feel of a girl clinging so tightly to him. Clumsily, he patted her back. "I will find out what happened to the watershifters, Alia, but you must go back to Aquataine."

She looked up at him through big blue eyes framed by long eyelashes. "Only if you promise me a stroll when this is all said and done."

"A stroll?"

"Yes, just you and me. Unless, of course, you have something against watershifters because wherever we go, I *will* have to have access to a lake or the ocean or even a bathtub."

Despite everything, he laughed.

She tilted her head and looked up at him. "You don't do that often enough."

"Do what?"

"Laugh."

"I know."

"Well, my Prince, what will it be? I am still waiting for your answer."

"You win, mermaid."

She smiled victoriously. "I will be looking forward to it."

He stepped back to let her go, but she lifted up onto the tips of her toes and brought his face down to hers. Their lips met and she smiled against his mouth. "I have wanted to do that for a very long time."

The kiss was over as soon as it started, but it was enough to ignite a fire in his young body. He was thinking of pulling her close for another, when a sardonic voice cut through the quiet of the night.

"Ah, young love!"

Kane turned to the voice. It was the group of four Ellvinians he had been following.

"Alia, you were just leaving, were you not?"

The girl squared her shoulders and stood up next to him. "No. I won't leave you, Kane." With a flick of her wrist, a puddle of water that had formed from the rain rose up from the ground in a long stream and settled between her hands. She twisted and rotated until she held a circular liquid ball.

Oddly enough, the Ellvinians began to sniff at the air. "Magic," one murmured.

Another licked his lips. "I would give anything to taste the blood."

Blood? Kane stepped forward. "Alia, go. Now."

"No."

An Ellvinian reached out and grabbed her by the waist. "We could have some fun with this one."

"Leave her alone," Kane hissed.

Alia took the water orb in her hand and smashed it on top of her aggressor's head.

His cohorts laughed. "You said you wanted feisty, Joff!"

"Alia! Go home!"

The wet Ellvinian smirked at Alia. "I don't have time to deal with you tonight, but I will find you. I promise you that." He ran a finger along her jaw. "Look in my eyes. You want to go home. You wish nothing more than to go home."

Alia nodded. "Did you hear that Kane? What a lovely song! Yes, I will go home." Without another glance his way, she turned and walked away down the pier.

A song? What was she talking about? How they were able to get people to do as they said? "Why are you here?" he questioned harshly.

"We ask the questions, young man. Let us start with why were you following us?" The dark Ellvinian stared at him with a sneer and when Kane didn't answer, the Elf backhanded him across the face. "Answer me! How much did you hear?"

Kane put the back of his fist up to his lip and it came back with blood. His first instinct was to summon his magic, but he did not do so. He had a theory to prove out. "I heard nothing."

One of the Ellvinians bent toward him. "That's right. You heard nothing. You know nothing. You will go home and forget this night."

"Yes, I will go home and forget this night."

"What a sheep." The Ellvinian cuffed him on the back of the head and laughed before he walked away with the others.

Kane turned and returned to the alleyway where Jain was hiding. Immediately, the white cat peeled away from the shadows of the buildings.

Can I kill them now, Prince?

No.

Well then, did you find your answers?

Yes.

What did you learn?

I learned that the Ellvinians use a form of mind control.

Jain growled. *Anything else?*

Yes. I learned that whatever power they possess, it does not work on me.

Chapter 13

Trapped

Frightened and confused, Izzy crouched in the corner of the room like a trapped animal. Frightened because she knew the two Elves in the room with her meant her harm and confused because she didn't understand why she followed them here in the first place. She remembered walking beside them willingly, but why? More importantly, why did everyone else abandon her?

Jala, Kellan, Kane, Elon. Even her parents. All those she cared about discarded her into the hands of these strangers. Jala promised not to let go of her hand, but she did.

The Ellvinians started to argue. Argue about who would have her first. Whatever that meant.

A tear trickled down her cheek as she pressed her body deeper into the corner wishing she could disappear like Kane or throw fire like Jala. She cast out with her magic searching desperately for any nearby animals she could summon to her aid, but found none. She assumed the Draca Cats were in the mayor's estate, but her magic did not work on them.

Maman! Father! Please help me!

Wiping away her tear, she stretched up from her crouch to search the room for anything she could use as a weapon. The tear turned to sobs and the dark Elves turned to look at her.

"Let's get this over with," one suggested.

The other glanced at her sideways, a frown on his face. "We're not animals, Oren. Maybe we should let her go."

"No," Oren responded. "You can leave if you want, but I have never seen anything like this white Elf, and I will have her."

"She is so young."

"Old enough for what I have in mind," Oren leered.

The other Elf looked at her once again with sadness in his eyes. For a hopeful moment, Izzy thought he might try and stop Oren from what he planned to do, but then he said, "Fine. I will wait outside."

"I won't be long."

The Elf nodded and left the room without a backwards glance.

Izzy stood and raced behind the sofa to put it between her and Oren. "Leave me alone!"

"Now, now, wildcat. Just be calm and do as you are told."

"Never!"

"I don't think I will use Ascendency on you, little one. I want you to enjoy this."

Izzy picked up a candleholder on the stand next to the sofa and threw it at him. He easily evaded the missile and laughed.

In a panic, she reached out with her magic once again. *Yes! There!* Her heart raced as she entered the mind of one of the mayor's hound dogs from the stables.

Come!

Izzy would have preferred an animal that could do more damage, but the dog would at least provide a distraction while she fought off the Ellvinian.

Come!

The hound bayed loudly outside of the window. It was coming closer.

Oren charged after her and jumped over the sofa. She ducked just out of his reach and ran for the door.

Come!

Her fingers closed on the handle and she managed to open it a few inches before Oren tackled her to the ground. She landed hard on the floor with a grunt, and the tall Elf fell on top of her and pinned her arms over her head.

"No! Get off me!"

The Elf ignored her pleas and leaned his face down close to hers as if to kiss her. She slammed her forehead into his face.

He screamed out in pain and released her arms, but still sat straddling her body with an angry glare as he fought off her attempts to claw at him with both hands. "I just might have to use Ascendency on you after all, wildcat."

A vicious growl sounded in the hallway.

Kill!

Outside the door, the hound's feet scrabbled for purchase on the marble floor as it rushed to do her bidding. Oren flinched in fright as the animal slammed through the partially open door and lunged for him. The Elf twisted off her and cried out as the dog tore a chunk of flesh from his arm.

Digging her heels into the floor, Izzy scrambled back as fast as she could.

Kill!

The animal tore into Oren with renewed frenzy at her command and blood splattered the floor as the dog carried out a relentless assault.

Thank the Highworld. Izzy got to her feet and ran to the door. She skidded to a stop when another dark Elf appeared in the open doorway, blocking her way to freedom.

"What is this?" the Ellvinian demanded.

Izzy recognized him as the Ship Captain, Chandal.

"Help me, please," she begged.

Oren groaned and writhed on the ground from the hound's vicious bites.

Chandal pulled out a small crossbow and aimed it at the dog.

"No!" Izzy screamed, but it was too late.

He let loose the bolt and it slammed into the hound, sending it into a violent roll. The dog came to rest against the legs of the sofa, where it lay still.

Chandal looked at her as though seeing her for the first time. "A white Elf? Why have I not seen you yet?" He reached out to touch her hair and sniffed the air. "And, a magic user. How delightful."

"Help me," Izzy pleaded once again. She pointed toward the Elf on the ground. "He was trying to hurt me."

Chandal smiled. "Do not worry, little one. I will not let him harm you. What is your name?"

Izzy breathed a sigh of relief. "Izabel Falewir."

"What a beautiful name for a beautiful child. Mine is Chandal and I will keep you safe." Chandal walked over to the prone Oren and kicked him. "Get out! You are reassigned back to the ships at once and you will not set foot on Massa again."

Oren held his bleeding arm and lumbered to his feet.

"Get out!" Chandal yelled.

Leaving a trail of blood on the floor, Oren sprinted through the door.

"My apologies, Izabel," Chandal said and moved back to her side. He gently lifted her chin. "You will come with me now. You do wish to go with me, Izabel, don't you?"

She smiled at the soothing inflection of his voice. "Yes."

He ran his hand slowly down her hair. "Do you like this, Izabel?"

"Yes," she murmured.

"Izabel, from this point on, whenever you think to use your magic, you will become violently ill. Do you understand? You must not use your magic."

"I understand."

"Aye, that is a good girl, because you are now mine, Izabel Falewir. All mine."

ତ

Kenley pulled her knees up close to her chest and let her head fall back against the wall of her prison. Loose clumps of dirt fell in her hair, but she ignored it. She struggled to stay awake as her mind fought for sleep. Sleeping would not allow her to find a way out of this earthen snare the Draca Cats set for her and Baya.

She knew it must be nearing dawn when the black of her world began to turn gray. Exhausted and dispirited, she could no longer fight the needs of her body. Her eyes grew heavy and closed.

Kenley twirled in front of the mirror, holding her white gown up at the sides as she admired her reflection.

She could hardly believe that it was finally happening. Today was the day she married the man she had loved all her life. By now, he would be standing at the altar of the church waiting for her in his red and black uniform, his unruly curls pressed into place.

The door opened and she knew it would be her mother.

Mother, how do I look? she asked breathlessly and turned to face the door. The smile melted from her face at the sight of her mother dressed in all black with a lace veil covering her face. What an odd choice for a wedding.

Kenley! Why do you have that dress on! Take if off right now!

Kenley blinked in confusion. But, it is my wedding day.

Through the veil, Kenley could see the pain in her mother's face. No, Kenley, it is not your wedding day. Your grief is playing tricks on your mind.

She rushed to her mother's side. It is my wedding day, mother!

No, Kenley.

Where is Kirby? He will straighten this out.

Her mother crumpled a white cloth in her hands and looked down. Kirby is dead.

What?

You are too late, daughter. Kirby is dead and today is his funeral.

The horror of her mother's words jarred her awake, and she sat up with a strangled cry. When she opened her eyes, a grateful breath escaped her lips at recognizing she was still trapped in her hole in the ground in Haventhal. If she was here, it meant Kirby was still alive.

What is it? Baya asked.

Nothing, she replied and leaned her head back against the wall. *Just a dream.*

Afraid to close her eyes again, she glanced up at the grate that had kept her up all night. At first, she couldn't understand why she could not blow it open with air. She had enough power to be able to drive that grate sky high with her airshifting.

After many hours of thought, she realized that her prison must be an abandoned entrance to Aquataine. It seemed that once the watershifters closed this portal, they magically sealed the grate from below, but hadn't bothered with the outside. Innate spiritshifters, the Draca Cats seemed to have no problem nudging it open from up top, but she did not have that same ability from below.

Once she gave up on the grate as a possible means of escape, she worked with Baya throughout the night attempting to carve out a tunnel in the wall. But, without a support system for the excavated channel, the dirt just continued to fall back in on the hole impeding any chance of success. She wanted to scream in frustration. The only other time she had ever felt this helpless was when she had been kidnapped by Avalon Ravener as a young child. She quickly shook her head to rid her mind of that event in her life. She didn't like to think about it. Ever.

Instead, she turned her thoughts to the Draca Cats and wondered what they could be doing at this moment. She knew that they wouldn't harm her family, but what about the people of Iserlohn? How would the cats react to resistance from her people? Nazar killed members of his own pride to start this revolution, so it was unlikely he would spare human life if they stood in his way.

She also wondered how her brothers would react to a possible threat by the Dracas. Had they gone as she asked with Kirby to Northfort to greet the Ellvinians? Were they now back home in Bardot? Her parents left her in charge of their well-being and all she managed to do was get herself in trouble. Her only source of comfort was the fact that at least Kirby was with the children, and in her mind, there could be no one more reliable than her austere Saber.

Thoughts of Kirby brought stinging tears to her eyes. *It was just a dream*, she reminded herself.

Do not cry, Princess.

She hastily wiped the back of her hand across her face. *I'm not.*

You are. Are you hurt?

No. Apart from the fact that I am hungry, cold and imprisoned while a pride of angry Draca Cats swarm toward Iserlohn, I am perfectly fine.

Yes, that is a problem. I promise you, Princess, Nazar will be very sorry when I next lay eyes on him.

How is Nazar able to do this to me with the oath? she asked Baya.

To be precise, he has not harmed you in any way.

He hasn't? I'm starving, I'm freezing and very, very angry. I would call that harmed.

In terms of the oath, I would probably call them inconveniences.

Kenley stood and began pacing the small space. *There has to be a way out, Baya!*

If there is, I cannot see it.

That was exactly the same conclusion she had come to over the past twenty-four hours. If they were to ever get out of here, help would have to come from outside.

She snorted.

An outside that knew absolutely nothing about her predicament.

Chapter 14

Blood Supply

"Wake up."

The voice was soft, but Kellan came awake with a startled jolt. Kane was standing over his bed, still in the same clothes he wore before leaving them last night. Jala was standing next to him.

"What is it?" he asked, sitting up.

"Izzy's missing."

Kellan swung his long legs to the floor and pulled his trousers on. "What do you mean Izzy is missing?"

"I let go, Kellan." Jala covered her face with her hands. "I let go."

Kellan guided her to the bed and knelt in front of her. "Tell me what happened."

"I...I don't know how we got separated last night, but we did. I...I remember going to bed last night, but as soon as I awoke, something didn't feel right. I ran to Izzy's room to check on her and she wasn't there."

"That's not all," Kane informed him. "There is no sign of any of the protectors or the watershifters that met with the Ellvinian ship yesterday."

A frown creased Kellan's face. "Gregor is not outside?"

"No."

Kellan reached back into his own memory of last night. He remembered walking down to the gala and then his face reddened when he remembered dancing with Samara. Did he just leave the girls behind to dance with the Ellvinian woman? He also remembered escorting Samara to her chambers and having a brief conversation with Maks along the way. *Maks!* Kellan stood in a rush and pushed by Kane to go into the sitting room.

The big white cat lifted his head. *Yes.*

Where is Gregor?

As I told you quite forcefully last night, he is missing.

You told me? Wait! Yes, I remember now.

It appeared as though you had other activities on your mind and you sent me away.

Kellan's face blazed once again when he realized he did just that. Once more, he tried to put together the missing pieces. Oddly, the last thing he remembered was Samara telling him to forget all that they had discussed. He scratched his head. She simply told him to forget and he did?

Kane produced an answer to his unspoken question. "The Ellvinians can use mind control."

Kellan whipped his head around to face his brother standing in the doorway to the bedroom. "Mind control? Are they mindshifters?" That would certainly make the situation much worse if not utterly hopeless.

"I don't believe so. Twice now, I heard comments about the quality of the Ellvinians' voices when they are using this control. You called it magic when you heard it, and Alia called it a song. It's almost as if they are putting their intended targets in a type of hypnotic trance."

"How do you know all this?"

"Ellvinian sailors attempted to use it on me down at the wharf last night. It didn't work."

"Why didn't it work?"

Kane's golden eyes glowed in the semi-darkness of the room. "I haven't figured that part out. Yet."

"Wait. Are you suggesting...? Did Samara use this mind control on me last night?"

"She must have!" Jala cried. "You walked away from me and Izzy without a word." Her eyes glistened and she turned her back on him, her voice growing softer. "And, I did the same thing to Izzy. I promised not to let go of her hand, but went to bed and left her with two of the dark Elves. I remember now that she was begging me to stay, and I just walked away!"

Kellan speared a hand through his hair and it took all of his willpower not to shed his own tears. Izzy was like a sister to him and his guard, Gregor Steele, had been a constant presence in his life ever since the day he was born. If the Saber wasn't outside of his door, he was most likely dead. And, not just him. Haiden, Elon, and Dallin were missing as well.

He had to think. What would his father and mother do if they were here? What would Kenley do? He never wanted so badly to see his sister.

"I already started an evacuation of the city."

Kane's casual statement stunned him. "You did?"

He simply nodded.

"Well done," he said, genuinely impressed.

"If the citizens follow my orders, by tonight, all that should be left in Northfort are those confined to this estate. In my estimate, counting guests from the gala and servants, there are close to two hundred people here."

"Not nearly enough to fight twelve hundred Ellvinians."

Kane raised a pale eyebrow. "Depends how many of those Massans are shifters."

"I like how you think, brother."

"So, we're trapped here?" Jala asked.

"For now. I suggest we play along with the Ellvinians. Act as though we don't suspect what is going on. That will give the people of the city the best chance of making it out. It won't take long for the Ellvinians to realize what is happening, but our ruse just might give us enough time to find Izzy before we show our hand. When that happens, all bets are off."

"Do what you must to deceive the Ellvinians, Kellan," Jala said, "but I am going after Izzy now. If I have to burn this building to cinders to find her, that is exactly what I'll do."

Kellan nodded. "Izzy is our first priority. Kane, check on the evacuation and make sure it is happening as discreetly as possible. Then, see if you can round up any shifters that are left in Northfort. We are going to need all the help we can get."

Now, you are sounding like a Prince of Iserlohn, Maks noted proudly.

"And, you?" Kane asked. "Where will you be?"

"I'm going to pay another visit to Samara and see what I can find out about the Ellvinians' plans or Izzy's whereabouts."

"I wonder if there is a way to counteract their mind control," Jala mused.

"Simple," Kane replied. "Don't listen to a word they say."

⁂

The Premier laid back on his cushions and stared up at the domed ceiling in a blood soaked haze. The world around him spun in a mesmerizing swirl of color, heightened senses reeling inside his mind and over his skin. The tips of his fingers and toes tingled with the blood pounding through his veins.

Magic blood.

He never felt so alive in all of his life!

With some effort, he lifted his head and peered through bleary eyes at his companions. Balder and Anah were wrapped together in a lazy sprawl, eyes open but not focused. Jarl was sitting up and mumbling to himself through his euphoria. In the corner of the room, Emile sat apart, clear-eyed and sober, refusing to partake in the blood.

A pale mound further along the wall caught his attention, but Hendrix wasn't sure what it could be. He struggled up on an elbow to look more closely. *What is it? Is that a leg?* It almost looked like...oh, aye, he remembered now.

A mound of dead bodies.

Watershifters, they called themselves.

The ship returned just that morning with the twelve Massans and Hendrix wasted no time setting the Vypir on them to extract their blood. Fortunately, the Vypir remembered exactly what he had been created to do and required no prompting once the shifters were led into its room.

The image of the creature striking out with its tail at the necks of the watershifters to siphon their blood played through Hendrix's mind in gruesome detail. One by one, he watched the shifters pound in desperation on the glass of the control room and beg to be freed. With each kill, the Vypir grew stronger and the bodies more mangled by the time they were drained.

Hendrix looked over at the pile once again and the three barrels used to collect the blood.

It was unfortunate that all had been killed. It had certainly not been the plan. He just hoped that the Massan representatives due to arrive in Ellvin also had the gift of magic. If so, the technicians would have to come up with a way to keep the Vypir from draining them so quickly.

I need to think. Sitting up, he stretched his hand along the floor looking for his goblet. He found it and raised it into the air. "Emile! More blood!"

"Aye!" agreed Balder, unwrapping himself from Anah's amorous limbs.

Emile walked over with a cold expression on his face. "May I speak honestly, Your Eminence?"

The look on Emile's face told him it would not be something he wanted to hear. "If you must."

"In a few hours, you have gone through the blood of twelve shifters. Not only that, you depleted them dry when you could have kept them alive to make more blood." He leaned down and lowered his voice. "Quite frankly, Your Eminence, you are not thinking clearly with so much of the magic in your system. You must stop."

"Stop?" Hendrix bellowed. "I am an Ellvinian, Emile!" He pitched to his feet in anger. "I WILL HAVE THE BLOOD!"

Emile stepped back, but pressed on. "At least keep them alive, Your Eminence. If you want a continual blood supply, you cannot kill them all!"

"It was the Vypir! It was your little pet that did this!"

"You ordered all of the shifters in the room at once," Emile pointed out.

He threw up his hands. "Well, how was I to know what that creature would do? Now, that I do know of its vicious nature, I can assure you that steps will be taken so that it does not happen again. The technicians are evaluating the proper protocol for harvesting, and it is something we will work out with time."

"I will not have you harm Tolah."

"Please! Do not attach a name to that thing."

"It is a human being."

"It is a beast, but I will not harm it. Why would I when it brings me so much pleasure?" Hendrix waved a clumsy hand in the air. "Do not worry so, Emile! There are plenty of shifters in Massa. I have complete confidence that Samara and Chandal will do all that is necessary to ensure our blood supply. And, in case you have forgotten, representatives from Massa will be here any day now."

"You cannot kill the representatives! It will be tantamount to declaring war!"

"If that's what it takes, so be it!"

Emile grabbed his arm roughly. "Your Eminence! The blood is addling your mind! Stop drinking and then make your decision."

Hendrix screeched and yanked his arm out of Emile's grip. "Let go of me! I have made my mind up and the decision is made! We have gone too long without, and I am through doing this the peaceful way with the Shiprunners. Take all the Battlearms to Massa, Emile!" With that final thunderous declaration, Hendrix slumped back down onto the pillows.

He was no longer looking at his Second, but could tell Emile's next words were forced out through gritted teeth.

"The Battlearms?"

"Aye, Emile, do I have to write it out for you?"

"And, once there, Your Eminence?"

"I want a steady well of magic users delivered to Ellvin, Emile! If anyone challenges your mission, kill them."

"Your Eminence! We do not have—"

"Are you disobeying an order, Emile? If you so much as speak one single word more of this heresy, I will have you whipped and executed. Do you hear me?"

Emile swallowed back his argument. "Aye, Your Eminence."

"Good, now prepare the Battlearms. I want you gone by tonight."

"As you command," Emile replied stiffly and walked toward the door of the Consulate.

"Wait!" Hendrix shouted at him.

The Second hesitated before turning back to him, a glimmer of hope in his eyes that Hendrix had changed his mind after all. "Your Eminence?"

Hendrix held up his goblet and wiggled it in the air. "You forgot my blood."

Chapter 15

A Tightening Web

Izzy pressed her fists into her stomach in an attempt to stay the vomit lodged in her throat. She took deep breaths in through her nose and tried to flood her mind with beautiful images of her deity, Elán, to prevent her from thinking about using magic. The Ellvinian named Chandal had warned her that trying to shift would cause her to be sick, but sometimes she couldn't help herself. Sensing out the animals around her was as natural to a feralshifter as breathing.

Feeling her nauseous belly finally subside, Izzy sat up on the large bed.

An Ellvinian guard stood unsmiling at the open door between the room she was in and the sitting room just beyond. *What a strange looking Elf.* He never smiled or acknowledged her presence. He just stood there and sniffed at the air every once in a while.

Izzy got out of the bed and strode to the window. The courtyard below the mayor's estate was empty. She had hoped to see someone outside that she could wave to, but quickly realized how improbable that was. She was on the third floor and it was not likely that anyone down below would look up this far or, even if they did, see her behind the thick windowpane.

She wondered where Chandal had gone. She hadn't seen him since he deposited her in his room last night, and she hoped she never saw him again. He made her skin crawl. Even though he had been nice to her, she wasn't fooled. She could tell that deep down, he meant her harm just as the other two Ellvinians had.

If only Jala, Kellan or Kane would find her before Chandal returned. Did they know she was missing? She knew her friends very well and under normal circumstances, they would stop at nothing to find her. But, she knew now that events surrounding these strange Elves were not normal. Her own actions since the night of the gala were hazy and indistinct so she could only assume the others were facing the same dilemma.

Izzy spotted a stray dog outside the window and quickly turned away, not wanting to call up the sickness again.

Instead, she glanced north and viewed the fleet of ships moored there. These Ellvinians would pay for their actions when her father returned. He wouldn't be pleased at all that they had locked up his daughter. If only he would come home today instead of weeks from now.

Turning from the window, she began to pace. How could she escape? Since she couldn't rely on her friends or her magic, she had to figure out another way.

Her gaze locked on a heavy candleholder on the stand by the bed. Ever since she was old enough to walk, Elon Aubry and other members of the Gladewatchers had instructed her in the art of defense. If brute force was all she had at her disposal, she would use it, and there was no time like the present.

She sat on the edge of the bed, making sure that the candleholder was within reach.

She cleared her throat. "Sir, can you please come here?"

The guard looked at her hesitantly.

"I am bleeding, sir, on the back of my leg and I need—"

The Elf crossed the room faster than she thought possible and knelt down to sniff at her leg. To her horror, his tongue darted out to lap up the blood he hoped to find.

She did not waste the opportunity. She grabbed the candleholder and slammed it into the side of his head. The tall Elf crumpled to the side, unconscious.

I can't believe it! It worked!

Izzy spared one fleeting second to hope that she had not killed the Elf, but then stepped around him and fled the bedroom. As she navigated the sitting room, she prayed to Elán that there wouldn't be any guards outside.

At the door, she stopped with her hand pressed against the frame. What would she do if there were? The element of surprise was crucial to any offense her father always told her. She was small and fast, so she could slam open the door and run before they realized she was escaping. Yes, that would work. Surely, they wouldn't hurt her once she was in the hallway and in view of others.

She took a deep breath to calm her racing heart. Clenching her muscles in readiness to act, she lowered her hand to the door handle.

Before she could turn it, the door opened and she stumbled back into the room.

It was Chandal.

"Going somewhere?" he asked, his black eyes furious.

⁂

Kellan stepped out of his room after Kane and Jala left, and it felt like he stepped into a nightmare. Ellvinians swarmed the hallway and a glance over the balcony showed that the lower floors and antechamber were flooded with them as well. There was not a single Massan in view.

What in the Highworld is going on here, Maks?

Maks lumbered to the railing and looked down. *An invasion.*

How did this happen? We allowed for a dozen Ellvinians only.

They disregarded your rules, but you have known this since yesterday.

I did?

Yes.

You're right, I did. Kane says that they have mind control abilities.

Just stay near me. I will protect you.

Kellan smiled at his friend and absently ran a grateful hand through his silky white coat. *Can you do something important for me?*

It depends.

His mouth twitched up once again. Draca Cats only performed the tasks they wished to perform, whether he liked it or not. *I want you to see if you can track the protectors. Find out what happened to them.*

I would rather not be parted with the enemy surrounding you in such numbers. I can already see how they are isolating us into small groups. *If I did not want to kill them so badly, I would be quite impressed.*

Are they really our enemy?

The snowy head peered down at the antechamber once again before answering. *Yes.* Maks spoke the truth. Even he could see that now. *But, I must find out what happened to the protectors, Maks. If harm has come to them, that is the proof I need for Kirby and the mayor.*

Maks nodded and then turned his blue eyes to look directly at Kellan. *I will go. Call out if you need me. I can find you anywhere.*

I promise. But, I am not without my own defenses, Maks. Remember that.

If the cat attached any value to his comment, he did not say. He simply turned and left, and the Ellvinians backed away hastily to give the enormous Draca room as he made his way down the stairs.

Kellan pushed away from the railing to pursue his own goals. He needed to talk to Samara, but he also wanted to find Kirby Nash and find out what the Captain of the Royal Guard was doing about this *invasion* as Maks put it. Or, was he, too, under the Ellvinians' influence?

The Elves he passed in the hallway made no attempt to hide their stares, and Kellan felt like an insect in a sea of hungry hawks. Instinctively, he stretched for the white fur that was always a reach away, but his hand came up empty. Maks was gone. Gregor was gone. It was up to him now to shoulder the cloak of responsibility to which he had been born. Kellan fingered the athame tattooed on his neck and drew strength from its presence and when he looked up again, he saw the hawks for what they truly were. Elves. Just

Elves. He on the other hand was a shifter. He was the child of *Savitars*, and he had the power to defeat them.

Shoulders squared, he strode through the throng of dark Elves and made his way toward the mayor's drawing room where he knew Lars held conferences with his deputies.

It shouldn't have been surprising to find white-robed Ellvinians standing before the double doors to the room as though on guard, but it was. He strode toward them prepared to fight his way in, but the Elves stepped aside as he neared and allowed him to enter without comment.

Kellan slammed open the doors harder than he intended and stepped inside.

Sunlight pooled in the center of the large room, casting its occupants in a halo of illumination. The laughter and gaiety of the six people sitting on a raised dais enjoying their midday meal broke off abruptly when they heard him enter.

It seemed such an innocent scene.

The mayor was there in the midst of delivering a toast to his guests. Samara, Chandal, and two other Ellvinians paused with their glasses raised. The sixth person in the room was Kirby Nash, and he immediately stood when he saw Kellan.

"Kellan! Come join us. I was just coming to look for you, but Lady Samara used her considerable charms to convince me to take part in this delicious repast." He waved his arms to draw attention to the elaborate spread of food before them.

Samara stood and opened her mouth. The beautiful song that drifted from her lips enticed him to approach, pulled him toward her.

Kellan smiled and took a seat at the table allowing the laughter and the toasts to resume.

Kane felt like he was running out of options. He spent most of the day simply attempting to leave the mayor's estate to check on the progress of the evacuation, but at every door, an Ellvinian turned him away, *suggesting* to him that he would rather stay inside and return to his room. He wanted the Ellvinians to think their mind control worked on him, so he abided by their words, but now it was getting late in the day and he had found out nothing useful thus far.

Not to mention that Jain, locked out of the estate when he slipped out to hunt, was becoming more and more anxious to reunite with him, and Kane didn't know how much longer he could hold the Draca Cat off from unleashing his fury on the Ellvinians.

Kane hugged the wall as he walked down one of the lesser-used corridors toward the kitchens. Except for the occasional servant scurrying about her workday, he hadn't seen another Massan all day.

That was why he picked the kitchens. If anyone knew what was happening within the walls of this estate, it would be the kitchen staff. He had already met the cook, Cora, yesterday before the gala and found her to be a spirited woman who bore her cooking utensil as though it were a bludgeon. And, for the servants not doing their jobs fast enough, it probably was.

Up ahead, he saw that the kitchen doors were open. With one last glance behind him, he darted to the entrance and...froze.

Inside were half a dozen Ellvinians, some sitting and eating at a makeshift table made from a butcher's block and others stirring the contents of Cora's pots.

Cora was nowhere in sight.

One Elf rose to his feet at Kane's sudden appearance. Not hurried. Not startled from being caught doing something wrong. More like the man of the manor being interrupted from his meal by one of his inferiors.

"Is there something I can do for you, Prince?"

"Where is Cora?" Kane asked softly. Softly, but tinged with enough threat that all heads turned his way.

"Who?"

"The cook. Where is the cook?"

"Oh, aye, Cora. Lovely lady. She took the day off." The black eyes dared him to challenge the statement.

Kane refused to bite and instead turned his full golden gaze directly at the dark Elf. It pleased him to see the Ellvinian recoil slightly. It was a familiar reaction. "Is that so? In that case, I think I'll just wander out to the gardens for some fresh air." He took a small step toward the back door of the kitchens, but knew with certainty that he wouldn't be allowed out.

He was right.

Several Ellvinians stood from the butcher's block to bar his way.

He thought of drawing his blade or shifting through them, but decided against it. There were too many, and he wasn't yet ready to show them what he was capable of. He needed to find Izzy first and ensure that the Massans evacuating had every advantage for success before the fighting started.

He smiled. "On second thought, maybe I'll take that walk another time." He turned and exited the kitchens.

"You do that, Prince!" he heard one of the Ellvinians shout, followed by mocking laughter.

Jaw clenched tight, Kane strode back down the hallway, but stopped in shock when he saw a woman round the corner up ahead. He immediately recognized the long red hair.

Alia!

What is she doing in the estate? Demon's breath, I thought she went back home to Aquataine. She must have found a way in before the Ellvinians locked down all of the doors.

He sprinted down the corridor to catch up to her. Whatever it took, he had to convince her to leave this place right now. His concern filling his thoughts, he didn't stop to look before turning the corner and slammed into someone coming from the other direction.

The girl fell backward with a grunt, but it wasn't Alia. It was Jala.

"Kane, what are you doing?" she asked angrily from her back on the floor.

He reached down to help her to her feet. "I was chasing after Alia and—"

"Alia is here?"

"Yes," he replied, searching up the corridor, but Alia was no longer in sight.

"What did you find out?" Jala asked, standing and brushing down the folds of her dress.

"Not as much as I would have liked," he replied. "I haven't encountered more than two Massans, let alone shifters, in the entire place. And, I can tell you that the Ellvinians are guarding all of the doors."

Jala nodded. "I know, I tried to get out once, but the next thing I knew I was walking back to my room before I stopped myself. I haven't had any luck finding Izzy." She grabbed Kane's hand. "I'm so worried for her."

Kane was worried for her, too. And, now, it looked like he had Alia to worry about as well.

Chapter 16

Predator and Prey

Gunther threw another piece of wood on the fire and poked at it with a long stick sending tiny sparks floating upward. He wanted the flames nice and hot just in case Harod had been more successful than he in bringing back meat for their dinner. If not, it would be cold beans again, and Gunther would be just as satisfied either way.

He took a slug from the skin of mead and sat back in contentment. Dear Highworld, but he enjoyed these annual hunting trips with Harod to the Du'Che Forest. As far as he was concerned, any chance to leave behind his wife and children and farrier business for some peace and quiet was one worth taking. Soon, he would be back home to the noise and never-ending stress of his life, but tonight, right now, he could appreciate doing nothing but drinking and prodding at a fire every once in awhile.

He set the stick aside and crossed his hands over his belly with a sigh. Maybe he could convince Harod to stretch out their trip for one more night.

Suddenly, a loud thrashing shattered the serenity of the still night as something tore through the forest toward him. *Harod?* He scrambled to his feet and grabbed the bow leaning against the tree behind his head. It was only when he was at full draw that he realized he had never nocked an arrow.

He let out a breath of relief at the sight of Harod. "What is wrong with you, man? I think you took five years off my life."

"Gunther! Come quick." Harod was panting from the exertion of the run.

"What is it?"

He shook his head. "You have to see it to believe it."

Gunther grinned and raced after his friend wondering what could have him so excited. A mantath? Now, that would be a trophy worth bringing home!

Up ahead, Harod waved him over to a hummock that looked down upon the long grasses of the Iserlohn plains. Together, they crawled to the top and peered over.

"Look, Gunther!" Harod hissed.

Gunther's eyes widened in surprise. Two enormous white felines stalked out of the Du'Che. "It's them cats the royals keep as pets!" he realized in excitement.

Harod brought his bow up. "I know and I'm gonna get me one, Gunther. Just don't move." Harold's arms shook as he brought the bowstring to his cheek.

The two large cats stopped suddenly and sniffed at the air.

"Hurry, Harod!" Gunther whispered.

The twang of the released arrow and subsequent hiss as it shot forward toward the unsuspecting cats seemed deafening in the twilight. The missile found its mark and pierced the flesh just beneath the shoulder blade of one of the animals. For a moment, the cat just looked down in surprise at the burgeoning red stain on its chest, but then it collapsed to the ground.

"You did it!" Gunther enthused softly, patting Harod on the back.

Gunther's elation soon turned to unease when the other, larger cat did not run away, but lifted its gigantic white head directly toward their hummock. There was unquestionable intelligence in those pale orange eyes and something else. Unmitigated fury.

With an ear-splitting growl, the cat sprang into an attacking sprint, his large paws eating up the distance between them in large gulps.

Harod screamed and ran.

Gunther ducked under the hummock and flinched when the body of the cat soared over his head and landed on the fleeing Harod. Large talons raked his friend's back ripping open his shirt and leaving deep gashes in the skin.

Gunther's whole body shook as he listened to Harod's terror-filled screams and watched the cat tear and shake him as though he were a toy. Blood soaked the ground, pooling in black puddles in the waning light.

The attack was too fast, too ferocious. There was nothing Gunther could do to help Harod escape the enraged animal. And, now, up close, Gunther could see what looked like scales all along the white body. This was not a creature to trifle with.

Slowly, he began to inch his way up the hummock. If he could just slip away from the occupied cat, he may be able to save himself. After seconds that seemed like hours, sweat coating his face and body, he made it over the small hill and rolled.

When he came to a stop, he quickly sprang to his feet and prepared to run, but then sat back down hard in shock. There was nowhere to go. The open space before him was filled with white cats. Hundreds if not thousands of them.

And, every single glowing orange eye was on him.

∽

Nazar licked his paws until satisfied that every last drop of blood had been cleaned away. He had not been the one to make the kills but had walked over the kill site to inspect the corpses of the men.

He rose to his feet and shook out his coat. The weakling humans caught them by surprise and killed one of his females, but it would not happen again. The next time men came seeking Draca blood, they would find his pride ready and waiting.

Rehka sat watching him.

How much farther to this Bardot, Nazar?

A few days of travel to the north. We must find Maks and Jain before we can continue to Nysa.

Will they willingly join with us, Nazar?

They will have no choice.

What of Baya and Princess Kenley?

I will have them freed as soon as we declare ourselves to the sons of Kenley.

Baya will be furious.

He shrugged. *I do what must be done, Rehka. Come, let us rest before resuming our journey with the new sun.*

Do you think we will encounter more battle here, Nazar?

I do. Unlike the Elves, man has just proven himself our enemy.

Chapter 17

Up in Smoke

Pure exhaustion sent Kane to his chambers the previous evening after a laborious game of cat and mouse with the Ellvinians, and he wasn't any closer to answers this morning than he had been last night. He stood up from the floor and stretched out the ache in his back. Jala was so distraught last night that he let her have his bed to sleep in. Since the Ellvinians' mind control worked on her, she didn't want to be alone.

With the exception of Chandal and Samara's personal guest chambers, which were heavily guarded, Kane and Jala searched the entire estate and had not found a single person that was not of Elven descent. Even Kellan and Kirby had now managed to disappear. It was all so bloody frustrating.

"Are you awake," Jala asked, sitting up and running a hand through her long chestnut hair.

"Yes."

"I am tired of this game, Kane. If we don't find Izzy today, these Ellvinians will find out what happens when you stir a blood oath." To back up her threat, a ball of fire flared into existence, and she rotated it back and forth between her hands.

"You remind me of your father right now."

Her smile was feral. "That's the nicest thing anyone has ever said to me."

Kane walked to the washbasin and filled it with water. Jala was right, but where to look that they had not already tried? Izzy, the protectors, servants, guests, the watershifters, Cora the cook, Kellan, Kirby and Alia, all gone. The thought of Alia and the kiss they shared brought a flare of heat to his cheeks but he pushed it away. Now, was certainly not the time to think about such whimsy. But, he did still wonder where she could be. After catching a glimpse of her yesterday, he had been unable to find her again.

How could two hundred people simply vanish overnight? He was overlooking something important, but couldn't figure out what.

"I was thinking," Jala said, letting the fireball disappear. She got out of bed and began tugging on her short leather boots. "Before we storm the guest chambers of our visitors, we should look for any rooms below ground. There must be a wine or root cellar we haven't checked yet."

"It's worth a try."

She walked into the sitting room and he followed. "I want to be sure that we have tried everything before using force." She paused. "It is what our parents would do."

"Agreed." Kane reached for the door handle, but before he could open it, Jala grabbed his forearm. "Kane, don't let any of them look at me or talk to me. Please."

Kane looked into her terrified eyes and placed his hand firmly over hers. "I won't."

She allowed him to open the door then and as soon as they stepped out, the Ellvinians in the hallway stopped to look at them.

"Good day, Prince!"

"Lady Jala, how was your sleep?"

All the banter sounded cordial and non-threatening, but Kane knew better. He nodded to each Elf that spoke to him, but kept walking toward the stairs. When they were halfway down, he spotted Kellan in the antechamber standing in a group.

About bloody time! "Kellan!"

His brother turned, lifted his head and waved him over. To Kane's dismay, he was standing with Samara and Chandal, but with some relief he also noticed Kirby Nash and Lars Kingsley there as well.

"Kane! Jala! We were just going out for a morning ride. One of the mayor's aides found a large patch of wormwood and Lady Samara wishes to see it for herself. Why don't you join us?"

"You're leaving the estate?" Kane questioned suspiciously.

"Of course. It's a beautiful day for a ride."

"Where have you been? We need to talk," he whispered urgently to his brother, but before Kellan could answer, Samara appeared at his side.

"We really must be going," she drawled. "Why don't you join us, Prince Kane?"

Jala nudged Kane and he knew what she was thinking. Kellan was being manipulated by the Ellvinians. He wanted nothing more than to shake his brother out of this farcical alliance and get him as far away from these creatures as possible, but knew he couldn't do that quite yet. Kane ignored the black-eyed glare from Samara. "No. I don't think so."

Kellan shrugged. "As you wish. I will see you when I return then."

With that, the small party departed for the horse stables outside.

A bump from behind caused Kane to turn. It was Maks.

Jain is worried for you.

Kane took a deep breath. *I know. Tell him I am fine for the moment. Will you stay with Kellan?*

Always.

Thank you, Maks. Kane turned to go.

Prince?

Kane looked back at the cat. *Yes?*

There is a door on a side corridor next to the kitchens. I detected a mixture of familiar scents at that door, but I could not get in.

Thank you, Maks! This is the best lead we've had in days, and now is the perfect time to go take a look.

Be careful. The enemy guards that corridor.

When Maks departed, Kane quickly explained to Jala what the Draca Cat told him. He put an arm around her shoulder and steered her toward a hallway off the antechamber. "Now, we are going to walk nice and slow until we get to the third corridor on the right up ahead. After that, we're going to run."

Her head turned sharply to look at him.

"We have to lose the two Elves following us. No! Don't turn around. Just keep walking and remember the third corridor on the right."

She nodded and when they arrived at their destination, they ran. Kane took the long way to the kitchens, sprinting through hallways he had come to know quite intimately during the night. Whenever they happened on one of the Elves, they slowed to a casual walk, but with the exception of the two that they lost from the antechamber, the other Ellvinians paid them little mind. He guessed they had no reason to be concerned about what happened within the estate since all of the exits were so well guarded.

Still, they kept up the deception until they arrived at the hallway near the kitchens that Maks told him about. Kane held up a hand to Jala and peeked into the short corridor. Three Ellvinians stood in front of the only door in the hall.

Kane pulled Jala to the side.

"What now?" she asked.

"It's time for a little fun."

✥

Fun? Did Prince Kane Atlan with the golden eyes just utter the word *fun*? Jala shook her head. She must have heard wrong. Kane Atlan did not joke. Even when they were having *fun* as a group, you would never know that he was. In fact, spending these past few days with him was the most she had ever heard the boy speak.

Yet, it was hard to miss the impish glint in his eye. He was up to something.

"I will create a diversion. As soon as the last Elf leaves the hallway, get to that door and see what is inside."

Jala nodded and crouched in readiness to run.

Kane took a deep breath and stepped out into the opening of the short hallway. "Hey, Elves, are any of you up for a game of tag? I heard that Elves can run pretty fast!" As soon as the words left his mouth, he sprinted away.

Jala pressed her body flat against the wall as one of the Ellvinians laughed and chased after him. What now, she wondered and then smiled when a shifted illusion of Kane appeared around the corner, whistling. At least she thought he was whistling. No sound ever issued from Kane's images.

One of the two remaining Ellvinians cursed. "What is this?"

"You better check it out," the other suggested.

Jala watched the Elf carefully come out into the hall and cautiously follow the whistling Kane headed in the opposite direction of the first.

She almost giggled out loud when a third image of Kane peeled away from the shadows of the hallway and stepped up to meet the lone Ellvinian still guarding the door.

This is fun.

The Elf, undaunted by the obvious magic he was witnessing, approached Kane. "Come here, boy. I have a song for you."

Kane backed away and ran, and the Ellvinian gave chase without looking at her.

After a quick glance both ways, Jala ran for the door and pulled it open. A musty scent filled her nose and all she could see was a set of stairs leading down into semi-darkness. Like her father, she did not like tight, closed places, but she promised Kane she would find out what was behind this door.

Taking a deep breath, she called forth a ball of light and started down, relieved when she saw Kane slip in the door behind her. She jumped the last few rungs of the steps, landed hard and rolled across a dirt floor.

Before she could get to her feet, someone with strong arms reached out and lifted her up. Someone with a long, black beard and thick braids on both sides of his head.

"Dallin!"

Overcome with emotion, it touched her to see tears in the Iron Fist's eyes as well. "Oh, Kali, thank the Highworld you are safe!"

She hugged him tight. "It's good to see you, Dallin."

Sensing movement behind Dallin, she peered around him into a root cellar filled wall-to-wall with people. Some sitting, some standing with their shirt sleeves rolled up and dirt covering their faces. Some even sleeping. Elon, Haiden, Gregor, servants and, if the silk trousers were any indication, visitors from the island of Hiberi. She even spotted a pair of giant Cymans standing in the back by the wall.

They finally found everyone, and her heart soared. "Where is Izzy?" she asked Dallin desperately.

He gave her a curt shake of his head. "Izabel is not here. I have not seen her."

Elon heard the exchange and her face fell. It was obvious that she had been hoping that Jala knew where her charge was.

Suddenly, the cellar door slammed shut, and she heard the sound of a bolt lock thrown closed.

Jala sprinted past Kane up the stairs and tried the door. "It's locked! We're trapped!" She hurried back down into the cellar and addressed the people. "We need shifters! How many shifters are here?"

"None," Dallin answered.

"None?"

"The Ellvinians took the shifters with them. They were able to somehow, for lack of a better word, *sniff* them out. Then, they persuaded all of us to go along with their orders through song. I can't explain it any better than that."

Jala held a hand up. "You don't have to. I know firsthand what the Ellvinians are capable of."

Haiden Lind rushed to Kane's side and knelt. "Your Grace, I should not be so bold, but I beg for your forgiveness in failing in my duty to you."

Kane just stood there with the sword of Iserlohn clenched in his fist, his face an unreadable mask.

The silence tore at Haiden. "Prince, I will renounce my position as your guard if that is what your wish. Just say the word." The Saber moved his shoulders uneasily, and the entire cellar went quiet as they waited to see what the Prince of Iserlohn would do.

Finally, Haiden could not take any more and reached out to grab Kane's arm.

The moment he did, Kane disappeared in a puff of smoke.

"Prince!"

⁂

Kane crouched in a hidden alcove on the second floor of the mayor's estate. Through his shifted illusion, he ran with Jala down into the root cellar. He watched her reunite with her guard, Dallin Storm, but his eyes were already scanning the rest of the faces. With relief, he found Haiden and Gregor and Elon. Cora the cook was there, looking very angry. He searched for Izzy or Alia, but neither was in the room. *Demon's breath!* The watershifters were not there either. If they had been, they would have been very ill by now from being out of the water for so long.

He listened in to Dallin explain to Jala about the Ellvinians taking the shifters from the cellar. What did they want with the shifters? It would make more sense to keep the most dangerous individuals locked up in the cellar not the other way around.

Haiden walked over to him and knelt. Kane wanted to reach out to him and tell the Saber that there was no reason to apologize. He wanted to assure his protector that he wasn't at fault for their separation, but Kane couldn't tell him any of these things. It was just an illusion that the people in the cellar were looking at.

"Prince!" Haiden reached out to grab Kane's arm and the contact destroyed his shifted image. The abrupt release from his magic caused Kane to fall back against the wall where he was crouched.

He rubbed his eyes with the heels of his hands. He knew they were glowing fiercely right now. It would take a few moments for them to resume their normal—if you could ever call his eyes normal—golden color.

Now, more than ever, he realized the immediate danger the island was in. If the Ellvinians were successful in occupying Northfort, it would give them a strategic advantage in challenging the royal seats of Bardot and Nysa next.

With Kirby and Kellan completely enthralled by the Ellvinians, Jala now confined to the cellars, and Izzy still missing, it was up to him to figure out a way to stop them.

Then, he swallowed as a sudden realization occurred to him. Since becoming caught up in the tightening tentacles of subterfuge from the Ellvinians here in Northfort, he neglected to remember an important detail. His parents were sailing directly for their sinister jaws.

Chapter 18

The Island of Ellvin

"There it is!" Beck announced over the shouted orders of Captain Wilden that sent sailors scrambling up into the rigging to manipulate the sails. "The island of Ellvin!"

Kiernan squeezed his arm. "It's beautiful."

Beck agreed.

The turquoise water leading up to the island was so still it looked as though you could walk along its surface. The port city itself was nestled in the midst of stunning white beaches and mangrove trees. Further inland, a mountainous array of sea caves that Beck guessed might have once been part of a large volcano, provided a stunning backdrop.

"Hey, fireball! Why don't you treat the Ellvinians to a display of your considerable talents?" Airron suggested.

Rogan crossed his arms at his chest and quickly shook his head. "No. We don't know how these people feel about magic. It is best not to flaunt it in their faces."

"What are you saying? If the Ellvinians choose to seek aid from a magical island, my friend, then they are going to see some magic."

Kiernan turned away and stifled a chuckle as Airron began to peel off his clothes.

"Stop that right this instant, Airron Falewir!" Melania yelled at him.

Airron ignored her as he hopped on one foot to pull off a leather boot.

"Almost forty years and he still acts like a child," Rogan groused.

"It is called fun, you little sourpuss, and it is something I have very little of these days. Oh, yes, I'm going in."

Melania continued to plead with her husband, but it was no use. Airron was determined to bodyshift.

Janin laughed out loud when he finally managed to shed everything he had been wearing and jumped up onto the ship's railing stark naked.

"What a bloody fool," Rogan murmured.

"Let him have his fun, Kal," Janin admonished.

Airron pointed a finger at Rogan. "See! I knew I liked your wife, and now I know why. She's brilliant!" With that, the Elf launched himself off the railing of the dinoque in a graceful dive into the tranquil blue ocean.

Beck looked over the side of the boat. The water was so clear that he could see Airron underneath the sea bodyshift into a dolphin.

Beck watched on in good humor as Airron leapt in and out of the water. Kiernan and Janin laughed out loud at his antics while Rogan and Melania scowled.

Captain Wilden took a moment from his critical watch over the sailors to approach Beck. "Your Grace. You better call the bodyshifter back on board. We have been given the signal to come ashore."

"Very well. Thank you, Captain. Will you be joining us on the island?"

The Captain's leathery face crinkled up into a smile. "I am a seaman, Your Grace. We will stay on the ship if that is acceptable to you. Never know when we might need a hasty retreat," he said with a wink.

Beck smiled. "I don't think we have anything to worry about here, Captain, but the choice is yours."

The Ship Captain bowed at the waist and went back to his duty.

Beck looked over the side again wondering how he was going to get Airron's attention, but it turned out he didn't need to. Beck ducked as the dolphin jumped straight into the air and landed on the deck. The gray mammal flapped around for a moment and made a strange keening noise before Airron shifted back.

Melania threw her cloak at him. "Hurry and get dressed. We're almost there."

"Aha! That's what you're worried about, isn't it? You don't want the women to see me naked!"

"It *has* been awhile," Janin commented to Kiernan.

"Over a year now and I've thought of little else," Kiernan teased back.

"You're not helping me here," Melania scolded the wives, hands on her hips.

Airron laughed and got to his feet. He unabashedly let the cloak fall from him as he picked his clothes up off the deck and walked behind one of the wooden food crates to dress.

Beck shook his head and turned back to watch the sailors expertly maneuver the ship to a dock that extended far out into the ocean. Ellvinian port workers rushed forward to assist the crew and while Beck waited for the gangplank to be lowered, he gazed toward shore and the large throng of people that awaited them there. Hundreds of Ellvinians shouted and waved excitedly. A smaller group of five stood before the crowd, and Beck assumed they were the higher-ranking Ellvinians.

Before departing, he had a lengthy conversation with Lars Kingsley and knew something of the Ellvinians' style of dress and physical appearance. Dark elves, Lars called them. The only question in Beck's mind was whether or not the darkness was confined to the outside.

※

"What do you mean it's missing?" the Premier hissed at his Adjunct.

The small Elf drew him away from the committee waiting to receive the Massan representatives. "The Vypir is nowhere to be found, Your Eminence. The glass of the observation room was found completely shattered and the Vypir gone."

"How could it get out of there? I thought that was reinforced glass? *Unbreakable*, the technicians assured me." He thought back to all of those times he stood at that very window thinking he was safe.

The Adjunct gulped nervously. "Since kill...I mean, draining the watershifters, the Vypir has grown extremely strong. We looked everywhere for it and cannot—"

Hendrix turned his back on the disembarking guests and grabbed the Adjunct by the throat. He knew that some of the people in the crowd could see him, but his control was gone. "If you looked *everywhere*, Adjunct, you would have found it.

Now, how in the Netherworld am I going to get my blood? Tell me!" He pointed behind him. "More magic users may be getting off that ship at this very moment and I have no way to extract their blood!" His eyes narrowed dangerously. "I should kill you for this."

"Aye, Your Eminence," the Adjunct managed to say around his constricted windpipe.

"Fortunately for you, I still need you. You will, however, execute the technician that allowed this to happen."

The Adjunct nodded, no longer able to speak.

Hendrix let go of the man's throat and his hands began to shake. "I need it, Adjunct. I *need* the blood."

The Adjunct placed his hands on his throat. "I'll find the Vypir," he said hoarsely.

"Go! Now!"

The Elf pulled up the sides of his tongor and raced away.

After taking a deep breath, he turned back to his Seconds, Anah, Balder and Jarl. "We need to talk. The Vypir is missing."

"What? We have to do something!" Anah cried in a panic. Hendrix looked into her gaunt face and red-rimmed eyes and wondered if his own appearance mirrored hers. It probably did. Since the blood, he couldn't remember the last time he had eaten. While the blood gave him sustenance and strength, his body still required food to survive. He would have to tell the Adjunct to make sure he ate on a regular basis once the blood supply resumed.

How ironic that after all these centuries of caring for that monstrosity, they finally find a land of magic and the Vypir escapes their grasp. If Emile were here, he would know how to find the Vypir he called Tolah, but Hendrix sent him and the Battlearms to Massa. Another cruel quirk of fate.

Balder started to question him further, but Hendrix cut him off. "Not now! We have guests."

Hendrix turned toward the dock and the six people walking toward him. He sniffed at the air and almost collapsed to the ground, quivering in excitement from the strength of magic these people possessed. Composing himself, he walked forward with his arms outstretched. "Welcome to the great island of Ellvin! You cannot begin to know how thrilled we are to have you here."

≈

Kenley smiled as she accepted the wild flowers Kirby handed to her. The strong breeze ruffled his blonde curls causing them to be even more disheveled than normal. This, along with his rosy cheeks from the wind-swept valley, made him look so young and carefree.

She loved this Kirby.

He grabbed her hand and they sprinted together over the hills and dips in the valley floor. At one point, Kirby abruptly stopped their headlong race to swing her into the air by her waist. She threw her head back and laughed, content to be in the arms of the man she loved more than anything. He kissed her forehead and desire flooded her body as he drew her down onto the carpet of verdant grass.

Kenley! Why do you have that dress on! Take if off right now!

Kenley rolled off Kirby and stood at the sharp words from her mother.

But, it is my wedding day.

No, Kenley, it is not your wedding day. Your grief is playing tricks on your mind.

It is my wedding day, mother!

No, Kenley.

She pointed behind her. Just ask Kirby! He will straighten this out.

Her mother crumpled a white cloth in her hands and looked down. *Kirby is dead.*

What?

You are too late, daughter. Kirby is dead.

Her head swiveled to the ground. Blood seeped from Kirby's mouth and his unseeing eyes glazed over as he lay in frozen death on the valley floor.

She screamed.

Bolting upright, Kenley covered her face with trembling hands and fought to get her breathing under control.

Another dream? Baya asked.

Yes.

Try to go back to sleep.

She sat unmoving for a long time, unwilling to surrender herself back to the dream. Finally, having no other choice, she groaned and fell back to the ground. Pulling her cloak over her head, she snuggled into its warmth and tried to empty her mind of all thought. Sleep eagerly made its claim on her once again. In her semi-conscious state, a noise jerked her back into awareness. It sounded like pebbles hitting a cobblestone road, but how could that be in a rainforest? Too tired to care about the answer, she closed her eyes but the noise continued to peck away at her consciousness until she could no longer ignore it.

With a growl, she lifted her head from out of the cloak. Baya sat in the middle of their prison with her eyes on the grate above.

What is that noise, Baya?

A crow.

A crow?

Yes. It is a type of black bird.

She snorted. *I know what a crow is. I hate crows.*

Why do you hate crows?

She shrugged mentally. *Everyone knows that when you see a crow, something bad is going to happen.*

Do you really believe that, Princess? There are many crows in the world. If each one was a portent of evil, we would have very little good in existence.

Diamond once told me to heed all warnings from crows.

Baya turned her green eyes on Kenley. *Heed all warnings does not mean that they are all dire.*

Kenley stood and peered up at the grate. Sure enough, a very large crow was perched in the center, pecking away at the iron grid.

"Unless you can open that grate, bird, get lost," Kenley shouted up at it.

The bird squawked angrily at her words.

The crow's appearance made her think back to the pier in Northfort when she saw one just like it and the old woman with white eyes.

She shuddered.

A tortured rasp cut through the quiet of the rainforest, and before Kenley could wonder at the sound, the grate ripped away from the hole.

Kenley gasped in surprise, but not wishing to waste the opportunity, she sprang into the air and shot out of her prison. Hovering several feet off the ground, she looked down in shock. Standing at the edge of the hole was the very woman she had just been thinking about and perched on her shoulder—the crow.

Baya scrambled out, her dragon talons easily allowing her to scale the dirt walls.

Kenley flitted down to the ground. "It would seem that my sincere gratitude is in order," she said to the woman with a bow of her head.

The old woman gave her a toothless smile. "I am wondering why you wallow in Haventhal, Princess, when others need your help."

Wallow? Really? Kenley dusted the dirt from her clothes. "What do you mean? Who needs my help?"

"An enemy has arrived on Massa's shores."

Her blood ran cold. "What enemy?"

"Dark Elves."

She quickly realized the woman must be referring to the Ellvinians. The same Ellvinians she sent Kirby and the children to Northfort to receive. "Are you sure, my lady? For what purpose would the Ellvinians attack Massa?"

"They have come for the blood of shifters."

"So, it is battle they seek?"

"Only as a means to an end. Pay attention. They have come for the blood of shifters. They wish to *drink* it."

Kenley stared at the old woman. "But, that doesn't make—"

"The Ellvinians are blood suckers. They crave the blood of magic users."

"They will kill Massans for their blood?" she asked incredulously.

"Worse. They will keep them alive."

Kenley snorted. "Unless they possess great powers, they will have a very difficult time obtaining the blood of a shifter."

"They do have a power of sorts. It is called Ascendency and it allows them to convince people how they should think."

How does this woman know so much? For that matter, how did she open the grate? Something her father spoke about a few years ago suddenly leapt into her mind. "Are you the Oracle?"

"I have been called by many names."

An enigma to solve another time Kenley decided as she thought about her brothers and the rest of the children in danger. "I must go." She bowed deeply at the waist. "Thank you, Oracle. I am indebted to—"

She looked up and the woman was gone.

With a shake of her head, Kenley swooped back down into the hole to gather her backpack. "Baya, I have to fly back to Iserlohn. It is the only way to get there in time."

Baya nodded. "I will follow from below."

"Baya, I must hurry. If we lose each other, I cannot wait for you."

"You will not lose me, Princess. I will keep up."

Kenley nodded, flexed muscles that had not been used in days and shot into the air.

Chapter 19

Shattered Innocence

"Take off your clothes, Izabel."

Izzy's body trembled at Chandal's words. She had known all along that this was what he wanted from her. His leering looks and furtive touches had finally built his confidence enough to act. Candlelight softened his angular features, but could do nothing for the iniquity that lurked behind his eyes.

"Please, sir, I need a moment," she told him softly. Crouched in the corner of the room, she needed time to build her own courage for what she was about to do. She needed to buy time so that he didn't use his mind control on her.

A fleeting image of her parents' loving faces brushed her mind, but she shook it away. She had to or else the emotional tide that hovered at the edges of her reason would overwhelm her.

She swallowed to regain some of her nerve. She was young, but she was also the daughter of Airron and Melania Falewir and a protector of her people. In the face of evil, it was her duty to destroy its existence utterly and without remorse.

She was staring at that evil.

Slowly, she stood.

Would her parents still love her after this act? Would they realize that she had no other choice? Deep down in her heart, she knew that they would. She had been taught from a very early age how to survive, and she would do what was necessary to live through this ordeal.

Chandal stared at her hungrily with eyes as black as night as her hands went to the front laces of her dress. Her hands were no longer shaking as she untied them and pulled the garment over her head.

Chandal rose fluidly from the bed and approached without hurry, most likely afraid she would dart away like a frightened animal if he moved too fast. "You are so beautiful, Izabel. I am utterly captivated by you." He reached out and ran the back of his fingers along her cheek. "I know you are young, but I will be gentle. I promise."

Standing before him in nothing but her shift, her composure almost shattered when he bent down and picked her up to carry her to the bed.

When he put her down, she scrambled as far away as she could and turned her head away when he began to remove his clothes. It didn't take him long, and she felt the mattress sink under his weight when he lay down next to her. She squeezed her eyes shut.

"Come here, Izabel," he whispered and dragged her close to him. He rolled his body on top of hers and pinned her arms above her head. *Oh, no. He must let go of my hand! I need my hand!*

She tried to wriggle away, but instead of angering him, it just seemed to excite him more. "That's right, Izabel," he said breathlessly. "Keep moving."

Finally, he let go of her one of her arms to trail his own hand down the length of her body.

She did not hesitate. She reached for the sharpened stick under her pillow and with both hands, plunged the makeshift weapon into the side of his neck.

He grunted, but did not scream out. Gulping back a sob, she pressed and pressed with all her might, not wanting to give the dark Elf an opportunity to sing his song.

The tears came now, flooding down her cheeks as she withdrew the weapon and stabbed it over and over into his neck. When he fell back, she rolled on top of him and straddled his body, all the while continuing to push the weapon deep into his neck.

She bit her lip to keep herself from crying out and tried to clear her mind of every thought except putting an end to the harm this Elf wanted to inflict on her and would inflict on others if given the chance.

The crude knife in her hands made a sickening sucking noise as she pulled it out and thrust it into the other side of his neck. Her mind shut down as she repeatedly hacked at his throat.

At some point, she realized he was no longer moving, but he continued to make a gurgling sound through lips coated in a red so deep it looked like black tar.

She lifted an arm to wipe her hair away from her face and suddenly became aware of the amount of blood dripping from her shaking hands. With a tortured cry, she jerked the knife free of Chandal and fell away from him onto the floor.

She scrambled back into the corner of the room and pulled her knees up close to her chest. Covered in the blood of the man she murdered, she glanced down at the weapon she fashioned from a stick and a piece of sandstone. Both pieces she pried from the toilet in the small privy off the bedroom, the only place she was allowed to go alone.

Her father taught her to how to make this knife once, and she silently thanked him for saving her life this day. But, thoughts of him broke the dam on her tightly-held emotions, and she fell on her side and began to sob uncontrollably.

&

Kane stumbled along the empty servant's quarter. He wasn't sure how much longer he could keep up the shifting needed to elude the Ellvinians. To make matters worse, more of them were coming in off the ships. All through the night, he suffered through their destructive ransacking of Northfort and the screams of the people still in the city. His only hope was that most of the inhabitants had followed his instructions and evacuated.

What he really needed was to find Kellan and Kirby. Together, the three of them would be able to free Jala and the others from the cellar and possibly even locate a bodyshifter messenger to fly to Nysa and inform his grandfather, King Maximus, of their plight so he could send troops to the region.

Jain!

All he received was a snarl in return.

I know, my friend. I want you by my side as well.

The pointy-eared cowards do not dare to show their faces outside. They know what awaits them.

When Kane glanced out of a window earlier, Jain had been prowling the courtyard outside. He couldn't imagine what the Ellvinians thought of him.

Have you been able to reach Maks?

Yes.

What did he say? Where is Kellan?

He said Prince Kellan will find you.

At least that means he is safe. I will continue my search, Jain. As soon as I find him, we will overpower the guards and let you inside.

Do not take long. My patience is wearing very thin.

Seemingly, out of nowhere, a pair of hands reached out, grabbed Kane by the shoulders, and rammed him against the wall. The breath rushed from his lungs in a loud grunt. "Let me see you use your magic now, Massan, with my nails dug into your flesh. It will not be so easy to fool me again."

Kane didn't bother with a reply. He just smashed his forehead into the Elf's nose. The Ellvinian stumbled back and Kane pushed away from him. Managing to put a few paces between them, he reached over his shoulder for the sword of Iserlohn. The quiet hall rang with a high-pitched whistle as the weapon emerged from its scabbard.

Unarmed, the Ellvinian stepped back even further with a hand cupped to his nose to try and stem the blood that seeped from his fingers.

Kane raised the sword out in front of him and stalked toward the Elf until the point was under his chin. "Where is Izzy Falewir?"

The Ellvinian glared at him. "I don't—"

Kane pushed until a pinpoint of blood appeared at the Elf's throat. "Last time. Where is Izzy Falewir?"

"You will not kill me if I tell you?"

"No."

"She...she is with Chandal. In his guest room."

Before he could question the Ellvinian further, the sound of running footsteps reached them. Kane spun, thinking to escape in the opposite direction, but Ellvinians appeared at both ends of the corridor.

"Don't move, Massan!"

Kane was trying to think of how he could use his illusions to escape so many when the Ellvinian who shouted pushed two men forward and forced them to their knees.

Kellan and Kirby.

The tall Elf held a sword of his own. "Put your weapon away. If you do not do as I say, I will kill these men where they kneel." From behind, he laid the tip of the sword on top of Kellan's shoulder.

Kellan stretched his neck back to look at the Elf behind him. "I am sorry, but it is very hard to hear you right now. Are you asking my brother to put down his sword? Do you know who he is? He is Kane Atlan, a Prince of Iserlohn, and he would never lay his sword at the feet of evil." Kellan looked Kane directly in the eye. "Not even for me."

Kane blinked slowly, but did not answer.

The Elf yanked Kellan's head back by his hair. "He *will* give up his sword, Massan. Whether the two of you are still alive by the time the steel reaches my fist remains to be seen."

"Tenderhooks?" Kellan asked his twin with his neck stretched back painfully.

Kirby snorted.

"Absolutely," Kane replied.

That single word sent everything in motion. Kellan and Kirby both slammed their elbows back into the tender lower belly of the Elves behind them. Kellan flipped the Ellvinian with the sword over his shoulder and hammered him with a blow that knocked him out cold. He pried the sword from the Elf's fingers and tossed it to Kirby, who caught it in midair.

Kane turned to his own fight. Two Ellvinians rushed him together and he called forth his magic and split into three images. He learned at a young age that whenever he did that, people always believed he was the one in the middle. He never was. The two Elves paid for that mistake with their lives.

Other Ellvinians came at him and he made little work of cutting them down. He derived no pleasure from killing. He simply did what had to be done to save his life and the lives of those he cared about. If an Ellvinian turned and ran, he lived. If he stayed to fight, he died.

When Kane's last opponent went down, he grimaced at the hall littered with dead Elves.

Kirby leaned down to wipe his sword on the white dress of one of the Ellvinians while Kellan strode over and embraced him. "Thank you, brother."

Kane pulled back. "Why are you thanking me? You are the one who came to my rescue." He grinned. "Tenderhooks? We haven't used that childhood move in years."

Kellan shrugged. "Seemed appropriate. But, you *are* the one who saved us."

"How?"

Kellan reached up and pulled wool out of his ears. "You told us not to listen to a word the Ellvinians said. It worked. Their song became muted with the wool and easier to cast aside."

Kane chuckled. "I didn't mean it so literally, but if it worked, I'm glad."

"It worked because at its core, the mind control they use is really just power of suggestion. Amazing what you can learn when people think you're not listening."

"Amazing what you can learn with a sword pointed to someone's throat as well. I found out where they are holding Izzy."

Kellan let out a sigh of relief. "And, the others?"

"Locked in a cellar below the first floor which you can get to off a short corridor behind the kitchens. Take Kirby and free them, and I will go after Izzy. The time has come to show our hand, Kellan. Use every resource you have and give no quarter. I'll meet you at the outer gates."

Kellan nodded grimly and turned to go, but Kane grabbed his arm. "Wait! Have you seen Alia?"

"Alia? She's here?"

"Yes. I don't know how she got in, but she is here." He thought of something. "Where is Maks?"

"Hiding with Lars, so Kirby and I could go with the Ellvinians and have them lead us to you or the others."

I do not hide.

Kane laughed at the rebuke from Maks in his mind.

Kellan threw up his hands. "Pardon me. Maks is waiting of his own free will for the right time to pounce on the unsuspecting Ellvinians."

I do not pounce.

"Fine. He's waiting for the right time to rip the Ellvinians to bloody hell."

Better.

"Come with us first, Kane," Kellan suggested. "Lars might know of a way to get past the Ellvinians guarding the guest chambers."

"If it gets us Izzy back, I'll try anything. Lead on, brother."

Chapter 20

Gifts

Hendrix Bane stood on a raised platform before the people of Ellvin and basked in the enthusiasm of their vocal adoration. At long last, he had become their beloved champion once again, and it was almost as intoxicating as the blood. The shouts and cries of praise and appreciation was deafening as the Ellvinians danced and cheered in complete abandon at the news he just delivered. Soon, word would spread to the outlaying areas of Ellvin and all would know that the rumors were indeed true. A life-saving supply of wormwood plants had arrived with the visitors and their ill loved ones would once again have access to the draught. All thanks to Hendrix Bane.

"Premier Bane!"

"Premier Bane!"

Hendrix lifted both arms to accept their ardent shouts and his action caused them to scream even louder.

For Hendrix, this momentous event in Ellvinian history was marred only by the fact that the Vypir was missing. Standing beside him with enough magic to render him unconscious were five Massan shifters. More were undoubtedly on their way here from Samara and Chandal, and he had no way to milk them.

His body trembled with need. The sudden withdrawal was affecting him much more than he realized it would. The plant-extracted drink that kept him alive now tasted bland and putrid. A poor substitute indeed for the blood.

He glanced behind him at his Seconds. If their sickly faces were any indication, they were feeling the same as he. Hendrix was about to turn back to his loving subjects when he noticed that the large man standing next to Jarl was looking directly at him with an unusually penetrating gaze. It was almost as though the man could read his thoughts and did not like what he found there. Hendrix turned away quickly and idly wondered what type of magic these newcomers possessed. Were they all watershifters like the Massans that were abducted previously? Out of the water, those shifters proved quite harmless and very easy to subdue. But, the six standing next to him did not have the same bodies as the watershifters, and they looked different. Bolder. Stronger.

Eventually, he would uncover the answers to all his questions and more, but first he needed that damn Vypir! If his Adjunct did not find it soon, the Massans would leave and Hendrix could very well be forced to go the rest of his life without the blood.

It was an unthinkable prospect.

A light hand on his arm startled him. He turned. It was Kiernan, the beautiful shifter with the light hair and green eyes.

"Premier Bane, I was wondering if it would be possible to be shown to our rooms. After more than a week on a ship, we would like to freshen up."

"Of course! How inconsiderate of me not to suggest it before. It is just that the news you bring to our island is of such staggering importance to our people. To show our appreciation, we have arranged an elaborate feast in your honor this evening."

She gave him a charming smile. "I am just very pleased that we could aid you in this matter."

Hendrix clapped his hands sharply and a servant hurried forward up onto the platform. "Please show our guests to their rooms at the compound." He turned back to Kiernan. "It is a full league walk from here so I will have horses readied for the short trip."

"Thank you, Premier, but that will not be necessary. After such a long journey on the ship, a walk would be a delightful change of pace. It will also give us the opportunity to explore your lovely island. The caves we saw from the sea are magnificent."

Hendrix hesitated as he thought of the Vypir on the loose. If the creature scented the magical blood of the shifters, there is no telling what it would do. But, there was no easy way to turn down Kiernan's simple request without arousing suspicion. He decided to send two Battlearms with the shifters just in case the Vypir reappeared.

"Very well. I will arrange an escort."

Kiernan smiled at the large shifter with the piercing gaze. "Do not bother yourself. My Mage husband is all the escort I will ever need."

Hendrix stumbled back and almost fell from the platform. Kiernan reached out to him with a steadying hand. "Are you all right?" she asked in a concerned voice.

Hendrix quickly recovered and fanned his face. "Aye, I think all of the excitement of the day is catching up to me. Did you say Mage?"

Her green eyes lit up. "Yes, my husband is a Mage."

Hendrix licked his lips at the unexpected gift. It seemed the makings of a new Vypir just landed squarely in his lap.

༄

"We are losing control!" Samara fumed at the two Shiprunners sitting at the table with her in the mayor's private office. They were Chandal's most trusted officers and she felt at ease speaking freely in front of them. She leaned forward and slammed both palms on the table. "Most of the people of the city have fled right under our noses! How in the Netherworld could that have happened? You do realize they will be returning with reinforcements?"

The more senior of the two flinched back from her. "Second Samara, we are sailors not fighters."

"You can secure a gate, can't you? Your delicate hands won't get bloodied standing in front of a closed gate!" She jabbed a finger at the Shiprunners. "This mess lies squarely at the feet of your caste! You have allowed your sailors to run amok in the city to frighten the citizens off before we could properly contain them!" She straightened from the table.

"When the Premier hears of this, I will not take the blame. No! This is Chandal's fault and his alone."

"What do you suggest, Second?"

Samara took a deep breath. "Have you found that boy with the golden eyes yet?"

He shook his head. "No, Second, not yet."

She pinched the bridge of her nose with two fingers in an attempt to repress the desire to kill these two officers where they sat. Once a bit calmer, she said. "Well, find him. Not only is he a powerful magic user, but a Prince of this land. We cannot afford to lose him." She cursed under her breath. The situation could not be worse. For the first time in centuries, they found a source for both the wormwood plants and the blood and now they were about to squander it all away. Discretion was what was needed, but instead they tromped over the Massans like arrogant swine. Did Chandal really think the sequester of the estate's inhabitants in the cellar would go unnoticed? Why was he not reining in his people? It was unlike him to be so careless in his duties. Speaking of which, "Where is Chandal?" she screamed at the top of her lungs.

One of the Shiprunners cleared his throat uneasily. "He...he is with the girl."

"He's still with that little Elf?" she shrieked at them. "How dare he? We are in the middle of a hostile takeover and he is enjoying a bloody bedroom romp? Go get him! If he is not in this room within a quarter of an hour, I will personally cut his—"

The door to the office opened behind her.

Samara twisted around and could hardly believe her eyes. "Emile!" As proof of her fragile state, she did the unthinkable. She ran to him and threw herself into his arms.

Emile returned the embrace rigidly, clearly uncomfortable with her demonstrative behavior. "Nice to see you, too, Samara. I think."

Red-faced, she pulled away from him. What was she doing? She was a high-ranking Second of the Ellvinian Empire, and an emotional outburst of this nature was far beneath her. Very far. Taking a deep breath, she smoothed out her tongor and raised her head to meet his gaze. "My apologies, Emile. It's just that it has not been going exactly as planned lately. I will admit that I am pleased to see you here."

He cocked his head to the side. "That much is obvious."

She turned away from him so he could not see her blush. "Please sit down. We were just discussing the problems at hand." Emile sat, and she described the events of the past few days making sure to highlight Chandal's inadequacies in controlling the Shiprunners. Emile might be a Second just as she, but everyone knew he was the Premier's right-hand man.

"Have you brought reinforcements?" she asked hopefully.

"At the moment, two hundred Battlearms, but in my wake another twenty thousand. Will that do?" he asked smugly.

Her body quivered in relief, but she managed to keep her excitement under control. Her lips twitched up into a smile. "Aye, I think that will do just nicely."

"I think it is time I had a talk with Chandal to see what he has to say about all this," Emile said and stood.

"Agreed," she said, still smiling. Because, although discretion was preferred, a Battlearm would do the job just as well. The only difference was the amount of blood involved. And, as an Ellvinian, that was pure magic to her ears.

Kane was glad he took the time to speak to Lars as the mayor did offer him a way to bypass most of the guards watching Chandal's room.

With the help of Kellan and Kirby, they stormed the kitchens and quickly dispatched the Ellvinians inside. From there, it took no time to locate the small lift Lars told them was built into the back wall by the hearth. It was nothing more than a wooden platform linked to a pulley system designed to carry dirty dishes from the guest chambers directly to the kitchens, but it was exactly what he needed.

Somehow, Kane managed to squeeze his bulk onto the platform and hand over fist began to haul himself up the chute. By the time he reached the third floor, his shirt was soaked through with sweat. His arms trembling with effort, he paused for a moment at the top to listen for any hint of noise outside of the lift. Hearing nothing, he slid the tiny door open and unfolded his cramped body free. The hallway was empty.

He moved silently down the corridor, unsheathing his sword as he went. Lars told him there were four Ellvinians guarding Chandal's room, and he would have to defeat them all to get to Izzy. Could Alia be in there as well? His heart hammered in his chest at the thought of seeing her. He promised her a stroll, and it was a promise he intended to keep.

Emboldened by his chivalrous desires, he turned the corner at a full sprint with his sword out in front of him. Skidding to an abrupt stop, he saw that there were not four guards. There were seven.

Having no other choice, he struck.

As a Prince of Iserlohn, he was born to the dance of the blade. His siblings disdained weaponry of any kind, and he couldn't blame them. A weapon would only weigh Kenley down when she took to the skies and Kellan's fists were deadlier than any weapon made of metal.

Not so for Kane. He relished the symmetry of movement in the swordfight. Every stroke found its mark and every parry was turned aside. Each forward movement he took meant death to the enemy because anything less meant he would die. That Izzy would die.

At the end of the dance, Kane stood alone.

He stepped over the body of the Ellvinian in front of the door and opened it, prepared to do battle once again, but the sitting room was empty. Hurriedly, he ran through to the bedroom. With a well-placed kick, the door flew open and he was inside.

He almost fell to the floor with relief at the sight of little Izzy sitting in the corner.

Then, he saw the blood.

Slowly, he walked forward, but she did not acknowledge him. As he advanced into the room, his gaze went to the bed and the naked dead man lying there.

A fury unlike anything he had ever felt in his life enveloped him. With stilted steps, he made his way to the bed. It was Chandal.

He sheathed his sword, moved to Izzy and squatted down in front of her. "Izzy, are you all right?"

Her lips began to tremble, but she nodded.

"Did you..."

"Yes, I killed him," she whispered softly.

He lifted her chin and waited until her violet eyes met his. "Good girl."

She glanced at him from underneath her eyelashes. "Do you really mean it?"

"Of course I do. Do not for one moment regret valuing your own life ahead that of a monster. He would never have returned the favor." He looked down at her state of undress. "Did...did he hurt you?"

"No."

Thank the Highworld.

"I will get you out of here safely, Izzy, I promise you that." Her back straightened a fraction at his words. "Can you walk?"

She nodded and got to her feet.

"I am sorry to rush you, Izzy, but someone will see the dead guards in front of this room very soon. We must leave at once before others come."

Her eyes widened. "You had to kill, too?"

"Yes. Hurry now and get dressed."

She quickly ran to the basin and washed the dried blood from her face and arms. Then, he turned away as she bent down and retrieved her dress from the floor and scrambled into it. She was just tying the laces of her boots when the door to the sitting room opened.

"Chandal! Chandal! Get out here now! We must speak with you at once."

Kane reached behind his back for his sword and it came free with a deadly rasp.

Lady Samara and another Ellvinian male appeared in the doorway to the bedroom and Kane stepped in front of Izzy.

He watched the Ellvinian woman's eyes take in the scene and her dead companion on the bed. "What is this? What have you done?"

"We have done nothing except protect our own lives. Now, step away from the door. We are leaving."

Samara opened her mouth and held a hand out to Izzy. "Come here, my darling. You wish nothing more than to come and be with me." Kane heard the words she said, but it did not have the same hypnotizing effect as it seemed to on others.

As Izzy started forward toward Samara, Kane grabbed her arm and held her back. "No!"

The shouted word seemed to confuse Izzy and she stopped.

The tall Elf with Samara stepped forward and when he opened his mouth and spoke, Izzy ran to him. He immediately hugged her to his body and put an arm around her neck. "Drop the sword or she is dead." There was no mistaking the menace in his voice. "Thus far, you have been dealing with the Shiprunners, lad, but I am a Battlearm and you do not wish to mess with me. I promise you that."

Samara held her arms out toward Izzy. "Give her to me, Emile." The Elf let her go and Izzy went willingly into Samara's arms. The Ellvinian woman promptly began stroking Izzy's hair and whispering in her ear.

"What is his magic?" The Elf Samara called Emile asked without taking his eyes from Kane.

"He creates illusions of himself and so is able to slip through our fingers like mist in the wind."

"Why is he not responding to Ascendency?"

"I have not figured that out yet. We learned the hard way that it does not work on the magic users who call themselves mindshifters either. They killed several Shiprunners before we were able to put them down."

The blood oath in Kane flared through his body.

Emile scratched his chin. "Interesting. It must have something to do with magic that originates in the mind.

Since this boy's magic is centered around his sight and mind, it seems he, too, is immune." Emile reached out and stroked Izzy's cheek. "We still have other ways to keep him under control."

"Get your hands off her," Kane seethed.

Emile smiled and leaned out of the doorway. "I would like you to meet two of my fighters. Zebin! Liam! Come here at once."

Almost instantly, two muscular Ellvinians stepped into the room. The crisp white frocks they wore bore an elegant gold trim Kane had not seen before on the others. Emile nodded toward Kane. "This boy here says that the Battlearms are weak."

Two pairs of black eyes snapped his way.

"He says you are lazy and slow. He thinks he can take the two of you on at one time and win the fight easily."

Samara ushered Izzy from the room. "Come now, darling. I believe the boys wish to have a little fun."

Kane stepped back to give himself room to fight.

Out of nowhere, one of the Battlearms flicked a metal star-shaped object through the air and before Kane could dodge out of the way, it embedded in his sword hand. He cried out, and the sword of Iserlohn dropped from nerveless fingers.

The Battlearms used the distraction to close the distance between them. One punched him in the jaw at the same time the other buried a fist in his stomach.

Kane doubled over in pain, but the Battlearms were not through with him yet. As it turned out, they were just getting started.

Chapter 21

Bloodbath

Kane's shoulders ached from the way the Ellvinian fighters carried him by his elbows, but he didn't have the strength to straighten his body and walk. Instead, his head hung low and his feet dragged feebly along the floor of the corridor.

His tongue glided over his swollen lip and then checked that his teeth were all still there. They seemed to be intact and he didn't think the fighters broke any bones, but by the way his body felt, they came close.

"Where are you taking me?" he croaked out and noticed that one of the Elves carried his scabbard and sword.

The two Elves ignored him and swept him down the hallway and through the doors to the ballroom. The tables and decorations from the gala had all been cleared and the two fighters dumped him unceremoniously in the middle of the large room.

"Don't move or you'll get your own sword through your back."

With a groan, Kane rolled over and stared motionless up at the ceiling willing the pain to subside. Slowly, he turned his head to the front of the room. Samara, Emile, and several other Ellvinians were sitting behind a long table covered in what appeared to be maps.

"We do not have any choice in the matter, Samara," he heard Emile say. "The Premier has commanded."

"But, declare war?"

"It is the only way. How else are we to meet the needs of our people?" Emile glanced over at Kane. "In any case, it is too late to turn back now."

Palpable grief raked Kane's body at the fate that awaited Massa. It was not likely that he would ever see his parents again either, trapped as they were on enemy land. Powerful though they were, anyone caught unawares would be vulnerable. Kenley was far away in Callyn-Rhe, but even she wouldn't be safe if war broke out. And, Izzy Falewir? After the nightmare she had been through with Chandal, he let her slip right through his fingertips.

He laughed bitterly at his incompetence. Not only did the children of *Savitars* invite the enemy onto their soil in unmanageable numbers, but they threw them a gala in the process! How would the Dwarves and Elves react to such outrageous naiveté? Would they blame magic users? Would it result in another segregation of the lands as had been the case after the Mage War? Until twenty years ago, the lands of Haventhal and Deepstone wanted nothing to do with each other or with Iserlohn. This mistake could have devastating and far-reaching consequences for the island of Massa.

If his father had been here, he never would have allowed any of this to happen. In good conscience, Kane could not even blame his youth. He was a Prince of Iserlohn and knew better.

"Kane, are you all right?" a soft voice asked.

He swallowed back the sting of failure when he saw familiar purple eyes peering down at him. Izzy. He turned his head away. "I am so sorry, Izzy. How can you even look at me?"

"Why wouldn't I look at you? I have never been happier to see anyone in my life."

"But, I let them take you again."

She tore a piece of fabric from the bottom of her dress and pressed it against his lip. "You did not *let* them do anything. You risked your life to come after me, and I love you for that. Thank you, Kane." She leaned down and planted a chaste kiss on his forehead. "Don't worry. Everything will be fine. You promised, remember?"

When he smiled, the cut on his lip caused him to wince. "I did promise, didn't I? On my life, Izzy, I will do whatever I can to keep you safe."

"I know."

The door to the ballroom opened.

"Second Emile! We found this girl soaking in a tub in one of the guest chambers."

Kane turned and his heart stopped beating in his chest. It was Alia and her clothes were soaking wet and clinging to her body. The fighter gripping her by her upper arm leaned down and sniffed her neck. "This one is quite full of the magic."

Emile strode forward. "Come here, girl. Where have you been hiding?"

Alia's mouth opened and then she saw Kane on the floor and frowned. "I...I was in the servant's quarters."

"You just happened to be bathing in your clothes?"

She lifted her chin. "I am a watershifter. It was either that or die." She glanced back at him. "What is going on here?"

"Are there others with you?" Emile asked instead of answering her question.

She quickly shook her head. "No."

Emile took a sniff. "Aye, she is one of the shifters. She should pose no problem out of the water. Take her to the cellar with the rest."

"No problem? I'll be happy to show you just how big of a problem I can—"

A high-pitched keening echoed from the hallway outside and interrupted Alia's tirade. Everyone in the room, including the Ellvinians at the table, went silent.

Click. Click. Shuffle. Click. Click.

Someone or *something* Kane amended to himself, lumbered toward the open ballroom doors.

Shuffle. Click. Click. Shuffle.

The distressed cry reverberated again, and the hair on the back of Kane's neck stood straight up. What in the Highworld was it? It reminded him of the sounds a dying animal might make. Instinctively, he pitched to his feet and stepped in front of Izzy. Despite the ominous atmosphere, his gaze sought out the fighter that held his sword. He would need that sword to get Izzy and now Alia to safety.

Click. Click. Shuffle.

A shadow appeared at the entrance to the ballroom and then the thing itself.

"Oh, dear Highworld," Izzy whispered.

The beast shuffled into the room hunched over and balanced on the knuckles of his hands. His muscled legs ended in claws that clicked on the tile when he moved, and a long appendage twisted sinuously in the air behind him.

White hair stood up in tuffs around its skeletal features, and the skin was pulled tight over a face and ears that looked remarkably Elven.

The creature's gaze locked on Emile and it stood to its full height, at least eight or nine feet tall, and let out a loud bellow.

"Tolah!"

The fighter holding the sword of Iserlohn immediately charged the beast.

"No! Leave him!" Emile shouted, but it was too late.

The creature lifted an elongated arm and backhanded the soldier with a swing so brutal, it lifted the Elf off his feet and he hit neck first onto the floor. The sword flew from his fingers and skidded across the marble floor of the ballroom.

The Elven creature sniffed the air and then snapped his head toward Alia still in the grip of the Battlearm.

"Tolah! No!"

Faster than Kane had ever seen anything move, the beast skittered toward Alia, claws scratching the slick floor. Alia screamed and tried to fight her way free of the Ellvinian holding her, but he pushed her out in front of him to shield himself.

Kane frantically searched for his sword, and spotted it up against the windowed wall of the ballroom and sprinted toward it.

Alia let out a bloodcurdling squeal.

Kane's hand clamped on the hilt of the weapon and he spun back around.

The Ellvinian that had been holding Alia was lying on the ground. At least he thought it was the same fighter. The head was missing.

The beast had Alia clutched in his long arms. Kane watched in horror as the beast's tail sprouted two fangs at the end of it and darted toward her. In an attempt to evade the menacing member, she arched her back so far away from the creature that her long hair brushed the ground. It was not enough. The tail struck her neck and latched on. A strange sucking noise issued from the tentacle and blood began to drip down Alia's throat.

Kane screamed and sprinted toward the ghastly spectacle, shoving his way past the Ellvinians in the room who stood staring transfixed as though in some kind of trance.

"Move!"

Kane cursed when he saw Alia's eyes roll up in her head. *I'm not going to make it!* With a cry, he lifted his sword and dove at the creature, but with uncanny speed it dropped Alia and flitted out of his reach.

"Alia!" Kane scrambled to his watershifter friend and cradled her head in his lap. Izzy dropped down next to him.

"Is she all right?"

He shook Alia gently. "Come on, Alia. You are going to be fine."

Her head lolled listlessly.

A sob tore from his throat. "Alia! Look at me!" Blood soaked Kane's trousers and he turned Alia's head to inspect her wound. Half of her neck was torn away.

Something inside him died.

"Kane, let's get out of here," Izzy cried, pulling on his arm.

Kane lifted his head and witnessed a bizarre scene playing out in the ballroom. The Ellvinians were trying to catch the blood-sucking creature with crazed looks in their eyes. One managed to get close, shoved the tail in his mouth, and began sucking out Alia's blood before the beast launched him off with a vicious kick.

"Leave the Vypir be!" Emile continued to scream at his Battlearms.

So, the beast had a name. Kane looked back down at Alia with a sad smile and brushed her red hair away from her face. "May the spirits of the Highworld take you gently into their embrace," he prayed over her softly. "I will miss you, mermaid." Then, he carefully moved from under her and stood.

Golden eyes radiated as he called forth the magic that was his to summon. "Izzy, go find Kellan and Kirby. Bring them and the others here to the ballroom."

"What are you going to do?" she asked worriedly.

"Just do as I say."

The little Elf looked at him with tears pooling in her purple eyes and then turned and ran.

Without emotion, Kane walked to the door and after Izzy went through, locked it. He turned back to survey the room with the sword of Iserlohn in his fist.

One of the Ellvinians finally noticed him and yelled out, but it was too late. Kane splintered his image into five replicas. "For Massa!" he cried and ran toward the Ellvinians in a wedge formation. "For Alia!"

Realizing the sudden danger, several Battlearms broke off from their chase of the Vypir to close with him. Of course, they attacked the point illusion first and Kane cut into them from the flank. He screamed as he fought and within seconds, he was covered in blood and three Ellvinians lay dead on the floor.

That left nine.

They came at him in a group now, the Vypir forgotten in the need to survive.

He split the replicas up to run in different directions and this fooled the Ellvinians for a time, but it soon became obvious who was the real threat. Still weakened by the beating he suffered, Kane began to tire and grunted in pain when more enemy thrusts snaked through his defenses and found their mark. The slices over his body were growing more numerous and soon the lion's share of the blood at his feet was his.

As he tried to defend against three attacks at once, he slipped to the floor and his sword fell from his grip.

"Finish him off!" he heard a feminine voice order. It had to be Samara.

A dark Elf standing over him lifted his sword and in that last second before death, Kane found that he had no regrets. He would go to the spirits in the Highworld knowing he fulfilled his oath. Knowing he fought to protect the people of Massa with his last breath. And, knowing that Alia would be waiting there for him.

He smiled and that modest act saved his life.

It caused the Elf standing over him ready to deliver the fatal blow to hesitate. And, in that hesitation, the room behind the Elves exploded into a million tiny razor-sharp shards as Jain crashed through one of the windows. The enormous white cat landed nimbly on the blood-soaked floor and let out a venomous roar.

A Kenley does not die lying on his back! On your feet, Prince!

Kane's chest swelled and an involuntary snarl erupted from his teeth at the authority in Jain's words. From the blood oath? The Dracan bond? Simple pride? It didn't matter. Kane smirked. *Let us die standing up then, my friend.*

Kane kicked out and sent the Elf standing over him to the floor. His golden eyes flared as he once again conjured five illusions into existence. The distraction gave him just enough time to get to his feet and retrieve his sword.

Together, Kane and Jain, upholding the promises of both of their ancestors, fought side by side to defeat the Ellvinians.

Kane cried out in frustration when he saw the Vypir, Emile and Samara escape through the broken window, but battling two Ellvinians, he couldn't give chase. Remotely, he registered the sounds of screaming and fighting out in the hallway, so Kane stepped up his efforts to end the battle and the two Ellvinians fell to his sword.

The locked ballroom doors shook from furious pounding from outside. Kane turned to see Jain make the final kill just as the doors exploded off their hinges and sailed backwards into the room.

It was Kellan.

Pouring in around him were all the people that the Ellvinians trapped in the cellar. Servants, mostly, but some were foreigner guests of the mayor. All had determined looks creasing their features as they ran in holding bloody knives or iron skillets. The cook, Cora, held a broom and she looked like she was more than capable of inflicting damage with it.

"We won back the estate," Kellan announced. "The Ellvinians are gone."

Chapter 22

The Feast

In the open pavilion on a portion of the beach cleared for the feast, Kiernan sat back on her pillow and smiled as she watched the Ellvinians fight for the pleasure of dancing with Airron and Melania. The dark Elves unabashedly admitted to their fascination with her white-haired friends. Airron seemed to enjoy the attention from the women, but poor Melania yelped as she was twirled from one Ellvinian male to the next in a lively dance. If it had been her, Kiernan knew she would have been sick to her stomach by now.

A young girl approached Kiernan shyly and held out a necklace she made from a string of flowers. "For you, my lady."

Kiernan lowered her head and allowed the girl to place the flowers around her neck. "Thank you. They are lovely."

In response, the girl giggled and ran off to join the energetic parade of dancers that swiveled their way through the festivities. The girl raced to the end of the line, placed her hands on the hips of the person in front of her and proceeded to kick her legs in unison with the others.

The Elf sitting next to Kiernan nudged her and offered her a pipe that emitted a sweet smelling smoke, but she politely declined. It seemed to make those who chose to imbibe a little wobbly on their feet and as exhausted as she was at the moment, it would most likely send her flat on her face right here in the sand. The soft moonlight and hypnotic undulation of the torch flames were not helping in keeping her awake and she stifled a yawn.

"You have made my people very, very happy this day," Hendrix Bane commented to their small circle that included Beck, Rogan and Janin as well as the three Ellvinian Seconds.

Kiernan sat up straighter, not wishing to appear rude.

"Yes, they do seem in good spirits," Beck answered.

"Why shouldn't they be? You saved their lives." The Premier took a long draw on the pipe. "So, what do you do in Massa, Master Atlan?"

"Please, just call me Beck."

"Very well, Beck."

"To answer your question, I am a simple man who enjoys living a simple life."

For some reason, Beck indicated on the journey that he didn't wish to disclose their royal status to the Ellvinians. She wondered now if her husband had reason to be suspicious of them. Kiernan gazed around at the celebrating Elves and did not feel the slightest bit of worry. In fact, the Ellvinians had done nothing except make them feel extremely welcome ever since they stepped foot on the island.

The Premier waggled a finger in the air. "Not so simple a man, Beck. Your wife tells me you are a Mage."

Beck conceded the statement with a small nod.

"Are there other Mages in Massa?" the Premier asked.

Beck shook his head. "No, but I confess to hoping that one day my sons will follow in my footsteps."

Kiernan snorted, but no one seemed to hear. Actually, she had no doubt that her husband heard, but he simply chose not to acknowledge her. She tried to suppress a second yawn, but wasn't so successful this time.

"Do not fall asleep just yet, Lady Kiernan," the Premier chided her. "I have yet one more surprise in store for you tonight."

Inwardly, Kiernan groaned at having to remain at the feast longer, but forced a smile on her face for Hendrix.

Beck stood. "It will have to wait until morning, Premier Bane. Surely, you can understand how tired we are from the day's activities."

Highworld bless that man, Kiernan thought to herself and accepted Beck's outstretched hand to help her to her feet.

Hendrix stood as well, waved a hand in Beck's face and in a singsong voice, said, "No, no, no. I'm afraid I must insist, Beck." Hendrix moved closer to her husband. "You would like nothing more than to receive that surprise right now, wouldn't you?"

Beck nodded. "I would like a surprise right now."

Kiernan snapped her head up to Beck. It was unlike him to give in so easily.

Anah turned to Rogan and said, "You wish to call your friends over so they can participate in the surprise as well."

She listened with even more confusion as Rogan opened his mouth in surprise. "What a lovely song, Anah!"

Song?

Anah repeated her request to retrieve Airron and Melania, and Rogan raced off toward the dancers.

Kiernan was suddenly alert. All was not right, but she didn't know why she felt that way. If she pried apart the conversations, they seemed innocuous, but her instincts were telling her something different.

When Rogan returned with Airron and Melania, Hendrix and the Seconds continued to suggest actions to her friends and they all complied without hesitation while commenting on the beautiful voices of the Ellvinians.

Kiernan had no idea what they were talking about. She heard no song from the dark Elves' mouths. It was the strangest thing.

"Come along now!" Hendrix intoned and led the way to an unoccupied portion of the beach. His dress, which the Ellvinians called a tongor, billowed around his ankles as he strode forward purposefully.

Kiernan threaded her arm through Beck's and glanced up at his profile, but he seemed as resolute as the Premier and kept his gaze forward as he walked. Still uneasy, Kiernan just wanted this surprise over with so she could go back to the compound and discuss her concerns in private with Beck.

The Premier led them off the beach and onto a narrow path that cut into a swampy copse of mangroves.

"Not much longer," Hendrix said and held out his hand, indicating he wanted Kiernan and Beck to step into the leafy tunnel ahead of him. The walkway through the groves was quite dry but off to the left and right of their path, Kiernan could see the moonlight reflected in water. A skittering sound drew her notice and she saw several crab-like creatures scrabble down a tree trunk and drop into the water below.

Strangely enough, she couldn't shake the feeling that she was walking to her execution.

"Ah, here we are now," exclaimed the Premier.

Their party emerged from the wooded grove and into a circular clearing. Several armed Ellvinians stood around six large stakes sticking up from the ground. Similar to the ambiance of the feast, torches on poles illuminated the eerie scene. Beck still had not said a word to her and that was making her even more nervous.

The Premier clapped his hands. "If you will all just step up to the stakes, we can begin the surprise."

Instinctively, Kiernan reached for the sword on her back and her hand came up empty. She no longer carried the sword of Iserlohn. Her son, Kane, wore it now.

The Ellvinians whispered words in the ears of Airron, Rogan, Melania and Janin and they all stepped up laughing to the poles.

"What an unusual party ritual," Airron commented, but happily stood against his stake.

The Ellvinians asked her and Beck to follow suit, and Kiernan watched in disbelief as Beck passively did as he was told.

"Come now, Lady Kiernan. You do not wish to spoil the surprise now, do you?" the Premier challenged.

"What is going on? I am not going to stand next to a stake in the ground. What absurdity is this?"

"Just do as they say, Kiernan," Beck instructed.

"Really? You want me to do this?"

"Yes."

"Beck! I refuse to—"

"Please."

Reluctantly, Kiernan stomped to the last remaining pole and stood against it. As soon as she did, she cried out in pain as her arms were wrenched behind her back and tied around the pole by one of the Ellvinian fighters.

She glared at her husband. "Happy?"

"This is not the time, Kiernan."

"No? Fine, I'll wait until they light the fire under my feet."

The Elf behind her yanked the ropes tighter and she grunted while wondering why her companions' demeanors showed none of the panic that gripped her. Airron, Melania, Rogan and Janin simply grinned as their hands were tied and and Beck's stony expression had all the animation of a rock. *What is he up to?* She knew her husband well, and he was holding something back. But, what?

"Surprise!" Hendrix cackled.

Chapter 23

Gooseberry

"Rogan, gooseberry."

"Gooseberry," Rogan repeated automatically.

Beck looked at Janin. "Gooseberry."

"Gooseberry."

"Airron, gooseberry."

"Gooseberry."

Melania said the word without the prompt.

Beck turned toward Kiernan.

"Are you serious?" she asked. "You want me to say *gooseberry*?"

Beck chuckled. "I knew you would be the difficult one."

"Gooseberry! There, I said it," she declared petulantly.

Airron looked around at the armed Ellvinians. "Am I right in assuming this is no longer a fun surprise?"

"It is not," Beck confirmed.

"Then, why are we standing here strapped to stakes?" Rogan demanded.

"The Ellvinians used what they call Ascendency on you. It is a potent form of power of suggestion."

"So, the Elves *convinced* me that it would be fun to let them tie me up and I believed them?" Rogan asked.

"Basically."

"Is it magic?"

"No. I believe this Ascendency is extremely effective in the Ellvinians because of the centuries they have had to perfect it, but it is not magic. Well, not entirely. I think innately, the Elves do have a small amount of inherent magic and this fact contributes to the strength of their control, but it is more of a learned skill."

The Premier simply stood and stared at them as Beck spoke.

"What's with the gooseberry?" Kiernan asked.

"The word was meant to break the hypnotic state the Ellvinians placed you in. Whenever the Ellvinians speak to you, I want you to think of a bright green gooseberry. This will neutralize their power of suggestion over you."

"Their power doesn't work on me," Kiernan stated.

"By the glares you have been giving me, I assumed that was the case."

"Gooseberry, huh?" Airron mused. "Is it really that simple?"

"Yes, it really is that simple. Think of a gooseberry and the Ellvinians will no longer be able to send you into a hypnotic state and control your actions."

"And, you have known this all along?" Kiernan accused.

He quickly shook his head. "No. Lars Kingsley mentioned a unique timbre to the voices of the Ellvinians and it prompted me to think of Ascendency, but all the pieces didn't slide together until the feast."

"If that is the case, then why are we still strapped to poles? Shouldn't we free ourselves?" Rogan asked.

The Ellvinian fighters shuffled their feet nervously.

"Not yet. I want to have a word with the Premier first."

Hendrix Bane wore a confident smirk on his face. "Your theories are very entertaining, Beck."

"Now that we are no longer friends, I would prefer that you address me as Mage."

The Premier tapped a finger on his chin. "Ah, aye, and while you mention it, that is the very reason for this little surprise I arranged. So, tell me, *Mage*, is this the extent of your powers? Mind over matter with a *gooseberry*?"

The Seconds laughed uneasily.

"The extent of my power? Good, Highworld, no. It was just the easiest solution to a problem. You do know what a Mage is, do you not?"

"Only in the form of a Vypir," the Premier commented snidely and the others laughed once again. Hendrix moved closer to taunt them. "What are you going to do? Flop around on the floor like a fish out of water like the kidnapped watershifters did before they died?"

The humor in Beck's face disappeared.

"Bah!" Hendrix said, turning from them. "How powerful can you be trussed up like animals?"

"We won't be for long."

Hendrix stopped and turned back. "There is no help coming for you, *Mage!* It will go easier for you if you accept that fact."

"I don't remember asking for help."

Hendrix snorted, but Kiernan noticed that he did take a step back behind the line of armed Ellvinians. "You are mad. How do you think you can get yourself out of this? I know the watershifters can swim well but they could not break the bonds of a good, sturdy rope."

"We are not watershifters."

"Then, how are you going to do it?"

"In order?"

"What does that mean, in order?"

"I was inquiring if you wished me to explain the order in which we will free ourselves."

"Oh, aye, I am looking forward to this." The Premier nudged Second Balder next to him, but Beck noticed the look he threw at the Ellvinian fighters that seemed to indicate they should be ready just in case the crazy Massans could actually break free.

Beck looked up for a moment. "Let me see. It will probably take two, maybe three, seconds for all six of us to be free. We are getting a little up there in age."

The Ellvinians laughed until the Premier cut them off with an angry look.

"Now, Airron, the Elf over at the end with the smirk, will shift into a small animal form that will seem to make him disappear into thin air. If I know his lovely wife, Melania, as well as I think I do, she has already summoned a squirrel or other rodent, and the creature is happily chewing through her ropes as we speak."

Melania nodded with a grin, and Kiernan noticed Hendrix Bane take another step further back.

"My friend, Rogan, is just waiting for the signal to call forth fire and burn through his bonds, and then he will free his beautiful wife, Janin." Beck paused to let his words sink in. "And, this magnificent woman to my left will enlist the help of your own fighters, Premier Bane, to free her. You see, her ability is similar to your Ascendency, but much, much more powerful. Anyone caught in her magical grasp will be powerless to do anything other than exactly as she commands, for as long as she commands it."

Hendrix wiped the sweat from his forehead. "And, you?"

"Me? For someone who covets our magic so much, you really do not know much about it. In addition to being a Mage, I am also an earthshifter. With the flick of a wrist, I could sink you into the very dirt on which you now stand and bury you until you suffocate in an agonizingly slow and painful death. And, these little strings holding me to this stake," he said, nodding behind him. "Almost too insignificant to mention."

"If that is true then what are you waiting for?" Hendrix shouted shrilly.

Beck took a deep breath. "The fact that you have restrained us should be proof enough, but I wanted to confirm your intentions."

"My intentions?"

"Yes. I do not make the decision to kill lightly. I wanted to make certain of your evil purpose before I committed myself."

The Premier's eyes bulged from his head. "Kill them!" he screamed and ran toward the path through the mangroves, his Seconds close behind.

The order of events happened almost as Beck predicted. He was the first one off the stakes with a quick snap of the ropes, and he knocked the nearest Ellvinians back with a sweep of his arm. But, he didn't allow any Ellvinian near her to untie her ropes. He did that himself.

By the time he was finished, the others were already free and engaged in holding the Ellvinians at bay.

"Now, what?" Kiernan asked her husband.

"We have to get back to the ship."

Kiernan grabbed Beck's arm. "Do you think the Premier was telling the truth when he said he killed watershifters?"

"Yes, I do. I think—"

Beck lurched forward with a surprised grunt, an arrow protruding from the middle of his chest.

"Beck! No!" His body slumped against her, but he was too heavy for her to hold up. As gently as she could, she let him fall to the ground at her feet.

No! Please, no.

Her eyes quickly scanned the woods and that was when she saw the archer, his bow trained on Rogan.

"Rogan, duck!"

The Dwarf did as he was told and the arrow missed him by a hairsbreadth.

At her shout, the archer turned her way. Big mistake. She slammed him with her magic and his bow turned, the arrows now seeking out his fellow soldiers.

She looked down at Beck. He wasn't moving.

Oh, Beck.

She searched out the two fighters closest to her and mindshifted them at the same time. The two Elves ran to Beck's side, picked him up by his legs and arms, and began running inland.

"Follow me!" Kiernan screamed to her friends and choking back a sob, followed behind the Elves. She ran quite a distance before realizing her friends were not behind her.

She mindshifted the Elves carrying Beck to stop and wait and then ran back as close as she dared to the clearing. Her friends were back under the Ellvinians' control and being led back to the beach. Not through Ascendency this time, but by the swords held to the throats of Janin and Melania.

Demon's breath!

Reluctantly, she went back to where her husband lay on the path. First, she had to get him to safety and back on his feet. Then, together they would save the others. Yes, she thought, scrubbing away the tears. Together. It was how they did everything and how it would always be. Even if she had to follow him into the Highworld to make it so.

Chapter 24

An Arrow Through the Heart

Despite their burden, the Ellvinians kept up a steady pace. Kiernan ran behind torn between her desire to stop and assess Beck's condition and her need to get him to safety.

She shifted a thought. *I will go where none will follow.*

The subjective mindshifted thought seemed to conflict in the minds of both Elves and they started to run in different directions before being yanked back together by their burden. Faces slack, the pair of fighters looked at each other in confusion.

Since their minds were hers to manipulate, she turned to the first one. "Where?"

"Rainforest."

She looked at the other. "Where?"

"Caves."

Not knowing the topography of the island, she had to take a guess. She thought for a moment.

I will go to the caves.

Without another word, the Elves took off again through the dense groves. It wasn't long before the path they were on grew steeper and Kiernan quickly realized their destination was the volcanic sea caves she saw from the ship. Running in a panic, she didn't recognize how high they climbed until she turned around and saw the tiny pinpoints of light from the port city spread out below her.

In Kiernan's unnerved mind, it was taking too long to arrive at their destination, and she was beginning to regret her decision when one of the caves opened up before them. The Elves ran right into the dark entrance and Kiernan followed.

I will lie him down gently.

The fighters lowered Beck to the cave floor on his side, the wicked arrow still protruding from his chest.

I will keep watch and give warning if anyone approaches.

Both Elves turned and walked out, and she dropped down to her knees next to her husband. "Beck, can you hear me?" She did not dare remove the arrow knowing that if she did, he would bleed to death. Her hands quickly roamed his body looking for any other injuries, but she did not find any. She leaned down and placed her cheek next to his mouth, but could not feel his breath. Alarmed, she looked at his face and noticed how deathly pale he was. Her shaking fingers searched out the artery on his neck, but could not find a pulse.

"Oh, no you don't, Beck Atlan!" she cried. "Don't you dare leave me!" She pounded on his chest in an attempt to get his heart started. "You know I can't do this without you, Beck!" Her fist struck down again. "Beck! Please! Please, don't leave me."

Her frantic efforts were not working.

"Beck!" She began to sob. Having no other option, she released the Elves from her magic. "Help me!"

The Ellvinian fighters responded immediately to her desperate plea and soft hands gently pulled her away. "Let me tend to him, Lady."

Kiernan could barely see the fighter standing above her through her tears, but she moved back to see if he could do anything to save her husband. She had no choice but to trust the dark Elf.

"Don't kill him," she begged. "Please, don't kill him."

A rueful frown appeared on his face. "You have my word, Lady."

The Elf bent over Beck and Kiernan watched while he blew air into Beck's lungs through his mouth. She had never seen such a thing, but she was willing to trying anything. Beck's chest rose and fell with each breath and Kiernan felt hope creep into her body. But, after a few moments, the Elf stopped, sat back on his heels, and looked at her with a small shake of his head.

"What are you doing? Don't stop! It's working!"

He shook his head. "I'm sorry."

"No! Move!" She pushed him out of the way and began to blow air into Beck's mouth the same way she saw him do it. Time lost all meaning as she did everything she could to save her husband. She only knew she had been at it a very long time when her body cramped up and pain shot through her lower back.

Fingers grabbed her shoulders once again. "He is gone, Lady."

"No! I won't give up! Don't you see? I can't...I can't give up." She leaned over Beck and rammed the heel of her palms into his chest. "Come on, Beck." She lowered her cheek to his mouth once again. Nothing.

"Beck!"

"Lady, please. You did all you could."

She sat back and covered her mouth. "Dear, Highworld, no!" Unbidden, the image that Avalon Ravener's conjured Sea of Void showed her of her family all those years ago sprang to her mind. The children, about the ages they were now, gathered around her as she sat on her throne. Beck missing.

The vision had come true after all.

She grabbed the kneeling Ellvinian by the front of his shirt, tears pouring down her cheeks. "Kill me, too."

He scooted back in shock. "What? No!"

"I am sorry, but you don't have a choice. I am a mindshifter, and you will do exactly as I say." She paused and shook her head regretfully. "I am sorry to have to put you through this, but you don't understand. I cannot live without him!"

"I...I can't, Lady, please don't make me do it."

She tugged him forward. "The Ellvinians want us dead, anyway, don't they?" she chortled madly. "You were given the order to kill us by your Premier and have already accomplished that task with my husband! What is one more dead Massan to you?"

The Elf's face hardened. "I cannot pretend to understand all that is going on here, but it is not the Ellvinian way to kill innocent people."

After a long, hard stare, she let go of his shirt front and pushed him back. "I am sorry, but you *will* kill me.

"I will never be able to live with myself if you make me do it."

Kiernan sniffed and ran a hand across her nose. "Please give me time alone with my husband, so I can say goodbye."

The Ellvinian rose to his feet. "Does this mean—"

"Leave me!"

Before he left, he removed his cloak and laid it gently across her shoulders. In return for his kindness, she mindshifted him and the other fighter. *I will stand watch outside and not leave.* It was the only way to ensure that the Ellvinians remained to do what must be done.

Alone now with Beck in the dark cave, she scuttled close to him and brushed the hair away from his forehead. She placed her lips on his, surprised at how warm they still were. Pulling back, she smiled down at his handsome face. The face that captivated her for over twenty years.

"We had a wonderful life together, didn't we, my love?" The burning lump in her throat threatened to clog her airway, so she cleared it nosily. "I don't think many people ever experience the kind of love we shared so I must be grateful for that much at least." A lifetime of memories flashed through her mind. "Beck, do you remember the day Kenley was born? Dear Highworld, was it really twenty years ago? You ran through the palace in Nysa like a fool, shouting and crying over the fact that you had your little girl." She paused wistfully. "I never loved you more than at that moment." She reached out to trace the athame on his neck. "Remember when the twins played that joke on you in the stables? I know you knew what they planned, but you walked right through the doors anyway and a pail of water dumped right over your head. Oh, Beck, we laughed for hours that day! Do you remember?"

Removing the Ellvinian cloak from her shoulders, she laid down next to Beck and covered them both with it.

"How about that time I dressed up in a Northwatch Legion uniform to follow you to The Crown Bluffs?" She laughed. "I thought I was being so clever but, of course, I never fooled you. And remember that time you saved me from the Gems in their castle in Elloree? What were you thinking, my love? Really? Marching directly into the witches' lair determined to sweep me away under your arm?" She reached for his lifeless hand and squeezed it tight. "You were my shining prince even back then. Remember saving me from that horrendous snake in the Puu Rainforest? You know how much I hate snakes." She shuddered. "My goodness, but you must have been bored from rescuing me all the time! But, it is the very reason that I cannot live without you, Beck Atlan."

A grey curtain of misery descended over her mind and heart. The silence of the cave clawed at her sanity. "It...it ended way too soon!" she wailed. "I hope you will forgive me in the end, but can't you see? My life only makes sense with you in it, Beck. I would fall apart without you. To go on without ever seeing your dimpled smile, to never hold your hand or kiss your lips? It's too much to ask! I would do anything for you, Beck, except live without you."

With that last avowal, she allowed the exhaustion and grief to pull her down, and she fell into a deep sleep curled up against the body of her dead husband.

Chapter 25

First Blood

"What are they doing?" Jala demanded.

Kellan glared out of the broken window of the ballroom at the Ellvinians outside lining up into battle formation in the wide boulevard directly east of the estate. "Preparing to attack."

"Where are the boards I requested?" Kirby Nash shouted. "Find whatever you can. It won't keep the Ellvinians out for long, but it will have to do for now."

I will keep them out, Maks growled in Kellan's ear. *I will take Jain and go to the courtyard. Any dark Elf that comes near this estate will die.*

Kellan nodded. *Be careful. I will see what I can do from the second floor.*

Maks and Jain leapt through the window just as two of the mayor's servants ran forward with loose wood and nails. Kellan looked around at the packed ballroom, but tried to avoid the spot where he last saw Alia. Lars Kingsley moved around the room and tried to reassure the scared and exhausted guests that all would be well, and Cora the cook, still scowling from this interruption to her duties, passed around cups of water.

Jala and Izzy stood by his side, but Kane had vanished. He was taking Alia's death very hard, as though he was personally responsible.

"Jala! Izzy! Come with me!"

Kellan took off at a sprint for the staircase. Kirby, Gregor, Dallin and Elon followed behind, naked swords at the ready. On the second floor, he crashed through the doors of the nearest guest chambers, strode through the sitting room to the balcony doors beyond, and flung them open.

The humid night air clung to his skin as he looked out over the estate grounds and assessed the enemy in the streets. The formation was made up mostly of whom he now knew the Ellvinians called the Shiprunners—basically, simple sailors with little fighting experience. Kellan dismissed them and his gaze landed instead on the Elves with the gold trimmed garments. It was these warriors that Kellan had to worry about the most. The Battlearms they called themselves, and he would strike there first.

Still, it was no secret that the Ellvinians had the strength of numbers. Eventually, the shifters would tire of using magic and the dark Elves would overwhelm their position. Any aid from the shifters in Bardot was close to a week away and military support from Nysa even longer.

How long could they hold out? That was the burning question in Kellan's mind. Certainly, not a week. Maybe not even the night.

He glanced down at Jain and Maks prowling aggressively below him in the courtyard. Jain saved his brother's life today and if Kellan had the opportunity after this night, he would let the Draca Cat know how grateful he was.

Someone squeezed in next to him at the balcony rail, and he was surprised to see Kane. "Are you all right?" he asked his twin.

Kane simply nodded.

"Tell me more about this creature you saw."

Kane was silent for a moment. Kellan knew he did not wish to relieve the horror of Alia's death, but Kellan had to know what they were dealing with.

Kane cleared his throat. "It looks like it may have once been an Elf. It is very tall, but walks on all fours instead of upright." He paused again. "It has a tail that sucks the blood from its victims."

Kellan reached out and put a comforting hand on Kane's shoulder. "Do you think the Ellvinians brought more of these beasts?"

His brother shook his head. "The Elf named Emile seemed just as surprised by its presence as we all were."

"Can it be killed?"

"It is very fast and very strong, but I think it can be done."

"Kellan!"

It was Izzy, and he quickly glanced to where she pointed. The line of Battlearms in the front row knelt to the ground, brought up long bows, and aimed them at the Draca Cats. After screaming a warning to Maks and Jain, Kellan threw his arm out and the ground in front of the Battlearms exploded in a hail of dirt and stones. Bodies flew backwards as the heaving ground tossed Elves into the air.

"First blood has been drawn," Kellan warned. "Be prepared. Now, they will come."

A ball of flame flared to life in Jala's hands, but she paused and looked questioningly at Kellan.

He gave her a grim nod of his head. "Yes, Jala, we must fight back. These people have already spilled Massan blood including that of Alia. It is hard to take a human life, I know, but we cannot falter now. As the children of *Savitars*, we have all grown up knowing that one day we may have to use our powers to kill. That day has arrived."

She looked down at the fire in her hands and nodded. Taking a deep breath, she straightened her back and threw her arm out toward the enemy.

Kellan tracked the fiery orb as it screamed away through the sky. The ball slammed into the Ellvinian lines setting clothes, bodies and hair aflame. Mournful cries lit up the night. Unable to rein in their abject terror, many of those on fire ran back through the ranks of their countrymen and created more damage by spreading the fire. Others simply fell to the ground in thrashing, flaming heaps. The smell of burnt flesh drifted unpleasantly on the night breeze.

Jala launched herself back into the bedroom, fell to her knees, and retched into the corner.

Despite the ruin inflicted by Jala, the Ellvinian line did not break. The Elves simply moved the dead or dying out of the way and formed up again for an attack. The archers were no longer out in front. Maces and swords were drawn by the Battlearms as they moved forward. The Shiprunners had only their bare hands to show. Together, they took up a battle cry that rang out into the night. Lifting their weapons and fists into the air, the dark Elves charged toward the estate.

We will not be able to stop them all, Kellan thought as he watched them come, floating over the ground like wraiths.

The Draca Cats roared out a challenge deep in their throats and leaned back on their powerful hind legs, ready to spring on the Elf foolish enough to reach the courtyard first. But then, all at once, Maks stood to his full height and jerked his head north in response to a foreboding sound.

Jain! Inside! Maks snarled.

The Elves also heard the noise and ground to an abrupt stop, unsure of what they were hearing.

Kellan knew and smiled.

High over the land, two tubular streams of water coiling like large snakes, slithered toward the enemy. A figure could be seen riding each liquid serpent with arms outstretched guiding the movements of the water.

Reilly Radek and Digby.

Jala must have also recognized the sound because she staggered to her feet and rushed to peer over the railing.

"Reilly!" she screamed at her brother.

Even over the sound of the gushing sea streams, Reilly heard her and waved with a grin on his face.

Kellan saw him motion to Digby who gave a curt nod in response. Reilly then made exaggerated circular movements with his hands similar to what Alia performed at the pier. The wave Reilly was riding flowed faster in response to his weaving and seconds before the water slammed into the Ellvinian Army, Reilly jumped away from his stream.

Kellan's breath caught in his throat as he watched Reilly fall through the air with legs and arms windmilling furiously. Just when Kellan thought for sure his friend was going to crash to the ground, Digby swooped in low with his wave and caught Reilly within the watery depths of his shifted water stream.

The jet carrying the two watershifters made an abrupt turn to the right and shot toward the open balcony where Kellan stood with the others. He sprang out of the way as the stream deposited the two soaking wet shifters into the bedroom and then collapsed into a lake-sized puddle in the courtyard below.

Kellan looked back outside to gauge the damage.

Reilly's rapidly flowing torrent cut a swath through the Ellvinians, and the Elves caught up in the onslaught of rushing water were swept away south. The Ellvinian line finally did break then and all those still on dry land retreated to escape the danger.

The siege was off. For the moment.

A chill raced up Kellan's spine when he heard the primal cry of Digby inside the guest chamber. It could only mean one thing. Someone just told him that his only daughter was dead.

Chapter 26

Surrender

Kane sat alone in the mayor's darkened office and gritted his teeth against the screams coming from outside the estate. Having recovered from the deadly watershifting, the Ellvinians stepped up their efforts to terrorize by ferreting out more citizens hiding in the city and using their torture as a tactic to get the shifters to surrender.

Every cry of a Massan was like an arrow directly to the heart for a shifter. The blood oath within Kane's body roared with the demand for vengeance and his body trembled from the strength of its resolve.

Twice more during the night, the Ellvinians tried to break past their defenses. Twice more they turned them back. But, the shifters were tiring. They wouldn't last much longer. All those trapped within the estate looked to the royals for orders on how to proceed, but when it came down to it, the fate of Northfort rested in the hands of children.

And, this child never felt more out of his element.

Kellan and Kenley were more suited to leading men than he was. His preference leaned toward a more solitary existence on the periphery of life—a proclivity most likely attributed to the existence of his golden eyes. From a very young age, other children shied away from his glowing orbs and gave him wide berth. For most people, anything different was to be feared and he was certainly different.

Instead, he sought solace in the shadows, seeking knowledge through observation and shunning personal entanglements. Except Alia. Alia was someone he could have walked out into the light for, only now she was gone.

He reached out and ran his hand through Jain's white coat. The Draca Cat was silent for once, and he was grateful.

Kane straightened when the door to the office slowly opened. His eyes, already accustomed to the darkness, had no trouble making out the old woman that shuffled inside and closed the door behind her. A gnarled hand thrust into the air toward the candles on the mayor's side table and they flared to life.

A fireshifter? If so, where did she come from? Even more strange, Jain didn't growl at her.

Kane got to his feet and cleared his throat so that he could make his presence known without frightening her.

She turned her gaze to him, and Kane took a step back. Her eyes were completely white.

She chuckled at his reaction. "It would seem that you are not the only one who carries around the yoke of an anomalous eye color, Prince."

Kane looked away, ashamed that he reacted in the same way he abhorred in others.

The old woman moved closer and stopped just inches from him. Without warning, her hand came up and slapped him across the face. Hard. "Snap out of it," she growled at him.

Kane ignored the stinging burn on his face and glared at the woman. "May I ask what I did to offend you, my lady?"

She pointed a crooked finger at his chest. "You offend me by sulking in a corner when the people of Massa require you to fulfill your oath! You offend me by your pity for a young girl who is happily in the arms of the spirits! And, you offend me, Prince of Iserlohn, by not realizing just how uniquely talented you are to end this battle with the Ellvinians."

"Me?"

"Yes, you are a sightshifter, are you not?"

"Yes."

"Then, do what you alone have the power to do!"

"Which is?"

"Surrender!"

ᕀ

Emile stalked through the muddy wet sand left behind by the twin tidal waves that crashed through Northfort with a snarl, his murderous glare locked on a circle of Battlearms tormenting two young Massan women by shoving them back and forth between them. Each time one of the girls was caught by a fighter, another piece of clothing was torn from her body.

The smaller of the girls lifted her hand to slap the fighter that held her and received a closed fist strike to the face for it. She crumpled to the ground in a senseless heap.

"Enough!" Emile hollered and the fighters immediately snapped to attention. He strode directly to the Battlearm who hit the girl and slammed his fist into the fighter's stomach and, when he doubled over, brought his knee up into his face. The Ellvinian grunted and fell to the ground beside the girl.

Emile pointed to two other fighters. "Take these girls back to their people. If any of you lay one more disrespectful finger on one of the prisoners, I will have your head!"

"But, Second Samara said—"

"Second Samara?" he roared. "Are you a bloody Eyereader now or a Battlearm?"

The fighter bowed at the waist. "Of course, a Battlearm, Second."

Emile glared at the circle of men in disgust. "Is this the way of Ellvinians? To debase innocent women outside of battle?"

"Well, no, Second, but the Massans struck first with the ground exploding, and the fire, and then those bloody waves! We lost good people!"

"Oh, they struck first, did they?" he snapped. "And, whose soil do we now stand on? Think on it and then tell me who struck first." He turned and walked away without waiting for an answer. It did not require one. "Get those girls back to their people," he shouted over his shoulder.

He cursed as his boots sank into the sand and headed toward the wooden pier built up around the merchant's district. As if he didn't have enough to worry about with Tolah on the loose and the Massans entrenching themselves within the mayor's estate, now he had Samara getting involved in affairs where she did not belong. She was an Eyereader for Netherworld's sake!

He scrubbed a hand down his face. He needed sleep, that's what he needed. He pulled his cloak tighter around his body.

The bitter cold temperature was something he was also not prepared for. Although only a few days ocean voyage to the west, the island of Ellvin did not experience the drastic fluctuation in the weather as here on Massa. He found himself longing for the balmy breezes of his homeland.

Emile stepped up onto the wooden platform and walked to the Salty Dog, once one of the more popular inns in Northfort and now the Ellvinian headquarters. He pushed open the door and stepped inside. He spotted Samara sitting at one of the inn's tables by the large fireplace in the back of the room. Emile strode up to the Massan bartender wiping down mugs behind the bar. "I will have spiced wine if you have it."

The burly Massan eyed him malevolently and turned to pour the wine without comment.

Emile thanked the fellow as soon as the drink was in his hands and made his way over to Samara. Ignoring the two Shiprunners sitting with her, he grabbed a chair, spun it around and straddled it. "Is it safe for me to turn my back on the fellow behind me?" he asked Samara, nodding toward the bartender.

She waved a hand. "Don't worry. We have his wife and son. He will not be causing any problems."

Emile glanced at the two Shiprunners. "Leave us."

The sailors glanced at Samara and she nodded her consent. He watched them go and pulled his long black hair away from his face to take a sip of his wine. "You are commanding the Shiprunners now, Samara?"

She shrugged. "With Chandal now gone, they need someone to direct them."

"Do what you must, but I will not have you giving orders to the Battlearms. Do you hear me?"

She leaned back from her study of the Massan maps and smiled. "Say what is on your mind, Emile."

"You will not abuse the Massan prisoners, and you will not give orders to the Battlearms. If you try to do either again, I will send you back to Ellvin to explain to the Premier why you have hampered my efforts here."

"Hampered your efforts? The Premier sent you here to conquer Northfort, Emile! You seem to be failing miserably in that regard."

Emile looked back over his shoulder at the Massan bartender, who made no secret of the fact that he was listening to every single word.

"Keep your voice down," he hissed at Samara. "The only reason we are having this conversation at all is because you had already given up every advantage we possessed before I arrived! I expected to find a cowered people, Samara, not a battlefield. Your orders were simple. Gain the trust of the Massans. Discretely send shifters back to Ellvin." He threw his hands up. "Even Anah's Coinholders could have accomplished that task."

Samara's face hardened into a beautiful mask. "What about the Vypir, Emile? Who let that thing loose onto foreign land?"

Emile leaned back and exhaled. "I don't know how that happened. Tolah must have boarded the ship somehow without anyone knowing."

She tilted her head. "It would seem that we have both made mistakes then."

He knew the Premier would be furious when he discovered the Vypir missing. "True enough."

The door to the inn opened and a young Battlearm rushed in. "Second!"

Emile turned. "Aye, what is it?"

"The Massans have just sent word! They are surrendering!"

A mug clanked to the floor from the bar behind them.

"Surrendering?" Samara questioned incredulously and scraped back her chair to stand.

"Aye, they have indicated that they will surrender at dawn."

"Well, then, Emile," Samara said with a smile. "It may be that our mistakes are not insurmountable after all."

Chapter 27

A Beacon of Hope

Her steady heartbeat against his chest represented his lifeline back to the world of the living. Beck concentrated only on that stirring sound as he worked to heal his injury. He wished that he could reassure Kiernan that he was still alive, but couldn't do so. If he spared the amount of energy required to fill his lungs with enough air to speak, he would die in truth. He had to reduce his lung capacity to almost nothing as he zeroed his magic in on his bleeding heart.

The arrow penetrated the right ventricle. In anyone else, it would have been an unrecoverable fatal injury. In him, it was still up for debate.

As soon as his mind registered what had happened, he forced his body to shut down just as he had learned to do during Mage training. In an agonizingly slow process, he went about repairing the damage caused by the arrow and in one infinitesimal step at a time, began to expel the shaft from his heart.

He knew it would take unwavering concentration to knit together the vital organ that kept him alive, so he had to tune out the frantic efforts of his wife to save him. He wished so much to be able to comfort her at this moment, but his desire to live for her was far stronger.

In spite of his best efforts to focus, he did hear Kiernan ask the Ellvinian fighter to take her life and his terror almost severed the flow of magic that kept him alive.

No! Please, Kiernan, hang on. I am doing everything in my power to get back to you. Have faith, my love!

Beck picked up the flow once again and went back to work, but still had the awareness to be overjoyed when the Ellvinian refused Kiernan's request. He cried tears of pain when Kiernan began to recall some of the special memories they had shared over the years and had to halt his efforts twice just to rein in his emotions.

When she finally fell asleep pressed tight to his body, a profound peace descended over him and he knew that now he could find the single-mindedness and endurance necessary to finish healing his wound.

Throughout the long night, with the beacon of her heartbeat serving as his guiding light, he inched the arrow further and further out of his body. With the arrival of dawn, he was at last able to allow more oxygen to fill his lungs, and his own heart began to pulsate more regularly as he started to work on the lesser muscle damage.

As the early morning sun peaked over the horizon, the arrow emerged fully from his body and clattered to the cave floor.

The small sound awakened Kiernan, and she threw the cloak off them and lifted her head in shock. "Dear, Highworld," she breathed and picked up the arrow. "Beck?"

He tried to answer, but the effort of using his diaphragm to form words proved too much just yet, so he simply nodded.

She leaned over and placed her lips on his and he felt hot tears fall on his cheeks. "Are you going to live? Please tell me you are going to live!"

He nodded again and she hugged him gently. "Don't you ever do that to me again, Beck Atlan! Do you hear me?"

He tried to smile, but it hurt too much. "I...I will...try."

She must have realized he was not yet fully healed. "Are you in pain? Is there anything I can do for you?"

"No. I just...need more time. Where...are we?"

"In one of the sea caves. I managed to get you away after you were shot, but the Ellvinians captured the others."

"All right. Give me...a few hours, and I will be as good as new."

She cupped his face in her hands and leaned in close. "Are you sure you are going to be all right? Promise me, Beck, that you are not going to leave me again. Please..." That last word was little more than a moan.

"You have...had that promise since the first day...I met you."

~

At dawn, Samara strode into the mayor's estate surrounded by Emile and a contingent of Battlearms. She didn't fully trust the Massans' offer of surrender and had to be prepared to act should it turn out to be an ambush.

"Give me your sword," she demanded of the Battlearm to her right. The fighter hesitated, but then removed his weapon from the scabbard on his hip and handed it to her hilt first.

As soon as her fingers encircled the leather grip, she felt more at ease, but she really had no cause. The more she learned about the capabilities of these Massan shifters, the more she realized just how useless their weapons were against them. Until they could get inside the shifters' magical defenses, all the swords in the world could not stop their destructive powers.

That was precisely why this sudden surrender was so suspect.

The doors to the ballroom stood open and she stepped inside cautiously. All of the Massans that had previously been locked in the cellar and the young royal shifters that had caused so much damage to her troops were sitting casually around the walls of the ballroom.

"Who will speak for you?" she asked the assembled Massans.

The infuriating young Prince with the golden eyes stood up from his position on the floor. "I will."

Samara narrowed her eyes. She thought it would be the other Prince who took the lead. He seemed the more political and outspoken of the two.

"What is this nonsense about a surrender?"

"It is not nonsense. We are surrendering to the Ellvinians."

"Why would you do such a thing when you have access to the magic you possess?"

Kane shrugged. "Our magic is not limitless. We cannot stand against your numbers forever. We have decided to surrender now before more innocent people are harmed."

"I see."

"I would ask for one concession, however."

Of course. "What would that be?"

"Let the citizens you are holding hostage go free. They are not soldiers. They are not magic users. As such, they hold no negotiating value for you. Let them go."

She laughed. "So, they can go and summon additional help for you? I don't think so."

"I am a Prince of Iserlohn, Lady Samara! You hold royal members of Deepstone and Haventhal as well! Help will come whether you are prepared for it or not. By your actions, I am assuming you mean to occupy Northfort for some time. Having royal children in your possession will help your cause."

"And, these *royal children* will go meekly along with all we say? I am finding that very hard to believe."

"What other choice do we have in order to avoid war?" He pulled down the shirt at his neck. "See this tattoo? Its presence on my neck demands that I protect the people of Massa. Inviting war would be contrary to that purpose, and I am confident the Kings will see it the same way."

Samara considered the Prince's words for several long moments. It made sense to go along, she finally decided. What were the citizens to her anyway except more mouths to feed? Still, if innocent Massans were what kept the shifters in line, she had to keep some of them around. She lifted a hand. "Free the prisoners." Several fighters ran from the room to comply with her order. "But, all these here in the estate will stay."

"As you say, Lady Samara," Kane said, bowing his head. "Now, that I am your prisoner, perhaps you will feel inclined to explain your hostile actions against my island. We would have given you all the wormwood plants you required if you simply asked."

She waggled a finger at him. "Ah, but the road to war is never as simple as that, young Prince. It is complex and winding and full of forks. Survival, greed, censure, addiction. These are but some of the factors that set the Ellvinians on this path, but I find now I can add another to the list."

"What would that be?"

"Retribution." Samara put a hand to her chin and began to circle the room. "You see I have a special concession of my own, Prince."

She noticed that Prince Kane moved his body to keep her in his sight at all times. She also remembered his skill at defeating the Battlearms in this very room and knew she could never let her guard down or underestimate this deadly young man.

"Yes? What concession can I offer you, Lady Samara?"

Samara stopped in front of the little Elf with the silver hair and pointed her sword at the girl's chest. "This Elf killed my friend, Chandal. I demand nothing less than her death in return."

&

Kane's hand shot out and grabbed Samara's wrist, stopping the sword that hovered inches from Izzy's chest.

Every Ellvinian in the room unsheathed his sword.

Samara's eyes blazed with fury. "I will have her blood, Prince. I demand it!"

"She is a child!" Kane retorted forcefully. "Chandal deserved to die for what he tried to do to her."

Samara tried to yank her sword arm from his grasp, but he held it firm. "I gave you the prisoners," she spit at him. "They are being freed as we speak. You *will* give me the life of this child. It will serve as a necessary reminder to the Massans of what will happen if they dare try to raise a hand to an Ellvinian again."

"Lady Samara—"

"All those lives for this one life, Prince! It is not so much to ask!" she screamed, trying to jab her sword toward Izzy once again. "Think on it. Otherwise, our deal is off. I can get those hostages back with very little effort!"

Kane felt hot breath on the back of his neck. "Let go of her."

He turned. It was Emile.

Kane glared at the tall Ellvinian for a long moment before finally releasing Samara's wrist. He moved toward the center of the room. "If you must do it, I cannot be witness."

Samara eyed him. "Very well, go hide in a corner if you must, but justice will be served here today."

Kane made his way to the door grateful that all eyes were on Samara and what she was about to do. He took full advantage of the inattention of the Battlearms and summoned his magic to create a replica right before he slipped outside.

While Kane made his way toward the kitchens, the replica turned back to the scene unfolding in the ballroom and he watched through its eyes.

Samara stood over Izzy ready to mete out the death she deemed just, but Emile put his hand on her arm and whispered in her ear. Whatever he said made her angry. With a resigned shake of his head, Emile brushed by the replica as he also left the ballroom.

Samara looked around at all of the Massans. "Let it be known that the death of a child does not please me, but I cannot allow her murderous act to go unpunished." The

Eyereader turned to Izzy, brought her arm back and plunged the sword directly into her chest.

When the sword did not bite into flesh as she had anticipated, the Ellvinian woman spun completely around, lost her balance and fell back into the crowd with a shriek. The moment her body made contact with the illusion of the seated Massans, it winked out of existence.

Samara looked around wildly at the empty room. "Somebody bring me that boy's head! Now!"

Chapter 28

Dark Legacy

Kellan frantically waved the prisoners toward the outer gates. "Hurry! Over here!"

As soon as their frightened eyes recognized him, they ran with every bit of energy they could muster. Women hiked up skirts and men scooped up children. Older adults wobbled as fast as they could toward safety.

The Ellvinians escorting them looked on in confusion. With orders to deliver the prisoners to the gates, they seemed unsure about the sudden frenzied behavior of the Massans.

Jala, Reilly, and Izzy and some of the servants from the mayor's estate ran out to help those struggling to make it. Poor Digby leaned against the wall, breathing heavily. Unlike Reilly, the subterranean watershifter couldn't be out of the water for long periods of time. Kellan tried to talk him into leaving, but he refused.

"Hurry!" Kellan shouted again, not sure how long Kane's ploy would keep the Ellvinians in the ballroom occupied.

He watched one of the fighters race back through the streets toward the mayor's estate, no doubt to report the odd behavior he witnessed. It didn't matter. The Ellvinians would come sooner or later. Kellan's only real hope was to get as many innocents as possible through the gates before that happened.

When the first Massan family ducked under the curtain wall, Kellan sighed in relief. One by one, the people of Northfort filed out of the city and hurried toward the relative safety of the Grayan Forest beyond.

But, no matter how fast they moved, the line just seemed to continue to grow longer. There had to be at least three hundred people or more. Quite a bit more than Kellan anticipated. They were never going to make it.

Come on! He urged silently while keeping an eye out for Kane. Then, he thought of a better way to see if his brother had made it out. "Keep them moving!" he screamed to Gregor and Haiden and sprinted to the curved stairs cut into the outer wall and led to a small gatehouse. Taking the steps two at a time, he raced up as fast as he could with Maks following closely behind. At the top, he pushed through the gatehouse door, crossed the narrow walkway, and leaned out over the parapet.

Kellan felt like he had been punched in the stomach and it left him winded. Dark-haired Elves flowed through the winding streets of the city toward the gates. Light and lithe, they were coming on fast.

༄

Beck pressed his lips to Kiernan's forehead. "I'm fine."

She leaned back to look at him. "Fine? By all rights, you should be dead right now. I still can't believe I have you back."

"Well, I am not dead and we have some friends that need our help."

She snuggled back into his chest. "Fine, but promise me something."

He stroked the back of her long hair. "Anything."

"No more of these goodwill ventures for a while. I would like to stay at home where I know my family is safe."

He closed his eyes tight against the pure elation of having his wife back in his arms. "You know how powerless I am to refuse any of your requests, Kiernan Atlan," he told her huskily.

"Good," she murmured contentedly.

A polite cough at the cave entrance drew Beck's attention. It was one of the Ellvinian fighters that helped carry him to safety. While he was healing, he heard the Elf offer some measure of comfort to Kiernan.

Beck gently put Kiernan aside and gestured the Ellvinian inside. "You have my eternal gratitude, sir, that, unlike me, you are able to resist the requests of my wife."

The Ellvinian's face colored. "She was not in her right mind, Master...?"

"Beck Atlan. Please call me Beck and this is Kiernan."

The dark Elf nodded. "I am Alric and the other fighter is Yurek."

"Alric, do you know why your Premier would want to harm us when we have come to help the Ellvinians?"

He was silent for a moment and then said, "I think I do. Why don't you sit and I will tell you what I know."

Beck and Kiernan sat cross-legged on the cave floor while Alric perched on a large piece of volcanic rock. "What do you know of my people?"

Beck shrugged. "From what I gathered at the feast by talking to several guests there, your ambassador, Chandal, lied to us. The wormwood plants the Ellvinians so desperately need are not for medicinal purposes at all. They are for sustenance."

Kiernan looked at him with raised eyebrows.

"It is true," Alric confirmed. "We must have the blood nectar in the plants to survive. We mix the nectar and other ingredients and prepare a draught that must be ingested or we will become very ill and eventually die."

"I didn't realize the plants were so critical to your survival," Kiernan commented.

"Aye, they are. In the past ten years or so, our own natural resource of wormwood was infested with a Titsu bug that destroyed almost all of our crops. As a result, the draught has become more difficult to obtain for every Ellvinian on the island. The Premier and the Seconds created eligibility lists to ration out the increasingly meager provisions, but it soon became apparent that only those who could buy their way onto the lists would receive the draught. The poor started dying off in staggering numbers."

"That is terrible," Kiernan said softly in shock.

"Aye, it has been a very difficult time for Ellvinians."

"But, we were bringing a new supply of wormwood plants and shoots here to the island. What would make the Premier act in such a way to people who are basically saving the lives of his people?"

Alric looked down. "Centuries ago, before the Ellvinians found a way to survive on the wormwood plants, we...they...drank human blood."

"Human blood?"

The Elf looked back up and met their eyes squarely. "More specifically, the blood of magic users. It is an intoxicating and life-sustaining elixir to the Ellvinian." His eyelids reduced to slits. "I can smell your magic where you sit and can only imagine what it would be like to drink it."

Beck moved his body closer to Kiernan. The implication was hard to dismiss. "So, in order to drink the blood of a human, you would have to kill them in the process?" Beck thought of the watershifters the Premier admitted to killing.

The dark Elf shook his head vigorously. "No, not necessarily. Humans make more blood every day. You can keep a person alive for a long time if..."

"If what?"

"If you do not become too greedy."

Kiernan stood up. "This is very hard to believe. Is the Premier after our blood?"

"Based on rumors I have heard, I am assuming those are his plans, but he does not share that kind of intelligence with the fighters." He hesitated again. "But, we hear things. We talk."

"What more can you tell me?"

Alric stood and began to pace the small confines of the cave. "The process for extracting magical blood has not been in practice for many, many years. It is said that our ancestors had...well, they had fangs for this purpose."

"Fangs?"

"Aye, fangs that allowed Ellvinians to not only drink the blood, but to siphon the magic. Just killing a magic user and drinking their blood is not sufficient. You have to have a way to draw out the magic."

"And, now Ellvinians no longer have these fangs?"

"No, as magic users became extinct and the wormwood solution became available, this physical trait was bred out of the Ellvinians."

"Then, how does the Premier propose to extract the magic from our blood?"

"He will use the Vypir." Alric held his hand up to indicate that he already knew what Beck's obvious next question would be. "The Vypir is a by-product of the experiments of the Mages of old and possesses the requisite fangs. When the capability began to breed out of Ellvinians, the Mages turned to the dark arts to try and recreate it. That is how the Vypir came to be."

"So, what is this Vypir? What are its organic roots?"

"It used to be a Mage," Alric replied, nervously picking at the pieces of volcanic rock on one of the walls. "The last experiment gone wrong I guess you could say."

"Used to be a Mage? What is it now?"

The Elf turned to look over his shoulder. "A beast."

Beck clamored to his feet at the word he had dreaded to hear for over a decade. The word that filled his every nightmare. "Where is this beast? I must destroy it at once!"

"Beck, what is the matter?" Kiernan asked anxiously.

"We have to go after it!"

"It's missing," Alric told him.

"Missing?"

"Ever since Emile left with the Battlearms to go to Massa—"

"What? The Premier sent fighters to Massa?"

"Aye, I thought you knew."

Beck's face paled. "I think I now know where your Vypir is."

Kiernan grabbed his arm. "What is going on?"

"It is the time, Kiernan! The time the Oracle prophesized about fifteen years ago."

She gasped in shock. "How do you know?"

He never told her about the beast because he didn't want to subject her to years of nightmares about a monster coming to the island. "The signs are there. This Vypir is in Massa, Kiernan, I'm sure of it. Come on! We have to get the others and get back to the ship." Beck grabbed Kiernan's hand and sprinted out of the cave.

Alric quickly took the lead. "Follow me."

It was much easier to run down the hill from the caves than it had been going up.

"What are we going to do, Beck?" Kiernan asked. "It will take time to ask around and find out where they are holding Rogan, Airron, Janin and Melania."

"I am not in the mood for subtle, Kiernan."

She glanced at her husband's profile and almost stumbled. She had never seen him look so determined—so deadly. "So...so, you are going to just barge right into the city and demand to be told where they are?"

He lifted one edge of his lip, but Kiernan wasn't sure if it was a smile or a snarl. "That is exactly what I plan to do, and Highworld help any Ellvinian that stands in my way."

Chapter 29

An Arrow Through the Back

Kiernan noticed Yurek look back uneasily at Beck's uncompromising words. Not for the first time since they arrived on Ellvin, her fingers twitched over her shoulder to reach for the sword of Iserlohn. "I need a sword," she whispered to Beck.

"I'll get you one."

Kiernan nodded and continued down the hill after the men. After what seemed like hours, they burst into the clearing where the Premier had them tied to stakes the evening before.

It was empty.

Beck stopped to look around, his face an inscrutable mask. Then, he gestured for Alric and Yurek to continue on the path through the mangroves toward the beach.

"Wait!"

Kiernan watched Beck spin around and peer into the swampy groves just outside of the clearing.

"What is it?" Kiernan asked.

"I hear something," he said and stood still as he scanned the area for the source of the noise.

"It's probably those crabs that are all over the trees," Kiernan murmured. "I just hope it's not a snake." Her whole body convulsed involuntarily at the thought.

Beck moved toward the swamp and used his earthshifting to move branches and tightly woven bramble away. At one point, he disappeared entirely.

Kiernan was growing impatient. "Beck, we have to go."

She heard him curse and instantly grew more alert. In the next instant, he was crashing back through the trees to the clearing.

Kiernan gasped.

He was holding a child.

Beck laid the boy on his side. A small crossbow dart stuck out of his back between his shoulder blades, and his small mouth was coated in red. Kiernan watched her husband lean in close to the boy. "I must remove the dart in your back and then I will heal your wound. You will not remember anything, I promise."

The boy's eyes fluttered nervously in response.

Beck then waved his hands over the boy's chest and whatever he did put the child to sleep. Gently, he extracted the short dart and threw it the ground in disgust.

"Who could do this to a child?" Kiernan asked. "Does he have any other injuries?" She knelt down beside the boy and watched as his small body convulsed and arched from Beck's healing ministrations.

Beck shook his head. "Shockingly, no, not even infection. Besides the wound to his back, extreme hunger pains, and dehydration, he seems fine." Beck wiped the red substance from the boy's lips and brought his fingers to his nose. "Berries. He must have been surviving on berries. It's fortunate that he did not try to remove the arrow. If he did, he would be dead by now."

Kiernan looked at Alric and Yurek who were crowding closer. "Do you know anything about this?"

Alric nodded. "I did hear about a missing child from the Ironfingers caste. It must be him."

"We'll find out soon enough. Stand back, I'm going to awaken him." Beck brushed his hand once more across the child's chest.

The boy's eyes popped open and he let out a strangled cry upon seeing the strangers leaning over him. He tried to scramble away.

Beck held out his hands. "It's all right. We are here to help you."

The boy started to cry when he saw Alric and Yurek. "Get away from me!"

Beck picked the boy up into his arms and held his flailing body tight. "Hush now, everything will be all right. What is your name?"

"I just want Papa," he moaned.

"I will bring you to him," Beck assured him. "But, first tell me your name."

"Tatum."

"Who did this to you, Tatum?"

Silence.

"You can trust me."

The boy shook his head, wiggled to get down, and sat on the ground.

Beck tried an easier question. "How long have you been out here in the swamp, Tatum?"

"Many days. Two weeks maybe." He looked up at Beck with a sudden question in his eyes. "Are you the foreigner who was to bring the wormwood plants?"

Beck smiled and knelt in front of him. "Yes. Your island now has plenty of plants and can begin to harvest them once again."

The boy covered his mouth. "Then, Mama will be well? She can have the draught?"

"Yes, Tatum. Your mother will be well now."

The boy stood and threw his arms around Beck's neck. "Thank you, sir! You cannot know what it means to me that you have come."

"I'm still trying to figure that one out, Tatum" Beck said cynically and picked the boy up in his arms once again. "I will take you back to the city."

"No! They will try to kill me again!"

Beck made sure that Tatum was looking directly in his eyes before he spoke. "I will not let anyone harm you, Tatum, I promise."

Kiernan put an arm around Beck's waist and looked up at the boy. "Trust me when I tell you, Tatum, that this man is very good at keeping his promises."

"You'll take me to my parents?"

"Yes. I will not leave you until you are in their arms."

"All right."

Beck led the way through the mangroves and onto the beach with the boy in his arms. He noticed that many people from the feast still lingered as they cleaned up the leftover debris, raked the beach or stood in small groups talking animatedly. Some still sported the elaborate costumes of the evening before. All stopped and stared as Beck made his way purposefully toward the wharf and the ship he hoped was still waiting there.

Kiernan and the two fighters trailed behind him silently.

A tall Ellvinian peeled away from one of the groups and started toward him, a scowl on his face.

Beck recognized him. It was Second Jarl of the Ironfingers.

"What is the meaning of this?" he demanded of the fighters behind Beck. "These trespassers are to be arrested at once! They are dangerous!"

Alric stepped forward. "With all due respect, Second Jarl," he said in a tone that implied he had none, "I would like an explanation as to why we are treating the Massans in this manner. What have they done to deserve such offensive treatment?"

Nervous murmuring echoed as the people on the beach gathered closer to the confrontation.

Jarl took a step closer. "I was not aware that Seconds had to clear their decisions through you, Battlearm."

Alric held his ground. "As a citizen of Ellvin, I think I have a right to understand your reasoning. That is all."

A few people in the quickly growing crowd shouted their agreement with Alric.

"I just want to see Papa," Tatum murmured in Beck's arms.

"Who is that? Who do you have there?" Jarl demanded, peering around Alric.

The boy lifted his face for all to see.

"It's Cullen's boy! Run and fetch him at once!"

"Tatum! It's Tatum!"

"I thought he was dead!"

Jarl's hard features softened. "Put him down."

Beck let the boy drop to his feet, and Jarl knelt and held out a hand toward Tatum. "We have been looking for you for a very long time, young man. Welcome back."

Tatum bit his lip nervously. Even though the Second seemed genuinely pleased to see the boy, Beck could tell that Tatum didn't trust Jarl.

Excited shouts in the crowd grew loud as a very large man with scars up and down his arms pushed through the line. As soon as his eyes fell on Tatum, he sank to his knees, covered his face and began to cry.

Tatum hurried over to the kneeling man. "Papa! Oh, Papa!"

The man grabbed Tatum around the waist and held him tight. "I thought I lost you, boy. They told me you died."

A woman came forward, her face haggard and tear-stained. "Mama! You had the draught?"

Tatum's mother nodded and fell in the sand beside her family. "Aye, darling. I am going to be all right now."

Alric lifted his hands to address the gathering. "I ask again! What have the Massans done except save the lives of Ellvinians?" He pointed to Tatum and his parents. "Look at this family! They have been reunited in health because of the Massans! What kind of people are we to arrest those that come to our island with such kindness?"

Jarl's face mottled with anger as his motives were called into question so publically.

"Papa, lift me up," Tatum asked his father.

The big man stood and did as his son asked. "This man," Tatum said in a shaky voice, pointing back to Beck, "not only saved Mama and so many others, but he also saved my life."

"What happened to you Tatum? Where have you been?" someone from the crowd asked.

Tatum choked back a sob. "I...I was shot in the back with a quarrel from a crossbow."

"What?"

"Who would do such a terrible thing?"

Tatum waited until the crowd grew silent once again. "I will tell you who. It was Premier Bane."

Beck was just as stunned by the admission as the Ellvinians.

Tatum looked at his father. "I'm sorry, Papa, but my curiosity got the better of me again, and I heard something I shouldn't have. So, the Premier waited until my back was turned, shot me, and dumped me in the swamp and left me for dead."

The crowd erupted in horrified gasps and murmurs of disbelief.

"It is the truth," Tatum said softly.

Even Jarl seemed shaken by the news. "Why would the Premier perpetrate such a heinous crime? Against a child?" the Second asked, voicing the question on everyone's lips.

"I thought about that when I was in the swamp and I think it's because he didn't want me to tell people about the blood. The Premier said that the people would not con...," his little face scrunched in thought, "aye, that's it, condone, his methods."

The wave of murmurs turned into outraged shouts.

An Ellvinian male stepped out from the crowd. "Why should we be surprised? Hendrix Bane has done nothing for the people of Ellvin. He bathes in the draught while innocent women and children die of starvation every day!"

"Not only that!" one shouted out. "I have heard that he is already dabbling in the blood!"

"The blood? But, how?"

Beck had had enough. "By killing Massans, that's how!"

"He's right," Alric told the crowd. "The Premier has been keeping the Vypir alive all these years and plans to use it to milk our saviors of their blood."

Beck held up his hands to quiet the vociferous debate set off by Alric's words. "I realize that you have issues to resolve amongst yourselves, but you will have to do it on your time, not mine. My family is in danger from your Battlearms and this Vypir creature you created, so I am leaving this island right now. If you want a fight, so help me I will give you one, but we have done nothing but show the Ellvinian people respect and compassion." His furious eyes scanned the crowd. "Tell me now, because I have important matters to attend to."

Commotion in the back caused a gap to open in the gathering of people.

"Oh, you shall have your fight, Mage Beck!" Hendrix Bane strode forward through the crowd. Four Battlearms prodding Airron, Melania, Rogan, and Janin just behind.

"Oh, this is ridiculous." Beck stepped forward, flicked a wrist and the four fighters cried out as they were lifted off the ground. Invisible bonds that no one but Beck could see, slithered over the Elves and pinned their arms and legs tight to their bodies as they hung suspended in the air.

The crowd backed away with frightened screams.

Rogan snapped his bindings with a quick flame. "Well, I could have done that! I was waiting for the signal. You know, a nod of the head or a coded word. You do remember *gooseberry*, don't you?"

Beck ignored him while Kiernan hurried over to help him untie the others.

The Premier waved his arms about. "Emile! Battlearms! Where are all my Battlearms?"

A bespectacled Elf next to the Premier coughed. "Uh, you sent them to Massa, Your Eminence. There are only a handful of fighters left on the island."

Hendrix Bane turned to the people of Ellvin. "Don't just stand there! Get them!"

Tatum's father, Cullen, was the first to respond, his face a thundercloud of rage. "No! This is not our way! We do not shoot children in the back and we do not kill innocent people who are here to help us!"

"Hear! Hear!" the crowd roared.

The Premier swung his elaborate robes and raced toward the people. "Don't you understand? We can have the blood again! That *is* the Ellvinian way!"

"The blood?" Cullen responded with disgust. "If drinking the blood makes you so despicable that you start killing innocents, I will drink the draught!"

"Take these people into custody!" the Premier raged.

"No!" Cullen shouted. "You are done, Hendrix Bane. We renounce you as our leader!"

Loud applause rippled through the bystanders.

Hendrix stumbled back in shock. "What?"

"Go find a new place to live out in the countryside. If you so much as step a toe in this city or seek to rise to power again, you will be executed." Cullen turned toward Jarl. "That goes for all the Seconds as well. The Ellvinian people will elect new leaders to help us recover from this dismal moment in our history."

"You will be sorry for this!" Hendrix screamed at him.

The big man towered over the Premier. "You will be the one sorry if I ever see you again. For what you did to my son, you are lucky I don't snap your neck right now. Now, go!"

The Premier looked around wildly for a shred of support, but found nothing. Finally, he gathered up his robes and, chin held high, walked away.

Cullen glanced at Beck and gestured to the hanging fighters. "Master Beck, if you will be so kind?"

Beck waved a hand and the Elves dropped to the ground at Cullen's feet.

"Where are your loyalties, Battlearms?" Cullen asked. "With Hendrix Bane or the people?"

They did not hesitate to answer. "The people."

"Good. Please escort Hendrix Bane, his Adjunct and Second Jarl to the city outskirts. When you are finished with that task, round up Seconds Anah and Balder and deliver the same message."

"As you command, Cullen."

Beck started toward the pier at a brisk pace. "Please come with me, Cullen!" he shouted over his shoulder. When the dark Elf fell into step beside him, he asked. "How many Battlearms are in Massa?"

"Almost all of them."

"Give me a number."

"Twenty thousand."

Beck's newly repaired heart skipped a beat. Twenty thousand enemy fighters and a blood-sucking beast stood between him and his children.

"Let's move!"

Chapter 30

The Short Stick

The black tide that raced forward seemed unstoppable. Kellan's heart hammered in his chest at the sight of the dark Elves flowing toward them. He jumped up onto the parapet and searched out Kirby Nash. "Captain! There's no more time!"

The Saber Captain gave him a grim look and flew into action, ordering the defenders into a protective perimeter around the fleeing citizens.

Kellan understood the meaning behind Kirby's look. The defenders were going to die. They had no chance to survive the battle at the gates. With only five shifters, five protectors, two Draca Cats and the sixty or so men and women from the mayor's estate who refused to leave the fight, they would be crushed underneath the onslaught. While he hoped fervently that they would be able to get the citizens out before the bloodshed began, there would be no such hope for the defenders. It was a foregone conclusion that all who stayed behind to hold the gates, were sacrificing their lives to allow the people of Northfort time to escape.

Kellan swallowed.

He would willingly give his life in protection of the people—that was never in question. It was just that he didn't wish to die with so much uncertainty surrounding the fate of his family. Kane was still out there somewhere. Kenley was facing who knew what kind of danger in Callyn-Rhe and his parents were in the hands of the enemy.

But, there was no further time for reflection as the first Ellvinian fighters appeared at the north end of the city square. More than half of the citizens were through the gates as the Massan defenders raced to close with the advancing host. The Ellvinians did not bother to establish a formal line of attack and the two opposing forces clashed with terrible force. With no room to bring weapons to bear, brutal hand-to-hand combat ensued and the grunts and screams of men filled the air.

Kellan looked for an opening, but the close quarter fighting made it difficult to direct his magic at the enemy. A quick glance at Jala where she stood along the wall, told him she was having the same difficulty.

Fortunately, Izzy could act and she did. Kellan heard petrified cries coming from directly below and looked down. Three black wolves from the Grayan Forest were slinking their way in through the horde of people storming out. Muzzles lifted in bone-chilling snarls, the three wolves burst out of the crowd and attacked.

Although, not quite as large as the Draca Cats, their formidable skill at pack killing wrecked havoc among the Ellvinians. Sharp canines sunk deep into flesh and ripped apart throats.

A hole opened up in the fighting as the Elves scrambled to flee the wolves, and this allowed one of the Battlearms to brandish his sword and sink it between the ribs of one of the wolves. The animal fell to the ground with a pained yelp.

The wounded cry sent the other wolves into a frenzied fury and they tore into the enemy with even more ferocious abandon. Several Elves brought their bows up and slammed arrows into the animals, but even with multiple shafts sticking out of each of the wolves, they continued their deadly slaughter for many minutes before finally going down. In the end, the wolves killed at least forty Elves. Considering the Ellvinian numbers, it was but a very small dent in their armor, but it did give the enemy pause at the powers of the shifters.

"They're through!"

Kellan peered over the wall and saw the gates close on the last Massan.

The attack of the wolves caused the Ellvinians to give ground, but it only served to aid the enemy as officers, taking advantage of the breach, bellowed out orders to bring fighters into cohesive battle lines.

The defenders, already exhausted and bloodied fell back to the gates for a moment to catch their breath.

When the Ellvinians made their next charge, it would be the end, Kellan knew, but at least the citizens had made it out safely. Any additional time the defenders could buy would allow them to make their escape through the forest and out of reach of any pursuers.

From there, the citizens would flock to Bardot with news that for the second time in twenty years, an enemy had infiltrated Massan shores.

Once that happened, the Ellvinians wouldn't stand a chance. Not against the combined might of the military and shifter magic on this island. The Ellvinians were capable fighters, but they didn't possess enough of their Ascendency powers to overwhelm the entire Massan nation. No, the Ellvinians would not gain much more ground into Massa then the land on which they now stood. At least there was that, Kellan thought as he prepared to meet the imminent charge.

All was suddenly silent for a moment as the Ellvinians and Massans stood across from each other in the city square. Wispy clouds of breath misted in the bitter cold of the morning. Feet shuffled in nervous anticipation. In just a few short seconds, men would die, but for this brief period of time, Kellan could believe that all was well. In the sounds of the gentle ocean waves slapping at the wooden pilings of the wharf and the mundane squawk of a seagull, he could imagine that there was still a chance that life could return to how it was before the Ellvinians came. He could hope for a miracle.

But, as soon as the Ellvinian in the center of the enemy line lifted his sword high above his head, Kellan scoffed at such wishful thinking. As soon as that blade dropped, the fighting would begin and lives would end.

He watched the quivering tip of the sword point and held his breath as he waited for the downward slice that would signal the charge. Muscles tense with restless energy, he vowed that not a single dark Elf would get through this gate. As long as he still lived and breathed, the gates of Northfort would hold.

A sudden roar shattered the tormented silence and all eyes turned north.

It is Jain!
Are you sure, Maks?
Of course.

Kellan felt his stomach drop. That had to mean that Jain was on his own. Kane was a shadow dweller. He would never give away his presence to the enemy.

From the harbor, avian screams joined Jain's roar. Small halos of white ripped through the sky as a convocation of bald eagles flew in a V formation straight for the city square. Kellan had never seen eagles fly in a flock. Immune from the threat of most predators, the large birds preferred a more solitary existence with a single mate.

The eagles approached low over the battlefield, but instead of soaring past, the large birds dipped from the air and with screeching yells, raked sharp talons across the faces and backs of the Ellvinians in their path. Cries of pain mingled with the shrieks of the eagles, and the Ellvinian archers quickly stepped forward and drew their bows.

The eagles shot back into the air before the Elves could release their arrows and banked toward the outer wall where they dove to safety behind the stone parapet.

Kellan watched the air shimmer and the eagles morphed into squatting men and women. Naked men and women. Shifters! But, how? He thought all of the shifters had been taken away!

Kellan's puerile miracle had arrived after all. More screams ripped through the early morning as a group of shifters cut a destructive path through the mass of Ellvinians. The earth shifted, great gouts of fire exploded upward into deadly columns of flame, and Ellvinians turned on each other in violent skirmishes.

The sudden assault from the rear created enough confusion and ruin in the ranks of Ellvinians to allow the attacking shifters to make it through the enemy horde. Eyes glinting with deadly resolve, the men and women burst through the line and sprinted toward the gates. There, in the middle of the cluster of shifters was Kane and Jain.

Sight of his twin brother and an overwhelming desire to protect him, bolstered Kellan into action. He leapt from the parapet and arched out over the heads of the running shifters. With bone-crushing force, he landed hard on one knee and drove a fist into the ground with all of the might of his elemental magic. The earth rippled outward in expansive rings from the depression he made in the ground. Ellvinians went flying through the air as the earth heaved and buckled from the impact. Forceful expletives and cries of pain rang out as bodies slammed into the ground and bones broke.

That single act of devastating power caused the improbable to happen.

The Ellvinians began to retreat.

*

Besides the scattering of black eyes that watched from the safety of the city buildings, the Ellvinians had left the square. Presumably to strategize on how best to use their numbers to combat the Massans' magic.

Kellan stood bemused as he listened to the strange story of the thirty shifters standing before him. According to them, they willing went aboard one of the Ellvinian ships. For some reason, they explained with a scratch of their heads, they thought it would be a good idea to visit Ellvin and happily followed the dark Elves into the hold.

The ship set sail and they were out to sea less than a day when fighting broke out on deck. When their three Ellvinian guards ran topside to investigate, the shifters, of course, followed closely behind. What they saw even now remained a source of such incredulity that they seemed reluctant to continue.

With firm prompting, they finally told Kellan that it was an old woman who saved them. She fought the Ellvinians with a magic that sent Elves crashing to the deck or overboard into the sea with a sweep of her arm. An old lady with white eyes! And, a crow perched on her shoulder!

When the fighting was over, she said the oddest thing to them. She said, "Massa needs you. Hurry now!" and once the words were delivered, she climbed onto the ship's railing and dove off into the ocean. That was the last any of them had seen of her.

None of the shifters knew how to sail the ship or turn it back toward Massa, but fortunately, they had several bodyshifters with them. Almost all had a dolphin form and they were able to transport everyone home.

Kellan didn't know what to make of it, but had no time to ponder the strange riddle when Kirby Nash waved him over. "I'll be right back," he muttered to the shifters and walked over to where the protectors were having a discussion.

"I wonder if any of the bodyshifters has a mantath form. That animal could do tremendous damage," Haiden said.

"Not likely. Airron Falewir is the only known shifter with enough power to call forth such a large form," Kirby answered. "But, don't be discouraged. With the addition of thirty shifters, I have much more optimism regarding our chances. Even though we're outnumbered, we can do this. I have faced odds such as these before with Kiernan Atlan and came out on top."

"We are not *Savitars*," Reilly pointed out.

Kirby smiled. "I know, but your skills are quite remarkable, and I will not be surprised if one day your abilities surpass those of your parents." Kirby looked around at the group. "To be honest, if I have to meet twelve hundred of these bastards in the field, there is no one else I would rather have at my side."

Kellan couldn't resist. "Except perhaps my sister."

For once, Kirby didn't blush. "You are wrong, Kellan. I happen to be very glad that Kenley is far from—"

A low, ominous battle horn sounded in the north, and Kellan froze. One of the defenders atop the crenellated wall shouted and pointed toward the sea. "Dear Highworld! Look!"

Kellan turned north, but couldn't see over the buildings. He turned and ran to the stairs that led to the gatehouse. He wasn't the only one that had the idea and he felt several people behind him pushing him ahead. He went through the gatehouse door and looked out to sea.

Kirby was wrong. Thirty shifters were not going to make a lick of difference. Not when the odds in their favor just shriveled to obscurity under the black stain appearing on the horizon. Ellvinian ships. Hundreds of Ellvinian ships. Tens of thousands of the enemy.

They were doomed. Kellan knew that Iserlohn alone did not have enough soldiers to meet this enemy and wondered if even combined with the military forces of the Elves and Dwarves it would be enough.

Kellan looked at the royal protectors and citizen defenders. "Go now to Nysa and my grandfather, King Maximus. Go to King Thorn in Haventhal and King Erik in Deepstone. Tell them to prepare the island for war. The shifters will hold the gates as long as we can."

"I'm not leaving!" Kirby declared. "Do you have any idea what Kiernan Atlan would do to me if I left her sons on the front line of battle? Trust me, my chances of survival are much better here. Probably less painful, too."

"None of the protectors are leaving," Dallin declared in complete contempt that Kellan would even suggest it.

Kellan looked down at the defenders from the mayor's estate on the ground in front of the wall. "We're not leaving, either, Your Grace," one shouted up and waved a pitchfork in the air.

"But, someone has to warn the Kings!" Kellan snapped.

"Send a bodyshifter," Gregor suggested.

Kellan could pick out the bodyshifters from the mismatched pieces of clothing they wore donated by whatever the defenders could spare. Most of it looked like small clothes, but at least they were no longer naked.

Gregor made his way to the gatehouse door. "I'll have them draw sticks. Whoever pulls the short one, goes to Nysa."

Kellan snorted. "Defending the gates is the better option?"

"Apparently to this lot it is."

After he left, Kirby pulled Kellan aside. "Look, if I don't make it today, can you tell Kenley...can you tell your sister that I loved her. Tell her I never loved anyone as much as I did her and I'm sorry we won't be together."

Kellan was taken aback. He knew there had been some flirtation between the two, but didn't know it was this serious. The Saber Captain must also realize that the chances Kellan walked away from this alive were just as nonexistent as his, but maybe he just needed to get it off his chest. Maybe he just wanted someone to know the depths of his feelings toward Kenley.

Kellan wasn't about to take that away from him. "I will."

Down below, one of the bodyshifters hollered out a curse and kicked angrily at the dirt.

It would seem the short stick had been drawn.

Chapter 31

Battle at the Gates

The defenders located torches and lanterns in the shops along the square to provide light as the night deepened. Heavy clouds blocked out any help from the stars. Kellan thought the Ellvinians might wait until dawn to strike, but Kirby felt confident it would happen under the cover of darkness.

The Massans were waiting.

Bodyshifters stood waiting to summon their most ferocious forms. Earthshifters, fireshifters, and mindshifters prepared to unleash lethal mayhem into the enemy lines. The non-magical defenders equipped with sword or makeshift clubs, organized into configurations that would allow them the greatest longevity against a much larger foe.

The rules of war were simple. Kill or be killed.

Kellan stood at the crenellated wall, scanning the darkness for any hint of movement when he felt a presence beside him. He turned. It was Reilly.

Kellan offered his friend a joyless smile. "Where are the girls?"

"Kane won't let Izzy out of his sight, and Jala is standing with the fireshifters." He grunted. "After Alia, that little sister of mine is quite literally burning for vengeance."

"How is Digby?"

Reilly shook his head. "He is soaking in a tub now, but he needs more water. He's just too distraught to care."

"What can we do for him?"

Reilly shrugged. "What he needs is beyond our ability to give him. He wants his daughter back."

Kellan nodded with a heavy heart. Digby, Liliana, and Alia were like family to him and it tore at his insides that such a thing could have happened so quickly—so violently.

He glanced sideways at the Dwarf. He knew what he had to say—the words were easy enough, yet his mouth felt uncomfortably dry. "We cannot let the Ellvinians through the gates, Reilly. Whatever happens, they cannot get through."

A long pause. "I know."

"What can you do?"

Reilly frowned. "A whole lot of damage, but only as a last resort."

Kellan turned his gaze back north and to the moonlit sea beyond, dreading the watershifter's answer to his next question. "How would you do it?"

"If I can get past the Ellvinians and closer to the ocean, I can create waves high enough to flood the entire city, but there are two problems with that. One, I will be in the midst of the enemy while shifting and would need some very heavy protection."

"The other problem?" Kellan asked.

"Water is a very powerful force, my friend. Anything I do will kill the defenders as well as the Ellvinians."

Kellan's grip on the parapet tightened until the stone cracked beneath his hands. "This must be how the shifters in Pyraan felt when they confronted Adrian Ravener. Over four thousand shifters perished, including my grandparents, when the Mage flooded the land. Are we really to share their same fate, Reilly?"

"I can see no other recourse," the watershifter admitted.

"Then, I think your last resort has arrived."

Reilly cursed and turned his head away.

Kellan blinked back hot tears that sprang to his eyes. "I wonder what our parents will think after we are gone."

"I hope they will understand that we did all we could," the Dwarf replied gruffly. "I hope they will be proud that we upheld our oaths."

"I think they will." Kellan wanted to say more to his friend, but the words escaped him in that moment. Instead, he resumed his watch and a breath hitched in his throat. Where a moment ago all was empty and dark, now Ellvinians filled his vision. Their eyes looked like ghastly black holes as they came forward from the shadows of the night. Together, this time, in perfect formation. Not hurried and disordered like the last time, but with measured, deadly grace. They made no noise as they poured out of the city and into the square, a merciless, relentless tide of dark Elves.

Kellan grabbed Reilly's arm. "Who will you take with you?"

"Jala and Dallin. They will give me the best chance to do what I have to do." Reilly squeezed Kellan's hand in his affectionately. "I'll see you on the other side, my friend."

"I'll be waiting."

Reilly turned and ran down the stairs.

"Fireshifters!" Kirby Nash cried out from below and the shifters standing along the bottom of the wall stepped up together and hurled fire into the advancing mass of Elves.

Shouts of terror echoed through the night and the smell of burnt flesh once again drifted to Kellan's nose. Elves flailed their arms as they attempted to put out the fire racing up their bodies, but just like the conflict outside of the mayor's estate, their movements only served to ignite their fellow fighters closest to them. One Ellvinian peeled away from the group and even though his entire body was engulfed in flames, attempted to reach the line of defenders. He took an arrow in the chest before he got close.

Mindshifters sought out the men on fire and directed them further back into the enemy line to cause as much damage as possible. It was a horrible, brutal use of magic.

Out of the now stalled horde of Ellvinians, a group of Battlearms bypassed the flaming center and with swords drawn prepared to catch the Massans unaware from the right flank. Kellan thrust out a hand and the earth pushed up through the cobblestones of the courtyard directly in the path of the oncoming Elves. Surprised cries rang out as their running feet stopped abruptly and they pitched forward. The rotating dirt swirled at their feet and sucked them into the ground to their knees.

Kellan turned away from the ensnared Battlearms. They would cause no further harm this night.

The enemy lines from the back finally broke through and trampled over their burning comrades. With no further obstacles between the two forces, there was no stopping them now and they clashed with terrible impact.

Kellan snarled at the sight of an Ellvinian smashing his fist into the face of a young female mindshifter. He launched himself from the rampart and directly into the melee with Maks landing next to him. The noise was deafening as four-legged animals ripped and tore at flesh, birds in the air dove down to rake sharp claws at exposed skin, fire raged, the earth heaved, and sparks flew as swords crossed.

Kellan knelt and crushed both fists through the cobblestones of the square. Reaching down into the dirt and sand, he shifted the earth. Filtering through the softer soil, he summoned the harder substances up through the loam and an earthen armor of stones and clay rolled up and over his arms and body. With a growl, he shot to his feet and swung his arms. Those who tried to take him down, died in the process.

Kellan and Maks fought their way toward where he last saw the embattled mindshifter. Out of the corner of his eye, he saw four different replicas of Kane and his breath caught every time a sword plunged through a chest made of air.

Izzy sat atop a Grayan wolf and slashed a dagger at any Elf who managed to get by the wolf's sharp jaws. Not many did.

There was no sign of the Radeks.

The cawing of a crow close by caused him to turn. Kellan blinked in disbelief. An old woman fought alongside the Massans with a crow perched on her shoulder. Despite her age, the woman moved deftly and with lethal consequence as she inflicted death to the enemy with every point of a twisted finger. Every so often, the bird would take to the air to slice at the eyes of the woman's opponents if they moved in too close and then it would settle back onto her shoulder.

He remembered the tale the kidnapped shifters told him and if he ever saw them again, he promised he would offer them an apology for finding their story unbelievable.

Kellan shook his head and continued on. Several swords licked out from the night at him, but they either bounced harmlessly off his armor or the wielder lost his arm to Maks. At last, he saw the mindshifter so brutally assaulted, but she already had the Ellvinian in her mental grasp, and he was now protecting her from his fellow fighters.

Sudden thunder boomed and fingers of light spread through the roiling clouds above. Kellan looked up in dismay as the first raindrops fell from the sky. It was the worst possible scenario. The rain would put out the fires continuing to rage through the enemy ranks and render the fireshifters useless. It would also hamper Kane's ability to cast his illusions.

With a muttered curse, he looked around at the battlefield helplessly. The Massan defenders were killing an exorbitant amount of the enemy, but they were dying as well and they had a lot less to lose.

Howling in rage, Kellan threw himself against the Ellvinians with unrestrained violence. Skulls caved in under his fists, legs broke under his powerful kicks. He became so lost in his anger-fueled rampage that he didn't see the Ellvinian behind him until it was too late. Sudden pain exploded behind his left ear and he was lifted off his feet by a crushing blow. A blood-crazed Elf brandishing a studded mace stood over him. The fighter heaved the heavy weapon over his head with two hands for another strike, but just as he began to swing, a flash of steel glinted through the air and a dagger sank deep in the Ellvinian's eye. Kellan rolled out of the way of the dropping mace and the dead Elf.

Still dazed from the attack, he looked up. Izzy appeared above him, squatted next to his assailant and yanked her dagger free. And, just like that, she was gone again.

Alarmed shouts came from the gates, and Kellan lurched to his feet in time to see several Ellvinians cut through the Massans guarding them. Defenders on top of the wall rained large rocks down on the heads of the Elves as they tried to wrench the gates open.

Kellan sprinted as fast as his armor would allow. It was pouring now and the ground dangerously slippery from mud and blood. He skidded to a stop in astonishment when a body dove off the outer wall directly into the Ellvinians at the gate.

"You're not doing this without me!" bellowed a familiar Dwarven voice before being buried under a knot of dark Elves. It was Iben Rydex, the protector for Reilly Radek! The Iron Fist had been left behind in Bardot when Reilly accompanied Kenley to Callyn-Rhe.

Kellan was relieved when the formidable soldier popped up among the taller Elves and slashed out with a long knife in each hand.

Then, Kane appeared at his side.

Kellan flashed his twin brother a bleak smile and they pressed their backs together. The sons of Beck Atlan and Kiernan Everard came together as one and the result was devastating to the enemy. Wherever they moved, they left incalculable ruin in their wake. Whereas Kellan was brute strength and raw power, Kane was speed and deadly timing, his blade a blur of whirling metal. One by one, the Ellvinians fell dead at the feet of the brothers. Fighting side by side, they were able to throw back the breach at the gates.

Breathing heavily, Kellan was able to pause for a moment as the Ellvinians pushed away from their circle of destruction. His arms burned from the effort of swinging his heavily-ladened arms.

He stretched back to look over his shoulder at Kane. His brother's hair was plastered to his head and the rainwater, mixed with blood, ran down his face in angry rivulets giving him a wild appearance.

Maks and Jain did all they could to protect them, but even the big cats were wearing down.

Suddenly, the Elves came at them again, and Kane yelled out as he slipped and went down on one knee. Kellan tried to protect him from above, but a sword point made its way through and punctured Kane in the left side of his chest. The man lost his life to Jain for the effort, but the damage was done. Kane lay on the ground, gasping in ragged breaths.

Kellan crouched over him protectively and suffered blow after blow, his earthen armor chipping away under a ruthless assault. Exhausted, Kellan could only lay over his brother and wait for the inevitable strike that would shatter his armor for good and end his life. Despondent, his thoughts turned to Reilly. Had he made it to the ocean? Was he at this very moment preparing the waves that would crash over all of their heads? He hoped so. At least then, he could go to his death knowing the gates held.

One particularly brutal clout to the head, scattered his senses and he fell on his back. It must have done real damage because when he glanced up at the outer wall, he saw rows of angels lining the parapet.

Beautiful, white glowing angels. Hundreds of them. Maybe even thousands! Was he dead already? Were these spirits here to guide him to the Highworld?

But, then the angels opened their mouths and let out a bestial roar that sent the Ellvinians running for their lives.

No, probably not angels.

Chapter 32

An Oath of the Children

Kellan rose up on trembling legs and let his earthen armor fall away from his body. He wiped the blood from his eyes and peered up through the curtain of rain.

Draca Cats.

A sea of white across the entire length and width of the wall and from the sounds, more gathered beyond the closed gates.

The Ellvinians left the field of battle, but continued to look on from the dark recesses of the city as they considered this new threat. After fighting Maks and Jain, they were well aware of the damage the dragon cats could inflict. And, now—there were a whole lot more of them.

Maks limped over to the newcomers. *Brothers and sisters, why are you here? What brings you out of Callyn-Rhe?*

A large male shook out his white mane and looked out over the devastation. *What is happening here, brother?*

An invasion of dark Elves. You came just in time to aid us in battle!

The Elves are friend to the Draca Cats.

Not these. May I ask your name?

I am, Nazar, and I am your new Sovereign. Show your respect, cub.

Jain came forward. *New Sovereign? What happened to Moombai?*

Kellan felt Kane's presence beside him and turned in shock.

"Jain healed me. What's happening?"

"Listen."

Moombai is dead. Bow to your Sovereign!

Maks and Jain let out agitated mewing sounds, but bent one foreleg out in front in a show of deference to this new ruler.

Better.

Maks straightened. *We need your help, Sovereign. The island of Massa is under attack.*

Let the humans handle it. We go now to the royal capital of Nysa. Tell the sons of Kenley that they must come with us. We will need their cooperation.

Nysa?

It is the seat of power of the Kenleys, is it not?

Yes.

Kellan peered over his shoulder to ensure that the Ellvinians were still holding back. He wondered what they thought of the silence since it was obvious that a form of communication was taking place.

Why Nysa? I don't understand.

To establish our rule, young cub! That is why we are here and why the Draca Cats have come out of hiding.

Kellan strode in front of Maks and nodded respectfully to Nazar. *Whatever is happening with the Draca Cats of Callyn-Rhe, I ask that you put those affairs aside for now.* He threw his arm backward. *We are fighting for our very lives here.*

You do not give the orders here, son of Kenley. I do.

Whatever it is you want, Nazar, we can work out a solution together. The Draca Cats do not deserve exile any more than the shifters of years ago did.

Nazar's amber gaze glowed with malice. *You know what I want? I want you to bow down to me, son of Kenley.*

The night turned deathly quiet. Kane rested a restraining hand on his arm. *I bow down to no one, Nazar.*

The new Sovereign growled and shook his head forcefully. *You will bow down and then we will travel to Nysa where you will be the voice of the Draca Cats!*

No! These Ellvinians have spilled the blood of my people and by my oath I will protect them from further harm. My duty is here, Nazar, and I ask you to uphold your oath to my family and fight beside me.

The cats on the wall swished their tails and screamed out in distress at their conflicting emotions between an old oath and a new order.

Kellan pressed on. *You will abandon a Kenley in his most desperate hour of need? Centuries of generations of Draca Cats and Kenleys have stood side by side in peace and in war and Nazar of Callyn-Rhe will break that oath?*

You will do as I say, son of Kenley, or you will never see your bondmate again!

Kellan spun toward Maks. *Maks?*

His friend's blue eyes so like his own welled with misery. *He is my Sovereign, Prince—*

Then, go and leave me if you must, but I will not break my oath! Go! Go join your oath breaker kin!

Maks' shook his head vehemently. *No! You did not let me finish. Nazar may be the new Sovereign, but our bond means far more to me. I would never leave you, Prince. Never.*

Kellan offered his friend a small smile of gratitude.

Nazar lifted his head and roared into the night. *Enough!* With a powerful leap, he jumped from the wall. *Call me oath breaker if you will, son of Kenley, but I will cower in the corner no longer!*

No one is asking you to!

I will take what is rightfully mine!

You are the child of oath, Kellan reminded him.

No more! I have already spilled the blood of my kin for this right and I will kill you, too! I denounce the oath!

Painful cries erupted from the Draca Cats as they recoiled from Nazar's dangerous words. Several cats fell from the wall, and Maks and Jain dropped to the ground and writhed in pain.

Kellan knelt next to Maks. *Maks, what is the matter?*

"The oath rises," Kane whispered.

Kellan stood when Nazar took a threatening step toward him. Over the plaintive wails of the Draca Cats, Kellan heard a bone break. Nazar's eyes widened in surprise and his gait took on a limp, but he kept coming. *I denounce the oath!*

More screams spewed from the Draca Cats as they twisted in mortal agony.

Kellan clenched his fists as he prepared to battle Nazar, but shrank back when another crack of bone echoed in the night. Nazar fell to the ground with a yelp of pain.

Nazar! You must stop!

The large cat struggled off the ground and came on, now dragging both hind legs behind him. *I denounce the oath!* The terrible howls of the Draca Cats were heartbreaking to hear. "Kane! What can we do?"

"There is nothing that can be done, brother."

A loud popping noise sounded and Nazar's ears and nose began to leak blood. Droplets of red splattered to the cobblestones. *I denounce the oath!*

Nazar! Save yourself! I am not your enemy!

Kellan heard a third snapping break, and Nazar fell to the ground once again. Crawling now, Nazar used one enormous paw to pull his body forward to try and get to Kellan. A river of blood left in his wake, he refused to stop.

I...denounce...the oath! The self-proclaimed Sovereign of Callyn-Rhe issued one last scream of defiance and then his massive snowy head, hit the cobblestones with a horrible thud just inches from Kellan's boots.

All went quiet.

Maks got to his feet shakily.

Are you all right? Kane asked him.

He nodded, but he looked furious as he stalked to the wall, his muzzle lifted in a snarl. *What of you, brothers and sisters! Does any other wish to try and harm my bondmate? If so, I promise you, I will kill you long before the oath!*

Another large male cat stepped forward and leapt from the wall to land next to Maks.

I am Muuki. I will address the pride.

Maks reluctantly nodded and stepped back. *Brothers and sisters! Nazar covered my eyes, but now I see! He deceived my heart, but now I feel the familiar oath beating there still. The son of Kenley is right. We are the children of oath!* The Draca paced before the wall. *This oath does not make us subservient* to the Kenleys, it makes us equals! It makes us whole! For I know that the Kenleys would give their lives to protect us just as we would do for them. They are the magic and we are the might! Let no one come against us and live! We are stronger by virtue of the oath! We are stronger together!

Muuki's words touched Kellan deep in his soul, and he threw his fist in the air. "We are the children of oath! Together we fight!" He said the words aloud so the Ellvinians would know what they faced.

Kane appeared at his side and lifted his fist. "The children of oath!"

While the recovered Draca Cats howled their agreement into the night, furtive movement behind Muuki caught Kellan's notice, and he watched a female Draca prowl forward from the stairs in the wall.

Muuki followed Kellan's gaze and spun around. *Rheka!*

Do not worry, Muuki, I will not hurt you.

No, you won't, Muuki replied with a low warning growl.

My mate is now dead, and I accept that. I come to ask if you will still allow me to be part of the pride.

I am not the Sovereign, Rheka, but all Draca Cats who follow our laws are part of the pride.

That is what I came to hear. The female swung her head toward Kellan. *I stand with you, son of Kenley. My oath beats firm.*

Kellan nodded.

Rheka bowed her head and retreated back to the wall.

It is as it should be, Muuki said to Kellan. *We stand united together.*

I am in your debt. While it is true that at the end of the Mage War, the Draca Cats chose seclusion, it was not imposed by humans. If you wish to now come out of hiding, it is up to you. *As long as you do not harm innocent people, you need not fight us for that right.*

Muuki nodded his acknowledgement.

Kirby Nash hurried to Kellan's side and grabbed his arm. "Your Grace, look!" Suddenly tense, Kellan swung his head to where he pointed. It was Emile. He was walking toward the center of the city square waving a white cloth with one hand and the other raised high in acceptance of defeat.

"Princes of Iserlohn! I come forward to offer our surrender!" He stopped halfway there. "We surrender!"

In unison, the Draca Cats growled out their frustrated disappointment.

Chapter 33

Calm Before the Storm

Kellan started toward Emile cautiously and sensed the others fall into step beside him to create a fearsome line. Kane, Izzy, Maks, Jain, Kirby Nash, and protectors Gregor, Haiden, Elon and the Dwarf, Iben, who, Kellan was pleased to see had survived his reckless dive into the enemy.

When he was within speaking distance, he stopped. "A surrender? Is it now your turn to use this tactic, Ellvinian?"

Emile dropped the cloth to the ground. "No tactic. I will not throw away any more Ellvinian lives fighting powerful beasts or your shifter magic." He snorted nervously. "If this is what a handful of shifters can do, I can only imagine at the might of your entire nation." He paused and Kellan could see emotion behind the Elf's eyes. "But, there is another reason I call a truce this night and it is a simple matter of what is right. The people of this island have never caused Ellvinians harm and, in fact, have done just the opposite." He shook his head. "There is no glory in this conflict! We do not fight over religion or for power or to resolve boundary disputes. We do not fight for civil rights or against oppression! Our Premier ordered us here so he can bask in the euphoria of your blood. Even as an Ellvinian who lusts for the blood, I say that is not just. I will fight no more."

Kellan had no idea what Emile was referring to when he spoke of the blood, but refrained from questioning the Elf when Kirby stepped forward with his hand firmly on the hilt of his sword. "Are all the Ellvinians with you in agreement?"

Emile blinked. "All but one." He gestured and two Battlearms brought forth a bound Samara.

The woman did not struggle, but directed an icy glare at Emile. "You will lose your head for this when the Premier learns of your cowardice."

"If I have my say, Samara, Hendrix Bane will not be the Premier of Ellvin for very much longer." Emile signaled again and Samara was led away.

Kirby strode closer to the Ellvinian Second. "We will grant your surrender with impunity, but our two nations will not be at peace until the ambassadors that sailed to your island are returned to us safely. Your Shiprunners and Battlearms are free to leave, but you will stay. If anything has happened to them, you will die first and then a campaign of war will be waged against Ellvin."

Emile nodded. "Under the circumstances, I can expect no less. For what it is worth, the Premier ordered almost the entire contingent of Battlearms here to Massa. If your ambassadors are as powerful as you have shown yourselves to be, the Ellvinians do not stand a chance."

Kirby eyes narrowed. "They are *not* as powerful as us, they are far stronger."

As Kellan listened in, he found it difficult to believe it was over. After days of relentless terror and making peace with his impending death, the threat to Massa was at an end. He was going to live after all. It would take time for the survivors to recover from the deaths that resulted from the battle, but they would get through it together. As though sanctioning this new chance at life, orange light appeared at the eastern horizon and pushed the rainclouds back. With a thankful smile, Kellan closed his eyes to soak in the comforting warmth of the awakening sun.

Click. Click. Shuffle.

What...?

He turned to the strange noise and a powerful blow sent his body flailing across the length of the square. The air rushed from his lungs as he smashed against the outer wall. Stunned from the impact, he first heard the warning screams and then the clicking of claws moving very fast on cobblestones.

He knew in that moment that it was the Vypir.

He tried to stand, but the beast was on him before he could pull himself upright. The Vypir pinned him to the ground by his shoulders, and Kellan watched in horror as a tail with sharp fangs reared up behind the beast and struck out at his neck.

"No!" He tried to struggle, but even with his strength could not dislodge the creature once it latched on and began to suck his blood. Sudden dread filled him. The vile beast wasn't just taking his blood, but his magic as well! Kellan felt his connection with the earth slipping from his control. He clawed desperately to grasp it back, but the link was growing smaller and harder to recognize.

"Tolah!" Someone cried out.

Through his panic, Kellan sensed others rushing across the square to come to his aid, could hear their boot strikes on the stone. His vision blurred. Blackness pushed seductively at the edges of his consciousness and beckoned him to let go. The temptation to leave everything behind and find refuge in the spirit world surged potently through his enervated mind and body. Death whispered and cajoled, urging him to seek release. Kellan parted his lips to accept the offer, but furious snarls in his ear startled him into full wakefulness once again. He felt his body jerked first one way and then another. Powerful teeth grabbed the back of his shirt and yanked him out of the grasp of the Vypir.

He looked up through heavy eyes and saw Maks and the Vypir rolling across the square in a white ball of struggling fury. It was his first look at the beast. A protracted ribcage and pale skin pulled tight over its skull gave the Vypir a skeletal appearance. Tuffs of white Elven hair poked up through its head in sickly patches. Lashing out with muscled legs that ended in claws, the Vypir managed to get loose from Maks, only to be surrounded by a hundred other Draca Cats, slinking around the beast as they searched for an opening to attack.

That was when Kellan noticed the beast's tail had been slashed off at the tip. He looked down in alarm. The portion of the tail with the fangs was still embedded in his throat. Still sucking the blood and magic from his body and spurting it out onto the cobblestones.

"Hold on!" Kane yelled and grabbed the offending appendage with two hands to try and yank it free. It would not budge. It just kept slurping and sucking.

"Get...it...off," Kellan said weakly and tried to lift his hand to help, but his arms felt like they were made of lead weights and he couldn't move them.

"It's not coming off!" he heard Kane scream.

Gregor Steele pushed Kane away and pressed his sword against Kellan's neck to try and pry the tail piece loose.

"Dracas," Kellan whispered.

Somehow, Kane heard his feeble appeal. *Jain! Come quickly!* A warm hand grasped his tightly. "Hold on, brother. Help is coming. Hold on!"

Kellan felt movement around him and then hot air on his face. Large golden eyes filled his vision.

Kane's eyes.

Jain's eyes.

The magic of the Healing Breath misted over his face and into his lungs. The benevolent vapor traveled through his body with purpose, healing small injuries, infusing him with energy. Then, the sinuous magic focused on the protrusion in his neck and attacked. Kellan gasped deeply and his chest rose in the air as the Healing Breath directed a forceful strike against the foreign object.

"Jain! What is happening?" he heard Kane shout.

I'm dying.

The magic struck again and he bucked off the ground under the intensity of the battle raging inside his body.

"Jain! You're killing him!"

From far way, Kellan could taste the froth at his mouth, could feel the violent convulsions.

I am doing what I must, Jain replied. *This beast is created of very ancient sorcery. But, then, so am I.*

Jain's Dracan magic assailed the quivering Vypir tail for a third time. *Grab it, Prince!*

Kellan felt Kane lean over and with a last vigorous pull and a revolting wet sound, the appendage popped free.

Quickly now, stem the blood flow from outside while I heal him from within.

Again, Kane followed his bondmate's orders and Kellan felt another strong breath on his face and a cloth pressed hard against his wound. Instantly, he felt the throbbing pain in his neck dissipate.

When the enormous head lifted away from him, Kellan took a long and ragged pull of air into his lungs and sat up against the outer wall. He tried to form the words to thank Jain for saving his life, but they came out garbled and incoherent. It didn't matter. The cat was already gone, back into the fight with the Vypir.

Kellan looked on in shock. The beast was so fast! The muscled creature took leaping bounds from one portion of the square to another somehow managing to avoid the spiked tails and sharp claws of the Draca Cats.

A group of defenders by the gates screamed out as the pouncing Vypir slammed into their position. Kellan leapt to his feet in horror as the beast ripped limbs from sockets and tore flesh from bone. Blood sprayed into the air in gruesome strings of red death.

Kirby Nash bellowed out a challenge and sprinted to the defense of the defenders. His curved Saber a slashing blur, he was able to cut two long gashes into the Vypir's abdomen. The beast shrieked in pain, turned, and leapt onto the outer wall. Digging sharp hind claws into the stonework, the Vypir scaled the wall with the agility of a spider. Fireshifters hurled fire at the creature, but none of the flames came close and it almost seemed to Kellan as though the creature had some sort of magical shield around it.

Then, the Vypir scrambled over the top of the wall and disappeared into the night.

Chaos erupted as demands for the gates to be opened filled the air. Ellvinians joined with the Massans as they prepared to go after the Vypir although if they couldn't kill it in the confines of this walled city square, it seemed unlikely they would be able to find it outside. Especially, if it managed to get to the Grayan Forest. The same forest where the citizens of Northfort were making their harrowing escape.

Over the cries of pain and shouted orders, Kellan suddenly heard a sound far more disturbing.

He put an arm out to Kane. "Listen!"

The rushing noise sounded distant at first and then grew louder. Like a violent clap of thunder directly overhead, it struck a spike of fear directly into Kellan's heart.

Reilly Radek made it the ocean and he was doing exactly what they discussed on the wall.

He was flooding Northfort.

Chapter 34

Airstrike

"Nooo!" Kellan took off at a sprint toward the wharf, pushing through the thousands of Ellvinians. Maks, realizing where he was going, dodged in front of him and growled out a threatening roar that scattered the dark Elves out of the way.

Kirby Nash, Gregor Steele and Kane chased after him.

"What is going on?" Kirby shouted as they ran.

"Reilly is flooding Northfort! He doesn't know about the truce! We have to stop him!"

Jain raced by and helped Maks clear the path. Unlucky Ellvinians who didn't see the Draca Cats coming paid dearly as they were trampled underneath their huge paws. Several times during their headlong flight, Kellan had to jump over the prone bodies left in their wake.

A sudden shift in the crowd caused Kellan to realize that those in the rear, closer to the wharf, were now pushing their way south.

"Run!

"Tidal wave!"

The Ellvinians' shouts of terror turned the mob en masse as they caught their first glimpse of Reilly's shifting. Masks of horror carved their faces as they wrenched at each other in desperation to flee the threat bearing down on them.

Now, even the Draca Cats were unable to make much progress through the massive number of Elves, and Kellan felt his body being carried away backwards under the press of bodies.

"Let go! I have to get to the wharf!" With two mighty swings, Kellan knocked away the Elves closest to him. Maks and Jain filled the gap and snapped at any who got too close.

Standing alone in a small island in the river of Ellvinians streaming past, Kellan looked up in sheer hopelessness.

The entire northern horizon was now a wall of blue water. Gushing straight up out of the sea at least two hundred feet in the air, a tower of ocean loomed over the ill-fated Northfort.

Large three-masted Ellvinian ships swept up in the swell looked like children's toys as they bobbed on the top of the wave's crest.

"Demon's breath!" Kirby cursed behind him. "What is he doing?"

"What I told him to do," Kellan whispered.

The panicked Ellvinians poured over their position, and Kellan was knocked to the ground under a crush of humanity. No one stopped to help, they just passed over him, their running feet pounding over his back and legs.

Incongruously, in the midst of the screams and shouts and the swelling waves, and with his cheek pressed into the cobblestone road, he heard laughter.

A great hearty bark of laughter.

What could possibly cause someone to laugh at a time like this, he questioned to himself as another passing boot struck him in the head. Who would laugh as their very life was about to be extinguished for all time?

It was Kane.

"Dear Highworld, that sister of mine sure knows how to make an entrance."

※

As Kenley soared toward Northfort, she tried to make sense of what she was seeing far below. Outside the gates, a thousand Draca Cats paced before the wall. Inside, tens of thousands of dark Elves blanketed three quarters of the northern portion of the city. Comparatively, only one hundred or so Massans stood at the southern end in front of the outer gates.

Dead bodies, almost entirely Ellvinian, lay between them.

She wondered if her brothers and the other children were down there. If so, how had they managed to hold off the enemy with so few?

Hurried movement in the north drew her attention. The Ellvinians were pushing forward. Were they attacking? Anger surged through her as she poured on the speed, the wind slicing forcefully over her body. She banked to the left to circle the city and that was when she heard the roar.

Her head snapped out to sea. A wall of water rose straight out of the ocean sending ships toppling—most, thankfully further out to sea, but some crashing into the pier. The deadly swell grew in size until the inevitable arc at the top shaped into existence and the water made a slow, terrifying descent toward the city.

Her heart pounding inside her chest, she plummeted downward toward the gigantic tidal wave. Grasping the windstream coming out of the west, she flattened the thermals into a solid wall of air and slammed it against the oncoming water. Teeth gritted in determination, she pushed. With hands thrust out in front of her and screaming with effort, she pushed with every bit of elemental power that rushed through her pureblood veins. Sweat popped out on her head from the strain, and her arm muscles trembled from the amount of strength necessary to hold the water back.

Her wall of air stopped the onward momentum of the wave, but it didn't fall back. No matter how hard she threw herself at the water, it stood firm.

She felt a sudden jolt and her body somersaulted backwards through the air. The water was pushing back! Quickly regaining her balance, she flew back to the wall, threw out her hands once again and pushed.

She was losing ground! How could that be?

An errant thought hit her. Could this be shifted water? But, that didn't make any sense. Why would a watershifter be trying to flood the city?

Her eyes scanned the wharf as she struggled to hold back the sea.

There! Standing on a stretch of beach out of harm's way with Jala and Dallin Storm was Reilly Radek! What in the Highworld was that boy doing? If she didn't stop him, he would kill everyone in Northfort.

Kenley had no choice, she had to release a bit of pressure on her wall of air to get to Reilly. Like an arrow, she shot toward the watershifter and hammered him with a blast of air.

The unsuspecting Dwarf flew into the air and rolled backwards in a violent tumble. If not for the quick grab by Dallin, he would have been sucked into the frothing sea.

With an angry scowl, Reilly got back to his feet and lifted his hands once again.

"Stop!" she screamed over the howling winds and raging waters. But, every effort she made to get closer to Reilly so he could hear her, the more ground she lost with the wall.

"Reilly!"

It was too late. The top of the water crested and crashed into Northfort harbor. The platform where they stood more than a week ago to see her parents away on their journey disappeared under the deluge.

Ellvinians screamed as they were swept out to sea.

Kenley swarmed down and hurtled more air at the dangerous gushing water.

"Reilly!"

Finally, Jala noticed her, and the fireshifter rushed to exchange urgent words with her brother, and just like that, Reilly dropped one arm and the wall of water fell back into the sea. With the other hand, he hastily created new and intricate movements that only another watershifter could understand. She watched in amazement as the water pouring into the streets of Northfort reversed its forward momentum and was sent careening back to the ocean.

Exhausted, Kenley plummeted back to the ground in a very ungraceful glide and collapsed onto the sodden sand. If the Ellvinians meant to attack now, they would find very little resistance from her. She couldn't move. She couldn't even think clearly.

A shrill caw pierced her foggy mind and with a knowing groan, she lifted her head.

The old woman and crow were back and standing over her, white and beady black eyes boring into her skull. It was the Oracle.

"I thought you would never get here," the woman remarked brusquely.

"Well, apparently, I cannot seem to move as fast as you can." Kenley let her head flop back to the ground and closed her eyes. "The Ellvinians?"

"Surrendered."

"Good."

The Oracle was silent for a moment, and Kenley said nothing either, refusing to open herself up to another taunt.

Finally, the woman said, "Well done, Kenley Atlan. Very well done."

Kenley lifted her lips in a smile, but didn't bother opening her eyes. She knew the woman would already be gone.

Then, Kenley remembered something that she had to do. She jumped to her feet and took to the skies once again. Fatigue raked at her insides, but this was too important. Gliding low over the city, Kenley flew past the dark heads of the Ellvinians and headed south. It didn't take long for her to pick out the distinctive blonde curls. She dreamt of those curls every night for over a week now and in every single dream, he was lost to her.

He stood apart from the others, watching her come.

She swallowed back a lump in her throat when she saw his bloodied face and torn clothing. It was then that she realized just how close she really did come to losing him forever.

She swooped down and grabbed his shirt in two fists and pulled him into the air. "Hang on and wrap your legs around me."

He did as he was told and she heard cheers from the Massans below as she flew with Kirby toward the beach. He smelled of leather and sweat, and it was the sweetest scent she had ever smelled in her life.

Her movements dipped and swayed as her strength finally gave out. The white sand came up to meet them harder than she intended and they rolled across the beach in a tightly tangled heap. When they finally stopped, he was laying on top of her, looking down into her eyes.

"Now, that was a homecoming I will not soon forget," he murmured.

Kenley's eyes blurred with sudden tears as the strength of her love for him washed over her. Her Kirby. Selfless, strong, honorable. He dedicated his entire life to keeping her safe, to loving her, and something deep inside her broke loose under the potency of that knowledge.

"What is this?" he said, and wiped away a tear from her face with a thumb.

"I just missed you," she whispered. Not trusting herself to adequately express the depth of emotion she was feeling at that moment, she simply said, "Let's do it."

"Do what?"

Hands still fisted in his shirt, she rolled him over until she was on top. "Let's get married."

"Married?"

"Yes, you still want me, don't you?"

His shoulders pulled up in a shrug. "Well...I don't know. You are quite difficult, you know."

"Kirby!"

"You do so love to torment me, Princess."

"Kirby Nash, if you don't agree to marry me right this instant, I will kill you!"

His blue eyes twinkled playfully. "Well, then I guess the answer is yes."

"Yes?"

"Yes, I will marry you, Kenley Atlan." He reached up and tucked a black curl behind her ear. "Don't you realize by now that there is nothing I want more in this entire world than to have you as my wife?"

She began to laugh through her tears. "I guess I do."

"Kiss me, my love."

She dutifully responded and lost herself in the intense pleasure of being back in Kirby's arms. "I cannot wait to tell mother," she said softly. "She will be thrilled for us."

Kirby's playfulness vanished. "I hope so. But, in interest of my personal safety, can you wrap your father in a shield of air when we tell *him*?"

Chapter 35

Release From Darkness

Since Kenley couldn't shift to save her life, she and Kirby made their way back to the gates on foot. Many of the Ellvinians cheered for her as she passed by and offered shouted words of gratitude for saving their lives. She accepted the praise graciously, but the attention slowed her progress and she was anxious to see the children.

At last, they made it through the vast throng of Elves and entered the city square. Kellan saw her first and rushed to her side only to swallow her in his enormous embrace. "So glad you made it, sister."

She hugged him back fiercely, but before she could reply, she was ripped from Kellan's arms and flung against Kane. This brother didn't say anything, just held her close, and that was perfectly fine with her.

She enjoyed enthusiastic reunions with Izzy, Jala and Reilly, who was a bit sore at her use of force. Fortunately, she was able to smooth things over with the watershifter, and was soon engrossed in a concerted tale of the mayor's gala when Kellan interrupted.

"Hate to break this up, but we have more work to do."

Kenley grabbed her brother's arm. "What now?"

"We have to track and kill the Vypir."

"What in demon's breath is a Vypir?"

"Oh, just a beastly Ellvinian creation that wants nothing more than to siphon the blood of magic users."

"Lovely. Where is it?"

"Outside the walls. We have to find it before it causes any more harm than it already has."

She sighed heavily. "What are we waiting for? Lead the way."

Kellan hurried across the square and she followed him along with the others.

"Prince! Prince!"

Kenley stopped when a tall Ellvinian intercepted their progress.

"Emile! What is it?" Kellan asked.

"Are you going after Tolah...I mean the Vypir?"

"Yes."

He shook his head in remorse. "I had hoped that we could save him, but I now know that is no longer an option. Not after the...the girl."

Kenley didn't know what he was talking about, but Kane made a tortured sound in his throat.

"How can we kill it?" Kellan asked.

"You will have to behead it. It is the only way." Emile visibly swallowed and continued. "It is—or once was—a talented wizard. While it is true that every year more of the man is lost to the beast, he will sometimes remember an old incantation and is able to utter the words necessary to cast a spell. After his recent intake of magical blood, I fear he is even stronger now. It will take your most powerful shifters working together to take him down."

"He could be halfway to Bardot by now," Reilly complained.

Emile shook his head. "No, he will not go far. He will not leave me."

Kellan thanked the obviously distraught Emile and they sprinted for the gates once again. Feeling stronger after her long walk from the pier, Kenley decided not to wait for the gates to be opened and took to the air. She thought she heard Kirby curse, but couldn't be sure.

She plunged into the low-hanging, cold mist and soared over the wall and the milling Draca Cats to scan the open land between Northfort's wall and the Grayan Forest. The first rays of dawn gave her plenty of light by which to see, but nothing moved on the plains below her.

Kellan, Kane, Reilly, Jala and Izzy sprinted out of the gates with their protectors—human and animal. Kenley swooped back down to the ground and walked over to Kirby.

"Kirby, you need to keep everyone back, including the Draca Cats. The shifters will come with me."

Not surprisingly, he opened his mouth to argue, but she held up a hand. "You heard Emile. We are dealing with a creature that was once a Mage, and it will take magic to defeat it. We cannot be distracted by concern for your safety."

His eyes flared in anger. "*Our* safety? Are you—"

Kenley leaned forward and planted a soft kiss on his lips. "Do not let your feelings for me cloud your duty. You know that the *Savitar* children have the best chance to end this nightmare. Let me go."

The words struck home as they were meant to. No one could ever accuse Captain Kirby Nash of shirking his duty.

He nodded reluctantly, but when she turned to go, he grabbed her from behind and leaned down to whisper fiercely, "Come back to me, wife."

Her mouth twitched up into a smile and she patted his hand on her shoulder. "I will."

Kenley motioned for the children to follow and they made their way through the host of Draca Cats. She was grateful Kirby didn't put up more of a fight. If she had her way, she would have many more years ahead of her to argue with Captain Nash. That settled, she put all thoughts of Kirby out of her mind.

She knew Baya was still making her way through the Grayan Forest. *Baya!*

I am here, Princess.

Have you seen anything out of the ordinary in the forest?

No.

Keep your eyes out for a strange beast.

I will.

Kenley stopped when she reached the center of the wet plains. She waved Izzy forward and tenderly stroked her cheek. The young feralshifter looked much older than when Kenley had seen her last. Her eyes more haunted. Battle would do that she supposed. Reaching out, she ran a hand down the back of Jala's hair and then smiled at each of the boys. She loved these children so much. More than friends, they were family, and she didn't think she could recover from the loss of any of them.

"We are going to do this just like we do in the games we play, except instead of me as your target, it will be the Vypir." The children nodded, but they looked so tired. She could only imagine what they had been through over the past few days and knew she had to do something to stir their blood oath. It was the only way to give them the enhanced strength and speed they would need to survive. "We can do this," she whispered ardently. "Yes, we are the children of *Savitars*, but more importantly, we are the defenders of Massa! We cannot fail in our duty this day!"

Eyes of every color swirled with the intensity of magic that dwelled behind them and she knew the green of hers matched theirs. She could feel her muscles strengthen, her vision sharpen, her hearing amplify.

She could feel the blood oath.

"Just like the games, but remember, this is, or was, a wizard. We cannot let up for a single moment."

Five heads nodded more eagerly this time.

I see it! It is coming, Princess!

Baya's warning sounded in her mind mere seconds before she heard a crashing movement from the Grayan. The Vypir was coming toward them. Fast.

As one, the six standing alone in the plains turned to meet the threat.

Kenley took a deep breath. "Kane, you are first."

Golden eyes glinted with deadly purpose as he took off at a sprint toward the oncoming Vypir without a word. The beast burst out of the woods running on all fours. Large knuckles helped to swing its body forward at an alarming rate. Even from the distance that separated them, she could see how muscular and strong the arms and legs were.

As soon as the Vypir saw Kane, it straightened into an upright position and began to take leaping bounds that brought him closer to Kane faster than Kenley would have liked. Kane replicated and five images of her brother tore toward the beast. But, instead of closing with the image in the lead position of the wedge as—without fail—all other opponents did, the Vypir veered off and slammed into the far right image on the wing. The real Kane.

With a powerful backhanded swat, the Vypir sent Kane reeling through the air.

Kellan screamed out in fury and advanced next, swirling his hands in a circle to soften the wet ground at the Vypir's feet to lock it in place before it could go after Kane.

The Vypir shrieked as it struggled to lift its legs. Kenley silently urged Kellan on as she watched the beast sink lower and lower into the ground. But, then the Vypir's lips moved in a silent chant and it burst up out of its snare.

Izzy crawled onto the back of a Grayan wolf and crept off to flank the creature, and Jala called fire to her palms and hurled it at the Vypir as she ran forward. The fire latched onto its white garment, similar to what the Ellvinians wore, and burst into flames. Again, she saw the Vypir's lips move and the fire was quickly extinguished.

Kenley realized then that if they continued to fight the Vypir one on one, the ancient wizard would use spell-casting to defeat their shifting. They would have to make it impossible for him to combat all at one time.

"Shifters! Together! All at once!"

Kenley lifted off the ground and watched as the children circled the Vypir.

"Now!" she screamed and they attacked.

Kellan opened the ground beneath the Vypir once again and it fell into the furrow created by the wet roiling earth. The beast started a chant, but Kenley slammed it hard with a direct force of air and pinned it to the ground.

Jala hurled another fireball into the creature and the bottom half its already charred garment flared.

Izzy directed the Grayan wolf close and the animal clamped its jaws on the Vypir's arm and, after a few violent tugs, ripped the limb from its body.

Reilly called forth water from the wet grass and a liquid stream slithered up the Vypir's face and transformed into a suffocating mask. As the water found its way into the beast's nose and mouth, the Vypir struggled in panic, but Kenley and Kellan kept it restrained with air and earth.

Finally, Kane unsheathed the sword of Iserlohn and the lethal ring sounded chilling in the dawn light.

Kenley alighted from the air and stood over the Vypir with the rest of the children. When it stopped moving, she gestured for Reilly and Jala to let go of their magic.

"Let me have the sword, Kane," she told her brother.

He handed the family heirloom to her and she held the point under the chin of the Vypir. Emile told her that it would have to be beheaded. If she didn't do it, given enough time, the beast could probably heal itself. She knew her father had such powers. Still, looking down at the pitiful creature, she hesitated. With an arm missing and his hair and clothes singed, it no longer looked like an evil beast. It looked like a wounded animal.

Suddenly, the Vypir took a loud, gasping breath and its enlarged chest rose off the ground. Instinctively, the shifters took a step back as they prepared to assault it again.

"No," Kenley said softly. It was up to her to end this now. She moved back toward the Vypir and the sword in her hand quivered as she held it against his throat.

The Vypir's eyes were open now, watery and filled with pain.

"No...more," it croaked out.

Kenley flinched at hearing it speak, but kept the sword close.

Through lips cracked and bleeding, the Vypir begged, "No more...don't want to live...no more."

Sympathy overwhelmed Kenley for what this creature, once an Elven Mage, must have endured during its transformation. She stood still for a long time, the sword tip hovering over the Vypir's throat, but found she couldn't do it.

A calloused hand gently reached for the sword and removed it from her fingers. She stepped back in a daze and watched as Kirby Nash lifted the sword of Iserlohn high over his head and took the Vypir's head from its shoulders.

CHAPTER 36

THE RETURN

Two days later, as Kellan stood up to swipe the back of his hand across his sweat-filled brow, he spotted the *The Wanderer* on the horizon. He looked around in satisfaction. Most of the debris and wreckage from Reilly's wall of water and from the battle had been cleared. Hammers rang out as carpenters worked to repair the wooden docks and shop fronts on the pier.

Several Ellvinians remained in Massa to help with the restoration, but most of the Shiprunners and Battlearms had already sailed back to Ellvin. Miraculously, only a handful of ships were destroyed. Most, were pushed out to sea with the tidal wave and the experienced Shiprunners on board were able to deftly sail them away from the danger.

Emile appeared at his side. "Your parents?"

Kellan nodded with a smile. "I hope so, Emile."

Kellan sent a young Massan to round up the children and protectors and within the hour, they all stood on the platform and watched as *The Wanderer* neared.

Despite the distance, Kellan could see clearly that the parents were distressed about something. In their agitated haste, they didn't even wait for Rafe Wilden to dock the ship. Kellan's father picked up his mother and shot toward shore using a hover spell, and Airron Falewir bodyshifted into a dolphin and cut through the water faster than any watershifter he had seen with Rogan Radek clinging to his back for dear life.

After Airron and Rogan pulled themselves from the water, all four *Savitars* strode down the extended dock with menace in their eyes and deadly power in their movements. The workmen that saw them coming dove into the ocean to get out of their way.

Even Kellan found himself taking half a step back.

His father pointed an imperious finger at the Ellvinians standing beside them on the platform. "Move aside, Ellvinians!" he thundered in righteous wrath. "We will not have you anywhere near our children! You may have had the upper hand here, but the deception is over. You now must deal with us! Stand back, everyone!"

Kellan saw the air around Airron Falewir shimmer, Rogan Radek called fire to his hands, and his mother reached for a sword that was no longer there.

"Father! Really!" Kenley exploded and threw her hands in the air.

Kellan could no longer smother his laugh.

His father's eyes narrowed. "I'll take care of this, Kenley. Don't you worry, darling."

"Father!" Kellan interrupted. "Everything is fine. The Ellvinians are our friends."

"Friends!" he roared. "These people tried to kill us!"

"Well, yes, they tried to kill us, too."

"But, we surrendered," Emile pointed out, stepping forward. "These *children* happened to defeat us pretty soundly."

The *Savitars* let go of their magic with stunned looks on their faces.

"Explain," Kellan's mother ordered.

"It is true that the Ellvinians declared war against us, but we have since come to a meeting of the minds and declared a truce," he told them.

Emile bowed at the waist. "If you wish to take action against my nation, you are within your rights. However, I can tell you that the Ellvinians have been under the leadership of greedy and immoral people." He flung an angry look at Samara tied up on the pier behind him. "If it is within my power, I plan to rectify that wrong when I return to Ellvin."

Kellan's father waved a hand dismissively. "It is already done. The Ellvin people have deposed your Premier and the Seconds."

The Ellvinians closest to the conversation let out excited gasps.

"Didn't the Ellvinians use their Ascendency against you?" his father asked.

Jala Radek laughed. "Oh, yes! You should have seen Kellan fawning over a woman twice his age!"

Now, Kellan glanced at Samara, the tips of his ears burning. "I did not fawn! I was under hypnosis!"

All on the dock laughed at his expense, and Izzy Falewir ran into her father's arms. She had the roughest time with all that happened. "You should have seen Kenley," the little Elf shared with the parents. "She pushed back a wall of water with her airshifting. It was incredible!"

His mother looked at Kenley with pride in her eyes. "That's my daughter."

"Oh, she's *your* daughter now?" his father asked with eyebrows that reached into his hairline.

"Always," Kiernan Atlan replied and his father's face crunched up in disbelief. Kellan thought it must be an inside joke between the two of them. It was something they did often.

His father suddenly noticed that Kenley had her hand on Kirby Nash's arm. "What is this?"

Kenley stepped forward. "Oh, Daddy, we have much to discuss when there is more time."

His father turned to his mother again. "She's calling me Daddy. That can't be good."

His mother shrugged and turned away. "Told you so."

Then, the tone turned somber when Kane said softly, "Not all turned out well."

Their mother rushed to his side. "What do you mean?"

"We lost Alia in the fight."

"Our Alia? Digby's daughter?" his mother cried.

"Yes."

She turned murderous eyes on the Ellvinians.

"It wasn't them," Kellan quickly clarified. "It was the Vypir."

"The Vypir! Where is it? I must destroy it at once!" his father declared and started a hasty stride down the pier.

"Oh, we killed that, too."

༺

Beck walked along the road with Kiernan having just completed a tour of the wharf to inspect the progress on the city repairs. Over lunch at the mayor's estate, the children regaled them with all that happened while they were away, and he was still in amazement over their feats of heroism.

They managed to head off a war with a much larger force, resolved a revolution of the Draca Cats, and saved the city of Northfort from annihilation. He shuddered as he was reminded of the destruction of Pyraan twenty years ago. The drowning deaths of his parents and all of the exiled shifters haunted him to this day.

At least now, a strong contingent of soldiers would be stationed here in Northfort. He would talk to Kirby Nash at some point to suggest adding shifters to each division of the army so that an event like this did not happen in the future.

The sound of galloping hooves thundered behind him, and he steered Kiernan to safety. From the side of the road, he stopped and watched a woman with long-blonde hair laying flat over her horse ride recklessly through the pedestrians and soldiers. It was the sorceress, Diamond.

"What in the Highworld is she doing here?" Kiernan questioned.

"Only one way to find out." Beck reached for Kiernan's hand and together they hurried after the racing sorceress. They came up on her just as she was dismounting from her horse.

Diamond strode angrily to where Emile and the bound Ellvinian woman waited to board a ship back to Ellvin.

"You!" Diamond pointed at the woman, her eyes furious. "How dare you!"

Beck hurried over to her. "Diamond! What are you doing?"

Diamond ignored him and put her hands on her hips. "So, you are the beast of prophecy! I will have you know that you have cost me *years* of good sleep waiting for you to show your face!" Her lip curled in disgust. "I have to admit, you are even uglier than I anticipated."

The woman gave her a contemptuous smile and in response, Diamond reached out and slapped her across the face. "An *Eyereader* you call yourself? You give seers a bad name. Get the hell off my island."

With that, the blonde witch strode to her horse, mounted and galloped away.

Kiernan's laugh echoed harshly, and Beck quickly hushed her and led her away. "Wonder what that was that all about," he mused aloud, hard pressed to suppress his own chuckle.

"Prophecy, my dear husband, that is what that was about."

He turned on the street that led back to the mayor's estate. The children were waiting for them there and he was eager to return. "Speaking of prophecy," he said, "I wonder why the Oracle never showed up. I thought for sure she would give me fair warning that the event she warned me about was approaching, and possibly even offer some kind of assistance. What if it turned out badly for the children? I must admit that I am very disappointed."

"It is also strange that Diamond mistook the Ellvinian woman as the beast instead of the Vypir."

"Prophecy can be tricky to interpret sometimes, Kiernan."

"Not with Diamond," Kiernan insisted.

"Well, at least now I can breathe easier. My family is safe and the prophecy is dead."

Kiernan gave him a sideways glance. "Unless..."

The hair on the back of his neck stood on end. "Unless what?"

"Unless, this is one of those prophecies that can have multiple outcomes. Maybe neither the Vypir nor the

Ellvinian woman was the prophetic beast the Oracle was referring to and that's why she hasn't showed up yet."

His gaze bored into her. "You're joking, right?"

She shrugged.

"Please, Kiernan! I just mended this heart and now you seem intent on stopping it once again!"

"But, Diamond said—"

"No! No more predictions! No more prophesy! I would like to spend the next few days at home appreciating my beautiful wife and family. As long as we live, Kiernan, there will be battles to face. We are defenders. We are shifters. I promise that you will have plenty of fights in the future to appease your warrior spirit. But, I beg of you, let us just enjoy this moment of peace while we can."

She tilted her head and gave him a smile to melt his heart. "Nicely said, Beck Atlan, nicely said. Very well, until the next time, then."

The End

RULING NOBILITY OF MASSA

ISERLOHN
King Maximus Everard
   House Colors - Black & Scarlet, Sigil - Golden Lions
Princess Kiernan Everard Atlan
Prince Mage Beck Atlan
Princess Kenley Grace Atlan
Prince Kellan Jaimes Atlan
Prince Kane Maximus Atlan

MEN AT ARMS
Sevant Kree - Personal Guard to King Maximus
Kirby Nash - Captain, Royal Guard, Personal Guard to Kenley Atlan
Gregor Steele - Personal Guard to Kellan Atlan
Haiden Lind - Personal Guard to Kane Atlan
Bo Franck - Captain, Iserlohn Army

COURT MEMBERS
Lady Lillian Knapp
   House Colors - Gray & Purple; Sigil - Shadow Panthers
Lord Gage Gregaros
   House Colors - Black & White; Sigil - White Tigers
Lord Johan Hamilton
   House Colors - Red & Yellow; Sigil - Red Dragons

DEEPSTONE
King Erik Rojin
   House Colors - Blue & Maroon; No Sigil
Kal Rogan Radek
Kali Janin Radek
Kal Reilly Radek
Kali Jala Radek

RULING NOBILITY OF MASSA

Men at Arms
Klay Arsten - General, Iron Fists, Personal Guard to King Erik
Iben Rydex - Personal Guard to Reilly Radek
Dallin Storm - Personal Guard to Jala Radek

Haventhal
King Thorn J'El
  House Colors - Brown & Green; Sigil - Ficus Tree
Airron Falewir
Melania Falewir
Izabel Falewir

Men at Arms
Raine Aubry - First Gardien, Gladewatchers, Personal Guard to King Thorn
Elon Aubry - Personal Guard to Izzy Falewir
Loren Faolin - Gladewatcher
Leif Oliver - Gardien

The Draca Cats of Iserlohn
Baya - Bondmate to Kenley Atlan
Maks - Bondmate to Kellan Atlan
Jain - Bondmate to Kane Atlan

The Draca Cats of Callyn-Rhe
Moombai - Sovereign
Felice - Mother to Baya
Nazar - Leader of the New Order
Rehka - Mate to Nazar
Muuki - Follower of the New Order

RULING NOBILITY OF ELLVIN

ELLVIN
Hendrix Bane - Premier
Samara - Second, Eyereaders
Emile - Second, Battlearms
Jarl - Second, Ironfingers
Balder - Second, Sagehands
Chandal - Second, Shiprunners
Anah - Second, Coinholders

ABOUT THE AUTHOR

Valerie Zambito lives in New York with her family. A great love of world building, character creation, and all things magic led to the publication of her first adult epic fantasy series, ISLAND SHIFTERS, in October, 2011. Since then, she has added five additional novels to her repertoire. Visit www.valeriezambito.com for the latest information.

Other Books Published by Valerie Zambito:

Book One: Island Shifters - An Oath of the Blood
Book Two: Island Shifters - An Oath of the Mage
Book Three: Island Shifters - An Oath of the Children
Book Four: Island Shifters - An Oath of the Kings
Angels of the Knights - Fallon
Angels of the Knights - Blane
Angels of the Knights - Nikki